THE
MILL MYSTERY

ANNA KATHARINE GREEN

1st WORLD
LIBRARY
Literary Society

The Mill Mystery

Anna Katherine Green

© 1st World Library, 2006
PO Box 2211
Fairfield, IA 52556
www.1stworldlibrary.com
First Edition

LCCN: 2007923732

Softcover ISBN: 978-1-4218-4224-0
Hardcover ISBN: 978-1-4218-4126-7
eBook ISBN: 978-1-4218-4322-3

Purchase *"The Mill Mystery"*
as a traditional bound book at:
www.1stWorldLibrary.com/purchase.asp?ISBN=978-1-4218-4224-0

1st World Library is a literary, educational organization
dedicated to:

- Creating a free internet library of downloadable ebooks

- Hosting writing competitions and offering book
publishing scholarships.

Interested in more 1st World Library books?
contact: literacy@1stworldlibrary.com
Check us out at: www.1stworldlibrary.com

1ˢᵗ World Library Literary Society

Giving Back to the World

"If you want to work on the core problem, it's early school literacy."

- James Barksdale, former CEO of Netscape

"No skill is more crucial to the future of a child, or to a democratic and prosperous society, than literacy."

- Los Angeles Times

Literacy... means far more than learning how to read and write... The aim is to transmit... knowledge and promote social participation."

- UNESCO

"Literacy is not a luxury, it is a right and a responsibility. If our world is to meet the challenges of the twenty-first century we must harness the energy and creativity of all our citizens."

- President Bill Clinton

"Parents should be encouraged to read to their children, and teachers should be equipped with all available techniques for teaching literacy, so the varying needs and capacities of individual kids can be taken into account."

- Hugh Mackay

CONTENTS

I

THE ALARM

Life, struck sharp on death,
Makes awful lightning.

—MRS. BROWNING.

I had just come in from the street. I had a letter in my hand. It was for my fellow-lodger, a young girl who taught in the High School, and whom I had persuaded to share my room because of her pretty face and quiet ways. She was not at home, and I flung the letter down on the table, where it fell, address downwards. I thought no more of it; my mind was too full, my heart too heavy with my own trouble.

Going to the window, I leaned my cheek against the pane. Oh, the deep sadness of a solitary woman's life! The sense of helplessness that comes upon her when every effort made, every possibility sounded, she realizes that the world has no place for her, and that she must either stoop to ask the assistance of friends or starve! I have no words for the misery I felt, for I am a proud woman, and—But no lifting of the curtain that shrouds my past. It has fallen for ever, and for you and me and the world I am simply Constance Sterling, a young woman of twenty-five, without home, relatives, or means of support, having in her pocket seventy-five cents of change, and in her breast a heart like lead, so utterly had every hope vanished in the day's rush of disappointments.

How long I stood with my face to the window I cannot say. With eyes dully fixed upon the blank walls of the cottages opposite, I stood oblivious to all about me till the fading sunlight—or was it some stir in the room behind me?—recalled me to myself, and I turned to find my pretty room-mate staring at me with a troubled look that for a moment made me forget my own sorrows and anxieties.

"What is it?" I asked, going towards her with an irresistible impulse of sympathy.

"I don't know," she murmured; "a sudden pain here," laying her hand on her heart.

I advanced still nearer, but her face, which had been quite pale, turned suddenly rosy; and, with a more natural expression, she took me by the hand, and said:

"But you look more than ill, you look unhappy. Would you mind telling me what worries you?"

The gentle tone, the earnest glance of modest yet sincere interest, went to my heart. Clutching her hand convulsively, I burst into tears.

"It is nothing," said I; "only my last resource has failed, and I don't know where to get a meal for to-morrow. Not that this is any thing in itself," I hastened to add, my natural pride reasserting itself; "but the future! the future!—what am I to do with my future?"

She did not answer at first. A gleam—I can scarcely call it a glow—passed over her face, and her eyes took a far-away look that made them very sweet. Then a little flush stole into her cheek, and, pressing my hand, she said:

"Will you trust it to me for a while?"

I must have looked my astonishment, for she hastened to add:

"Your future I have little concern for. With such capabilities as yours, you must find work. Why, look at your face!" and she drew me playfully before the glass. "See the forehead, the mouth, and tell me you read failure there! But your present is what is doubtful, and that I can certainly take care of."

"But—" I protested, with a sensation of warmth in my cheeks.

The loveliest smile stopped me before I could utter a word more.

"As you would take care of mine," she completed, "if our positions were reversed." Then, without waiting for a further demur on my part, she kissed me, and as if the sweet embrace had made us sisters at once, drew me to a chair and sat down at my feet. "You know," she naively murmured, "I am almost rich; I have five hundred dollars laid up in the bank, and—"

I put my hand over her lips; I could not help it. She was such a frail little thing, so white and so ethereal, and her poor five hundred had been earned by such weary, weary work.

"But that is nothing, nothing," I said. "You have a future to provide for, too, and you are not as strong as I am, if you have been more successful."

She laughed, then blushed, then laughed again, and impulsively cried:

"It is, however, more than I need to buy a wedding-dress with, don't you think?" And as I looked up surprised, she flashed out: "Oh, it's my secret; but I am going to be married in a month, and—and then I won't need to count my pennies any more; and, so I say, if you will stay here with me without a care until that day comes, you will make me very happy, and put me at the same time under a real obligation; for I shall want a great many things done, as you can readily conceive."

What did I say—what could I say, with her sweet blue eyes looking so truthfully into mine, but—"Oh, you darling girl!" while my heart filled with tears, which only escaped from overflowing my eyes, because I would not lessen her innocent joy by a hint of my own secret trouble.

"And who is the happy man?" I asked, at last, rising to pull down the curtain across a too inquisitive ray of afternoon sunshine.

"Ah, the noblest, best man in town!" she breathed, with a burst of gentle pride. "Mr. B—"

She went no further, or if she did, I did not hear her, for just then a hubbub arose in the street, and lifting the window, I looked out.

"What is it?" she cried, coming hastily towards me.

"I don't know," I returned. "The people are all rushing in one direction, but I cannot see what attracts them."

"Come away then!" she murmured; and I saw her hand go to her heart, in the way it did when she first entered the room a half-hour before. But just then a sudden voice exclaimed below: "The clergyman! It is the clergyman!" And giving a smothered shriek, she grasped me by the arm, crying: "What do they say? '*The clergyman*'? Do they say 'The clergyman'?"

"Yes," I answered, turning upon her with alarm. But she was already at the door. "Can it be?" I asked myself, as I hurriedly followed, "that it is Mr. Barrows she is going to marry?"

For in the small town of S— Mr. Barrows was the only man who could properly be meant by "The clergyman"; for though Mr. Kingston, of the Baptist Church, was a worthy man in his way, and the Congregational minister had an influence with his flock that was not to be despised, Mr. Barrows, alone of all his fraternity, had so won upon the affections and confidence of the people as to merit the appellation of "The clergyman."

"If I am right," thought I, "God grant that no harm has come to him!" and I dashed down the stairs just in time to see the frail form of my room-mate flying out of the front door.

I overtook her at last; but where? Far out of town on that dark and dismal road, where the gaunt chimneys of the deserted mill rise from a growth of pine-trees. But I knew before I reached her what she would find; knew that her short dream of love was over, and that stretched amongst the weeds which choked the entrance to the old mill lay the dead form of the revered young minister, who, by his precept and example, had won not only the heart of this young maiden, but that of the whole community in which he lived and labored.

II

A FEARFUL QUESTION

Nay, yet there's more in this:
I pray thee, speak to me as to thy thinkings,
As thou dost ruminate; and give thy worst of thoughts
The worst of words.

—OTHELLO.

My room-mate was, as I have intimated, exceedingly frail and unobtrusive in appearance; yet when we came upon this scene, the group of men about the inanimate form of her lover parted involuntarily as if a spirit had come upon them; though I do not think one of them, until that moment, had any suspicion of the relations between her and their young pastor. Being close behind her, I pressed forward too, and so it happened that I stood by her side when her gaze first fell upon her dead lover. Never shall I forget the cry she uttered, or the solemn silence that fell over all, as her hand, rigid and white as that of a ghost's, slowly rose and pointed with awful question at the pallid brow upturned before her. It seemed as if a spell had fallen, enchaining the roughest there from answering, for the truth was terrible, and we knew it; else why those dripping locks and heavily soaked garments oozing, not with the limpid waters of the stream we could faintly hear gurgling in the distance, but with some fearful substance that dyed the forehead blue and left upon the grass a dark stain that floods of

Anna Katherine Green

rain would scarcely wash away?

"What is it? Oh, what does it mean?" she faintly gasped, shuddering backward with wondering dread as one of those tiny streams of strange blue moisture found its way to her feet.

Still that ominous silence.

"Oh, I must know!" she whispered. "I was his betrothed"; and her eyes wandered for a moment with a wild appeal upon those about her.

Whereupon a kindly voice spoke up. "He has been drowned, miss. The blue—" and there he hesitated.

"The blue is from the remains of some old dye that must have been in the bottom of the vat out of which we drew him," another voice went on.

"The vat!" she repeated. "The vat! Was he found—"

"In the vat? Yes, miss." And there the silence fell again.

It was no wonder. For a man like him, alert, busy, with no time nor inclination for foolish explorations, to have been found drowned in the disused vat of a half-tumbled-down old mill on a lonesome and neglected road meant—But what did it mean? What could it mean? The lowered eyes of those around seemed to decline to express even a conjecture.

My poor friend, so delicate, so tender, reeled in my arms. "In the vat!" she reiterated again and again, as if her mind refused to take in a fact so astounding and unaccountable.

"Yes, miss, and he might never have been discovered," volunteered a voice at last, over my shoulder, "if a parcel of school-children hadn't strayed into the mill this afternoon. It is a dreadful lonesome spot, you see, and—"

"Hush!" I whispered; "hush!" and I pointed to her face, which at these words had changed as if the breath of death had blown across it; and winding my arms still closer about her, I endeavored to lead her away.

But I did not know my room-mate. Pushing me gently aside, she turned to a stalwart man near by, whose face seemed to invite confidence, and said:

"Take me in and show me the vat."

He looked at her amazed; so did we.

"I must see it," she said, simply; and she herself took the first step towards the mill.

There was no alternative but to follow. This we did in terror and pity, for the look with which she led the way was not the look of any common determination, and the power which seemed to force her feeble body on upon its fearful errand was of that strained and unnatural order which might at any moment desert her, and lay her a weak and helpless burden at our feet.

"It must be dark by this time down there," objected the man she had appealed to, as he stepped doubtfully forward.

But she did not seem to heed. Her eyes were fixed upon the ruined walls before her, rising drear and blank against the pale-green evening sky.

"He could have had no errand here," I heard her murmur. "How then be drowned here?—how? how?"

Alas! that was the mystery, dear heart, with which every mind was busy!

The door of the mill had fallen down and rotted away years before, so we had no difficulty in entering. But upon crossing

Anna Katherine Green

the threshold and making for the steps that led below, we found that the growing twilight was any thing but favorable to a speedy or even safe advance. For the flooring was badly broken in places, and the stairs down which we had to go were not only uneven, but strangely rickety and tottering.

But the sprite that led us paused for nothing, and long before I had passed the first step she had reached the bottom one, and was groping her way towards the single gleam of light that infused itself through the otherwise pitchy darkness.

"Be careful, miss; you may fall into the vat yourself!" exclaimed more than one voice behind her.

But she hurried on, her slight form showing like a spectre against the dim gleam towards which she bent her way, till suddenly she paused and we saw her standing with clasped hands, and bent head, looking down into what? We could readily conjecture.

"She will throw herself in," whispered a voice; but as, profoundly startled, I was about to hasten forward, she hurriedly turned and came towards us.

"I have seen it," she quietly said, and glided by us, and up the stairs, and out of the mill to where that still form lay in its ghostly quietude upon the sodden grass.

For a moment she merely looked at it, then she knelt, and, oblivious to the eyes bent pityingly upon her, kissed the brow and then the cheeks, saying something which I could not hear, but which lent a look of strange peace to her features, that were almost as pallid and set now as his. Then she arose, and holding out her hand to me, was turning away, when a word uttered by some one, I could not tell whom, stopped her, and froze her, as it were, to the spot.

That word was *suicide!*

I think I see her yet, the pale-green twilight on her forehead, her lips parted, and her eyes fixed in an incredulous stare.

"Do you mean," she cried, "that *he* deserves any such name as that? That his death here was not one of chance or accident, mysterious, if you will, but still one that leaves no stigma on his name as a man and a clergyman?"

"Indeed, miss," came in reply, "we would not like to say."

"Then, *I* say, that unless Mr. Barrows was insane, he never premeditated a crime of this nature. He was too much of a Christian. And if that does not strike you as good reasoning, he was too— happy."

The last word was uttered so low that if it had not been for the faint flush that flitted into her cheek, it would scarcely have been understood. As it was, the furtive looks of the men about showed that they comprehended all that she would say; and, satisfied with the impression made, she laid her hand on my arm, and for the second time turned towards home.

III

ADA

For, in my sense, 't is happiness to die.

—OTHELLO.

There was death in her face; I saw it the moment we reached the refuge of our room. But I was scarcely prepared for the words which she said to me.

"Mr. Barrows and I will be buried in one grave. The waters which drowned him have gone over my head also. But before the moment comes which proves my words true, there is one thing I wish to impress upon you, and that is: That no matter what people may say, or what conjectures they may indulge in, Mr. Barrows never came to his end by any premeditation of his own. And that you may believe me, and uphold his cause in the face of whatever may arise, I will tell you something of his life and mine. Will you listen?"

Would I listen? I could not speak, but I drew up the lounge, and sitting down by her side, pressed my cheek close to hers. She smiled faintly, all unhappiness gone from her look, and in sweet, soft tones, began:

"We are both orphans. As far as I know, neither of us have any nearer relatives than distant cousins; a similarity of condition that has acted as a bond between us since we first knew and loved each other. When I came to S— he was just settled here, a young man full of zeal and courage. Whatever the experience of his college days had been—and he has often told me that at that time ambition was the mainspring of his existence,—the respect and appreciation which he found here, and the field which daily opened before him for work, had wakened a spirit of earnest trust that erelong developed that latent sweetness in his disposition which more than his mental qualities, perhaps, won him universal confidence and love.

"You have heard him preach, and you know he was not lacking in genius; but you have not heard him speak, eye to eye and hand to hand. It was there his power came in, and there, too, perhaps, his greatest temptation. For he was one for women to love, and it is not always easy to modify a naturally magnetic look and tone because the hand that touches yours is shy and white, and the glance which steals up to meet your own has within it the hint of unconscious worship. Yet what he could do he did; for, unknown, perhaps, to any one here, he was engaged to be married, as so many young ministers are, to a girl he had met while at college.

"I do not mean to go into too many particulars, Constance. He did not love this girl, but he meant to be true to her. He was even contented with the prospect of marrying her, till— Oh, Constance, I almost forget that he is gone, and that my own life is at an end, when I think of that day, six months ago—the day when we first met, and, without knowing it, first loved. And then the weeks which followed when each look was an event, and a passing word the making or the marring of a day. I did not know what it all meant; but he realized only too soon the precipice upon which we stood, and I began to see him less, and find him more reserved when, by any chance, we were thrown together. His cheek grew paler, too, and his health wavered. A struggle was going on in his breast—a struggle of whose depth and force I had little conception then, for I dared not believe he loved me, though I knew by this time he was bound to another who would never be a suitable companion for him.

"At last he became so ill, he was obliged to quit his work, and for a month I did not see him, though only a short square separated us. He was slowly yielding to an insidious disease, some said; and I had to bear the pain of this uncertainty, as well as the secret agony of my own crushed and broken heart.

"But one morning—shall I ever forget it?—the door opened, and he, *he* came in where I was, and without saying a word, knelt down by my side, and drew my head forward and laid it on his breast. I thought at first it was a farewell, and trembled with a secret anguish that was yet strangely blissful, for did not the passionate constraint of his arms mean love? But when, after a moment that seemed a lifetime, I drew back and looked into his face, I saw it was not a farewell, but a greeting, he had brought me, and that we had not only got our pastor back to life, but that this pastor was a lover as well, who would marry the woman he loved.

"And I was right. In ten minutes I knew, that a sudden freak on the part of the girl he was engaged to had released him, without fault of his own, and that with this release new life had entered his veins, for the conflict was over and love and duty were now in harmony."

"Constance, I would not have you think he was an absolutely perfect man. He was too sensitively organized for that. A touch, a look that was not in harmony with his thoughts, would make him turn pale at times, and I have seen him put to such suffering by petty physical causes, that I have sometimes wondered where his great soul got its strength to carry him through the exigencies of his somewhat trying calling. But whatever his weaknesses—and they were very few,—he was conscientious in the extreme, and suffered agony where other men would be affected but slightly. You can imagine his joy, then, over this unexpected end to his long pain; and remembering that it is only a month previous to the day set apart by us for our marriage, ask yourself whether he would be likely to seek any means of death, let alone such a horrible and lonesome one as that which has robbed us of him to-day?"

"No!" I burst out, for she waited for my reply. "A thousand times, no, no, no!"

"He has not been so well lately, and I have not seen as much of him as usual; but that is because he had some literary work he wished to finish before the wedding-day. Ah, it will never be finished now! and our wedding-day is to-day! and the bride is almost ready. But!" she suddenly exclaimed, "I must not go yet—not till you have said again that he was no suicide. Tell me," she vehemently continued—"tell me from your soul that you believe he is not answerable for his death!"

"I do!" I rejoined, alarmed and touched at once by the fire in her cheek and eye.

"And that," she went, "you will hold to this opinion in the face of all opposition! That, whatever attack men may make upon his memory, you will uphold his honor and declare his innocence! Say you will be my deputy in this, and I will love you even in my cold grave, and bless you as perhaps only those who see the face of the Father can bless!"

"Ada!" I murmured, "Ada!"

"You will do this, will you not?" she persisted. "I can die knowing I can trust you as I would myself."

I took her cold hand in mine and promised, though I felt how feeble would be any power of mine to stop the tide of public opinion if once it set in any definite direction.

"He had no enemies," she whispered; "but I would sooner believe he had, than that he sought this fearful spot of his own accord."

And seemingly satisfied to have dropped this seed in my breast, she tremblingly arose, and going for her writing-desk, brought it back and laid it on the lounge by her side. "Go for Mrs. Gannon," she said.

Mrs. Gannon was our neighbor in the next room, a widow who earned her livelihood by nursing the sick; and I was only too glad to have her with me at this time, for my poor Ada's face was growing more and more deathly, and I began to fear she had but prophesied the truth when she said this was her wedding-day.

I was detained only a few minutes, but when I came back with Mrs. Gannon, I found my room-mate writing.

"Come!" said she, in a voice so calm, my companion started and hastily looked at her face for confirmation of the fears I had expressed; "I want you both to witness my signature."

With one last effort of strength she wrote her name, and then handed the pen to Mrs. Gannon, who took it without a word.

"It is my will," she faintly smiled, watching me as I added my name at the bottom. "We have had to do without lawyers, but I don't think there will be any one to dispute my last wishes." And taking the paper in her hand, she glanced hastily at it, then folded it, and handed it back to me with a look that made my heart leap with uncontrollable emotion. "I can trust you," she said, and fell softly back upon the pillow.

"You had better go for Dr. Farnham," whispered Mrs. Gannon in my ear, with an ominous shake of her head.

And though I felt it to be futile, I hastened to comply.

But Dr. Farnham was out, attending to a very urgent case, I was told; and so, to my growing astonishment and dismay, were Dr. Spaulding and Dr. Perry. I was therefore obliged to come back alone, which I did with what speed I could; for I begrudged every moment spent away from the side of one I had so lately learned to love, and must so soon lose.

Mrs. Gannon met me at the door, and with a strange look, drew me in and pointed towards the bed. There lay Ada, white as the driven snow, with closed eyes, whose faintly trembling lids alone betokened that she was not yet fled to the land of quiet shadows. At her side was a picture of the man she loved, and on her breast lay a bunch of withered roses I could easily believe had been his last gift. It was a vision of perfect peace, and I could not but contrast it with what my imagination told me must have been the frenzied anguish of that other death.

My approach, though light, disturbed her. Opening her eyes, she gave me one long, long look. Then, as if satisfied, she softly closed them again, breathed a little sigh, and in another moment was no more.

Anna Katherine Green

IV

THE POLLARDS

There's something in his soul,
O'er which his melancholy sits on brood.

—HAMLET.

Fearful as the experiences of this day had been, they were not yet at an end for me. Indeed, the most remarkable were to come. As I sat in this room of death—it was not far from midnight—I suddenly heard voices at the door, and Mrs. Gannon came in with Dr. Farnham.

"It is very extraordinary," I heard him mutter as he crossed the threshold. "One dying and another dead, and both struck down by the same cause."

I could not imagine what he mean, so I looked at him with some amazement. But he did not seem to heed me. Going straight to the bed, he gazed silently at Ada's pure features, with what I could not but consider a troubled glance. Then turning quickly to Mrs. Gannon, he said, in his somewhat brusque way:

"All is over here; you can therefore leave. I have a patient who demands your instant care."

"But—" she began.

"I have come on purpose for you," he put in, authoritatively. "It is an urgent case; do not keep me waiting."

"But, sir," she persisted, "it is impossible. I am expected early in the morning at Scott's Corners, and was just going to bed when you came in, in order to get a little sleep before taking the train."

"Dr. Perry's case?"

"Yes."

He frowned, and I am not sure but what he uttered a mild oath. At all events, he seemed very much put out.

I immediately drew near.

"Oh, sir," I cried, "if you would have confidence in me. I am not unused to the work, and—"

His stare frightened me, it was so searching and so keen.

"Who are you?" he asked.

I told him, and Mrs. Gannon put in a word for me. I was reliable, she said, and if too much experience was not wanted, would do better than such and such a one—naming certain persons, probably neighbors.

But the doctor's steady look told me he relied more on his own judgment than on anything she or I could say.

"Can you hold your tongue?" he asked.

I started. Who would not have done so?

"I see that you can," he muttered, and glanced down at my

dress. "When can you be ready?" he inquired. "You may be wanted for days, and it may be only for hours."

"Will ten minutes be soon enough?" I asked.

A smile difficult to fathom crossed his firm lip.

"I will give you fifteen," he said, and turned towards the door. But on the threshold he paused and looked back. "You have not asked who or what your patient is," he grimly suggested.

"No," I answered shortly.

"Well," said he, "it is Mrs. Pollard, and she is going to die."

Mrs. Pollard! Mrs. Gannon and I involuntarily turned and looked at each other.

"Mrs. Pollard!" repeated the good nurse, wonderingly. "I did not know she was sick"

"She wasn't this noon. It is a sudden attack. Apoplexy we call it. She fell at the news of Mr. Barrows' death."

And with this parting shot, he went out and closed the door behind him.

I sank, just a little bit weakened, on the lounge, then rose with renewed vigor. "The work has fallen into the right hands," thought I. "Ada would wish me to leave her for such a task as this."

And yet I was troubled. For though this sudden prostration of Mrs. Pollard, on the hearing of her young pastor's sorrowful death, seemed to betoken a nature of more than ordinary sensibility, I had always heard that she was a hard woman, with an eye of steel and a heart that could only be reached through selfish interests. But then she was the magnate of the place, the beginning and end of the aristocracy of S—; and when is not such a one open to calumny? I was determined to reserve my judgment.

In the fifteen minutes allotted me, I was ready. Suitable arrangements had already been made for the removal of my poor Ada's body to the house that held her lover. For the pathos of the situation had touched all hearts, and her wish to be laid in the same grave with him met with no opposition. I could therefore leave with a clear conscience; Mrs. Gannon promising to do all that was necessary, even if she were obliged to take a later train than she had expected to.

Dr. Farnham was in the parlor waiting for me, and uttered a grunt of satisfaction as he saw me enter, fully equipped.

"Come; this is business," he said, and led the way at once to his carriage.

We did not speak for the first block. He seemed meditating, and I was summoning up courage for the ordeal before me. For, now that we were started, I began to feel a certain inward trembling not to be entirely accounted for by the fact that I was going into a strange house to nurse a woman of whom report did not speak any too kindly. Nor did the lateness of the hour, and the desolate aspect of the unlighted streets, tend greatly to reassure me.

Indeed, something of the weird and uncanny seemed to mingle with the whole situation, and I found myself dreading our approach to the house, which from its old-time air and secluded position had always worn for me an aspect of gloomy reserve, that made it even in the daylight, a spot of somewhat fearful interest.

Dr. Farnham, who may have suspected my agitation, though he gave no token of doing so, suddenly spoke up.

"It is only right to tell you," he said, "that I should never have accepted the service of an inexperienced girl like you, if any thing was necessary but watchfulness and discretion. Mrs. Pollard lies unconscious, and all you will have to do is to sit at her side and wait for the first dawning of returning reason. It may come at any moment, and it may never come at all. She is a very sick woman."

"I understand," I murmured, plucking up heart at what did not seem so very difficult a task.

"Her sons will be within call; so will I. By daybreak we hope to have her daughter from Newport with her. You do not know Mrs. Harrington?"

I shook my head. Who was I, that I should know these grand folks? And yet—But I promised I would say nothing about days now so completely obliterated.

"She will not be much of an assistance," he muttered. "But it is right she should come—quite right."

I remembered that I had heard that Mrs. Pollard's daughter was a beauty, and that she had made a fine match; which, said of Mrs. Pollard's daughter, must have meant a great deal. I, however, said nothing, only listened in a vague hope of hearing more, for my curiosity was aroused in a strange way about these people, and nothing which the good doctor could have said about them would have come amiss at this time.

But our drive had been too rapid, and we were too near the house for him to think of any thing but turning into the gateway with the necessary caution. For the night was unusually dark, and it was difficult to tell just where the gate-posts were. We, however, entered without accident, and in another moment a gleam of light greeted us from the distant porch.

"They are expecting us," he said, and touched up his horse. We flew up the gravelled road, and before I could still the sudden heart- beat that attacked me at sight of the grim row of cedars which surrounded the house, we were hurrying up between the two huge lions rampant that flanked the steps, to where a servant stood holding open the door. A sense of gloom and chill at once overwhelmed me. From the interior, which I faintly saw stretching before me, there breathed even in that first moment of hurried entrance a cold and haughty grandeur that, however rich and awe-inspiring, was any thing but attractive to a nature like mine.

Drawing back, I let Dr. Farnham take the lead, which he did in his own brusque way. And then I saw what the dim light had not revealed before, a young man's form standing by the newel-post of the wide staircase that rose at our left. He at once came forward, and as the light from the lamp above us fell fully upon him, I saw his face, and started.

Why? I could not tell. Not because his handsome features struck me pleasantly, for they did not. There was something in their expression which I did not like, and yet as I looked at them a sudden sensation swept over me that made my apprehensions of a moment back seem like child's play, and I became conscious that if a sudden call of life or death were behind me urging me on the instant to quit the house, I could not do it while that face was before me to be fathomed, and, if possible, understood.

"Ah, I see you have brought the nurse," were the words with which he greeted Dr. Farnham. And the voice was as thrilling in its tone as the face was in its expression. "But," he suddenly exclaimed, as his eyes met mine, "this is not Mrs. Gannon." And he hurriedly drew the doctor down the hall. "Why have you brought this young girl?" he asked, in tones which, however lowered, I could easily distinguish. "Didn't you know there were reasons why we especially wanted an elderly person?"

"No," I heard the doctor say, and then, his back being towards me, I lost the rest of his speech till the words, "She is no gossip," came to salute me and make me ask myself if there was a secret skeleton in this house, that they feared so much the eyes of a stranger.

"But," the young man went hurriedly on, "she is not at all the kind of person to have over my mother. How could we—" and there his voice fell so as to become unintelligible.

But the doctor's sudden exclamation helped me out.

"What!" he wonderingly cried, "do you intend to sit up too?"

"I or my brother," was the calm response, "Would you expect us to leave her alone with a stranger?"

The doctor made no answer, and the young man, taking a step sidewise, threw me a glance full of anxiety and trouble.

"I don't like it," he murmured; "but there must be a woman of some kind in the room, and a stranger—"

He did not finish his words, but it seemed as if he were going to say: "And a stranger may, after all, be preferable to a neighbor." But I cannot be sure of this, for he was not a man easy to sound. But what I do know is that he stepped forward, to me with an easy grace, and giving me a welcome as courteous as if I had been the one of all others he desired to see, led me up the stairs to a room which he announced to be mine, saying, as he left me at the door:

"Come out in five minutes, and my brother will introduce you to your duties."

So far I had seen no woman in the house, and I was beginning to wonder if Mrs. Pollard had preferred to surround herself with males, when the door was suddenly opened and a rosy-cheeked girl stepped in.

"Ah, excuse me," she said, with a stare; "I thought it was the nurse as was here."

"And it is the nurse," I returned, smiling in spite of myself at her look of indignant surprise. "Do you want any thing of me?" I hastened to ask, for her eyes were like saucers and her head was tossing airily.

"No," she said, almost with spite. "I came to see if you wanted any thing?"

I shook my head with what good nature I could, for I did not wish to make an enemy in this house, even of a chambermaid.

"And you are really the nurse?" she asked, coming nearer and looking at me in the full glare of the gas.

"Yes," I assured her, "really and truly the nurse."

"Well, I don't understand it!" she cried. "I was always Mrs. Pollard's favorite maid, and I was with her when she was took, and would be with her now, but they won't let me set a foot inside the door. And when I asked why they keep me out, who was always attentive and good to her, they say I am too young. And here you be younger than I, and a stranger too. I don't like it," she cried, tossing her head again and again. "I haven't deserved it, and I think it is mighty mean."

I saw the girl was really hurt, so I hastened to explain that I was not the nurse they expected, and was succeeding, I think, in mollifying her, when a step was heard in the hall, and she gave a frightened start, and hurried towards the door.

"So you are sure you don't want anything?" she cried, and was out of my sight before I could answer.

There was nothing to detain me, and I hastened to follow. As I crossed the sill I almost started too, at sight of the tall, slim, truly sinister figure that awaited me, leaning against the opposite wall. He was younger than his brother, and had similar features, but there was no charm here to make you forget that the eye was darkly glittering, and the lip formidable in its subtlety and power. He advanced with much of the easy nonchalance that had so characterized the other.

"Miss Sterling, I believe," said he; and with no further word, turned and led me down the hall to the sick-room. I noticed even then that he paused and listened before he pushed open the door, and that with our first step inside he cast a look of inquiry at the bed that had something beside a son's loving anxiety in it. And I hated the man as I would a serpent, though he bowed as he set me a chair, and was careful to move a light he thought shone a little too directly in my eyes.

The other brother was not present, and I could give my undivided attention to my charge. I found her what report had proclaimed her to be, a handsome woman of the sternly imposing type. Even with her age against her and the shadow of death lying on her brow and cheek, there was something strangely attractive in the features and the stately contour of her form. But it was attraction that was confined to the eye, and could by no means allure the heart, for the same seal of mysterious reserve was upon her that characterized her sons, and in her, as in the younger one of these, it inspired a distrust which I could imagine no smile as dissipating. She lay in a state of coma, and her heavy breathing was the only sound that broke the silence of the great room. "God help me!" thought I; but had no wish to leave. Instead of that, I felt a fearful pleasure in the prospect before me—such effect had a single look had upon me from eyes I trembled to meet again or read.

I do not know how long I sat there gazing in the one direction for that faint sign of life for which the doctor had bid me watch. That he who inspired me with dread was behind me, I knew; but I would not turn my head towards him. I was determined to resist the power of this man, even if I must succumb a trifle to that of the other.

I was, therefore, surprised when a hand was thrust over my shoulder, and a fan dropped into my lap.

"It is warm here," was the comment which accompanied the action.

I thanked him, but felt that his sole object had been to cover his change of position. For, when he sat down again, it was where he could see my face. I therefore felt justified in plying the fan he had offered me, in such a way as to shut off his somewhat basilisk gaze. And so a dreary hour went by.

It was now well on towards morning, and I was beginning to suffer from the languor natural after so many harrowing excitements, when the door opened behind me, and the electric thrill shooting through all my members, testified as to whose step it was that entered. At the same moment the young man at my side arose, and with what I felt to be a last sharp look in my direction, hastened to where his brother stood, and entered into a whispered conversation with him. Then I heard the door close again, and almost at the same instant Mr. Pollard the elder advanced, and without seeking an excuse for his action, sat down close by my side. The fan at once dropped; I had no wish to avoid this man's scrutiny.

And yet when with a secret bracing of my nerves I looked up and met his eyes fixed with that baffling expression upon mine, I own that I felt an inward alarm, as if something vaguely dangerous had reared itself in my path, which by its very charm instinctively bade me beware. I, however, subdued my apprehensions, thinking, with a certain haughty pride which I fear will never be eliminated from my nature, of the dangers I had already met with and overcome in my brief but troubled life; and meeting his look with a smile which I knew to contain a spice of audacity, I calmly waited for the words I felt to be hovering upon his lips. They were scarcely the ones I expected.

"Miss Sterling," said he, "you have seen Anice, my mother's waiting-maid?"

I bowed. I was too much disconcerted to speak.

"And she has told you her story of my mother's illness?" he went on, pitilessly holding me with his glance. "You need not answer," he again proceeded, as I opened my lips. "I know Anice; she has not the gift of keeping her thoughts to herself."

"An unfortunate thing in this house," I inwardly commented, and made a determination on the spot that whatever emotions I might experience from the mysteries surrounding me, this master of reserve should find there was one who could keep her thoughts to herself, even, perhaps, to his own secret disappointment and chagrin.

"She told you my mother was stricken at the sudden news of Mr. Barrows' death?"

"That was told me," I answered; for this was a direct question, put, too, with an effort I could not help but feel, notwithstanding the evident wish on his part to preserve an appearance of calmness.

"Then some explanation is needed," he remarked, his eyes flashing from his mother's face to mine with equal force and intentness. "My mother"—his words were low, but it was impossible not to hear them—"has not been well since my father died, two months ago. It needed but the slightest shock to produce the result you unhappily see before you. That shock this very girl supplied by the inconsiderate relation of Mr. Barrows' fearful fate. We have taken a prejudice against the girl, in consequence. Do you blame us? This is our mother."

What could I feel or say but No? What could any one, under the circumstances? Why then did a sudden vision of Ada's face, as she gave me that last look, rise up before me, bidding me remember the cause to which I was pledged, and not put too much faith in this man and his plausible explanations.

"I only hope death will not follow the frightful occurrence," he concluded; and do what he would, his features became drawn, and his face white, as his looks wandered back to his mother.

A sudden impulse seized me.

"Another death, you mean," said I; "one already has marked the event, though it happened only a few short hours ago."

His eyes flashed to mine, and a very vivid and real horror blanched his already pallid cheek till it looked blue in the dim light.

"What do you mean?" he gasped; and I saw the doctor had refrained from telling him of Ada's pitiful doom.

"I mean," said I, with a secret compunction I strove in vain to subdue, "that Mr. Barrows' betrothed could not survive his terrible fate—that she died a few hours since, and will be buried in the same grave as her lover."

"His betrothed?" Young Mr. Pollard had risen to his feet, and was actually staggering under the shock of his emotions. "I did not know he had any betrothed. I thought she had jilted him—"

"It is another woman," I broke in, jealous for my poor dead Ada's fame. "The woman he was formerly engaged to never loved him; but this one—" I could not finish the sentence. My own agitation was beginning to master me.

He looked at me, horrified, and I could have sworn the hair rose on his forehead.

"What was her name?" he asked. "Is it—is it any one I know?" Then, as if suddenly conscious that he was betraying too keen an emotion for the occasion, pitiful as it was, he forced his lips into a steadier curve, and quietly said: "After what has happened here, I am naturally overcome by a circumstance so coincident with our own trouble."

"Naturally," I assented with a bow, and again felt that secret distrust warring with a new feeling that was not unlike compassion.

"Her name is Ada Reynolds," I continued, remembering his last question. "She lived—"

"I know," he interrupted; and without another word walked away, and for a long time stood silent at the other end of the room. Then he came back and sat down, and when I summoned up courage to glance at his face, I saw that a change had passed over it, that in all probability was a change for life.

And my heart sank—sank till I almost envied that unconscious form before which we sat, and from which alone now came the one sound which disturbed the ghostly silence of that dread chamber.

V

DOUBTS AND QUERIES

And that well might
Advise him to a caution, to hold what distance
His wisdom can provide.

—MACBETH.

At daybreak the doctor came in. Taking advantage of the occasion, I slipped away for a few minutes to my own room, anxious for any change that would relieve me from the gloom and oppression caused by this prolonged and silent *tete-a-tete* with a being that at once so interested and repelled me. Observing that my windows looked towards the east, I hastened to throw wide the blinds and lean out into the open air. A burst of rosy sunlight greeted me. "Ah!" thought I, "if I have been indulging in visions, this will dispel them"; and I quaffed deeply and long of the fresh and glowing atmosphere before allowing my thoughts to return for an instant to the strange and harrowing experiences I had just been through. A sense of rising courage and renewed power rewarded me; and blessing the Providence that had granted us a morning of sunshine after a night of so much horror, I sat down and drew from my breast the little folded paper which represented my poor Ada's will. Opening it with all the reverent love which I felt for her memory, I set myself to decipher the few trembling lines which she had written, in the hope they would steady my thoughts and suggest, if not reveal, the way I should take in the more than difficult path I saw stretching before me.

My agitation may be conceived when I read the following:

"It is my last wish that all my personal effects, together with the sum of five hundred dollars, now credited to my name in the First National Bank of S—, should be given to my friend, Constance Sterling, who I hope will not forget the promise I exacted from her."

Five hundred dollars! and yesterday I had nothing. Ah, yes, I had *a friend!*

The thoughts awakened by this touching memorial from the innocent dead distracted me for a few moments from further consideration of present difficulties, but soon the very nature of the bequest recalled them to my mind, by that allusion to a promise which more than any thing else lay at the bottom of the dilemma in which I found myself. For, humiliating as it is to confess, the persistency with which certain impressions remained in my mind, in spite of the glowing daylight that now surrounded me, warned me that it would be for my peace to leave this house before my presentiments became fearful realities; while on the other hand my promise to Ada seemed to constrain me to remain in it till I had at least solved some of those mysteries of emotion which connected one and all of this family so intimately with the cause to which I had pledged myself.

"If the general verdict in regard to Mr. Barrows' death should be one of suicide," thought I, "how could I reconcile myself to the fact that I fled at the first approaching intimation that all was not as simple in his relations as was supposed, and that somewhere, somehow, in the breast of certain parishioners of his, a secret lay hidden, which, if known, would explain the act which otherwise must imprint an ineffaceable stain upon his memory?"

My heart and brain were still busy with this question when the sound of Mr. Pollard's footsteps passing my door recalled me to a sense of my present duty. Rising, I hurried across the hall to the sick- chamber, and was just upon the point of entering, when the doctor appeared before me, and seeing me, motioned me back, saying:

"Mrs. Harrington has just arrived. As she will doubtless wish to see her mother at once, you had better wait a few moments till the first agitation is over."

Glad of any respite, and particularly glad to escape an introduction to Mrs. Harrington at this time, I slipped hastily away, but had not succeeded in reaching my room before the two brothers and their sister appeared at the top of the stairs. I had thus a full opportunity of observing them, and being naturally quick to gather impressions, took in with a glance the one member of the Pollard family who was likely to have no mystery about her.

I found her pretty; prettier, perhaps, than any woman it had ever been my lot to meet before, but with a doll's prettiness that bespoke but little dignity or force of mind. Dressed with faultless taste and with an attention to detail that at a moment like the present struck one with a sense of painful incongruity, she advanced, a breathing image of fashion and perhaps folly; her rustling robes, and fresh, if troubled face, offering a most striking contrast to the gloom and reserve of the two sombre figures that walked at her side.

Knowing as by instinct that nothing but humiliation would follow any obtrusion of myself upon this petted darling of fortune, I withdrew as much as possible into the shadow, receiving for my reward a short look from both the brothers; the one politely deprecating in its saturnine courtesy, the other full of a bitter demand for what I in my selfish egotism was fain to consider sympathy. The last look did not tend to calm my already disturbed thoughts, and, anxious to efface its impression, I impulsively descended the stairs and strolled out on the lawn, asking myself what was meant by the difference in manner which I had discerned in these two brothers towards their sister. For while the whole bearing of the younger had expressed interest in this pretty, careless butterfly of a woman thus brought suddenly face to face with a grave trouble, the elder had only averted looks to offer, and an arm that seemed to shrink at her touch as if the weight of her light hand on his was almost more than he could bear. Could it be that affection and generosity were on the side of the younger after all, and that in this respect, at least, he was the truer man and more considerate brother?

I could find no more satisfactory answer for this question than for the many others that had suggested themselves since I had been in this house; and being determined not to allow myself to fall into a reverie which at this moment might be dangerous, I gave up consideration of all kinds, and yielded myself wholly to the pleasure of my ramble. And it was a pleasure! For however solemn and austere might be the interior of the Pollard mansion, without here on the lawn all was cheeriness, bloom, and verdure; the grim row of cedars encircling the house seeming to act as a barrier beyond which its gloom and secrecy could not pass. At all events such was the impression given to my excited fancy at the time, and, filled with the sense of freedom which this momentary escape from the house and its influences had caused, I hastened to enjoy the beauties of walk and *parterre*, stopping only when some fairer blossom than ordinary lured me from my path to inspect its loveliness or inhale its perfume.

The grounds were not large, though, situated as they were in the midst of a thickly populated district, they appeared so. It did not, therefore, take me long to exhaust their attractions, and I was about to return upon my course, when I espied a little summer-house before me, thickly shrouded in vines. Thinking what a charming retreat it offered, I stepped forward to observe it more closely, when to my great surprise I saw it was already occupied, and by a person whose attitude and appearance were such as to at once arouse my strongest curiosity. This person was a boy, slight of build, and fantastic in his dress, with a face like sculptured marble, and an eye which, if a little contracted, had a strange glitter in it that made you look and look again. He was kneeling on the floor of the summer-house, and his face, seen by me in profile, was turned with the fixedness of an extreme absorption towards a small opening in the vines, through which he was intently peering. What he saw or wished to see I could not imagine, for nothing but the blank end of the house lay before him, and there could be very little which was interesting in that, for not one of its windows were open, unless you except the solitary one in my room. His expression, however, showed that he was engaged in watching something, and by the corrugation in his white brow and the peculiar compression of his fresh red lip, that something showed itself to be of great importance to him; a fact striking enough in itself if you consider the earliness of the hour and the apparent immaturity of his age, which did not appear to be more than fourteen.

Resolved to solve this simple mystery, I gave an admonitory cough, and stepped into the summer-house. He at once started to his feet, and faced me with a look I am pondering upon yet, there was so much in it that was wrathful, curious, dismayed, and defiant. The next moment a veil seemed to fall over his vision, the rich red lip relaxed from its expressive curve, and from being one of the most startling visions I ever saw, he became—what? It would be hard to tell, only not a fully responsible being, I am sure, however near he had just strayed to the border-land of judgment and good sense. Relieved, I scarcely knew why, and remembering almost at the same instant some passing gossip I had once heard about the pretty imbecile boy that ran the streets of S—, I gave him a cheerful smile, and was about to bestow some encouraging word upon him, when he suddenly broke into a laugh, and looking at me with a meaningless stare, asked:

"Who are you?"

I was willing enough to answer, so I returned: "I am Constance

Sterling"; and almost immediately added: "And who are you?"

"I am the cat that mews in the well." Then suddenly, "Do you live here?"

"No," I replied, "I am only staying here. Mrs. Pollard is sick—"

"Do they like you?"

The interruption was quick, like all his speech, and caused me a curious sensation. But I conquered it with a laugh, and cheerily replied:

"As I only came last night, it would be hard to say"—and was going to add more, when the curious being broke out:

"She only came last night!" and, repeating the phrase again and again, suddenly darted from my side on to the lawn, where he stood for an instant, murmuring and laughing to himself before speeding away through the shrubbery that led to the gate.

This incident, trivial as it seemed, made a vivid impression upon me, and it was with a mind really calmed from its past agitation that I re-entered the house and took up my watch in the sick-room. I found every thing as I had left it an hour or so before, with the exception of my companion; the younger Mr. Pollard having taken the place of his brother. Mrs. Harrington was nowhere to be seen, but as breakfast had been announced I did not wonder at this, nor at the absence of the elder son, who was doubtless engaged in doing the honors of the house.

My own call to breakfast came sooner than I anticipated; soon enough, indeed, for me to expect to find Mr. Pollard and his sister still at the table. It therefore took some courage for me to respond to the summons, especially as I had to go alone, my companion, of course, refusing to leave his mother. But a glance in the hall-mirror, as I went by, encouraged me, for it was no weak woman's face I encountered, and if Mrs. Harrington was as beautiful as she was haughty, and as haughty as she was beautiful, Constance Sterling at least asked no favors and showed no embarrassment. Indeed, I had never felt more myself than when I lifted the *portiere* from before the dining-room door and stepped in under the gaze of these two contradictory beings, either of which exerted an influence calculated to overawe a person in my position. The past—But what have I promised myself and you? Not the past, then, but my present will and determination made the ordeal easy.

Mr. Pollard, who is certainly a man to attract any woman's eye, rose gravely as I approached, and presented me with what struck me as a somewhat emphasized respect, to his sister. Her greeting was nothing more nor less than what I expected—that is, indifferently civil,—though I thought I detected a little glimmer of curiosity in the corner of her eye, as if some words had passed in regard to me that made her anxious to know what sort of a woman I was.

But my faculty for observation was very wide-awake that morning, and I may have imagined this, especially as she did not look at me again till she had finished her breakfast and rose to quit the room. Then, indeed, she threw me a hurried glance, half searching, half doubtful in its character, as if she hesitated whether she ought to leave us alone together. Instantly a wild thrill passed through me, and I came perilously near blushing. But the momentary emotion, if emotion it could be called, was soon lost in the deeper feeling which ensued when Mrs. Harrington, pausing at the door, observed, with a forced lightness:

"By-the-way, where is Mr. Barrows? I thought he was always on hand in time of trouble."

I looked at her; somehow, I dared not look at her brother; and, while making to myself such trivial observations as, "She has not been told the truth," and, "They took good care she should overhear no gossip at the station," I was inwardly agitating myself with the new thought, "Can *she* have had any thing to do with Mr. Barrows? Can she be the woman he was engaged to before he fell in love with Ada?"

The expression of her face, turned though

It was full upon us, told nothing, and my attention, though not my glances, passed to Mr. Pollard, who, motionless in his place, hesitated what reply to give to this simple question.

"Guy has not told you, then," said he, "what caused the shock that has prostrated our mother?"

"No," she returned, coming quickly back.

"It was the news of Mr. Barrows' death, Agnes; the servants say so, and the servants ought to know."

"Mr. Barrows' death! Is Mr. Barrows dead, then?" she asked, in a tone of simple wonder, which convinced me that my surmise of a moment ago was without any foundation. "I did not know he was sick," she went on. "Was his death sudden, that it should affect mother so?"

A short nod was all her brother seemed to be able to give to this question. At sight of it I felt the cold chills run through my veins, and wished that fate had not obliged me to be present at this conversation.

"How did Mr. Barrows die?" queried Mrs. Harrington, after waiting in manifest surprise and impatience for her brother to speak.

"He was drowned."

"Drowned?"

"Yes."

"When?"

"Yesterday."

"Where?"

This time the answer was not forthcoming. Was it because he knew the place too well? I dared not lift my eyes to see.

"Was it in the mill-stream?" she asked.

This time he uttered a hollow "No." Then, as if he felt himself too weak to submit to this cross-questioning, he pushed back his chair, and, hurriedly rising, said:

"It is a very shocking affair, Agnes. Mr. Barrows was found in a vat in the cellar of the old mill. He drowned *himself.* No one knows his motive."

"Drowned *himself?*" Did she speak or I? I saw her lips move, and I heard the words uttered as I thought in her voice; but it was to me he directed his look, and to me he seemed to reply:

"Yes; how else account for the circumstances? Is he a man to have enemies?—or is that a place a man would be likely to seek for pleasure?"

"But—" the trembling little woman at my side began.

"I say it is a suicide," he broke in, imperiously, giving his sister one look, and then settling his eyes back again upon my face. "No other explanation fits the case, and no other explanation will ever be given. Why he should have committed such a deed," he went on, in a changed voice, and after a momentary pause, "it would be impossible for me, and perhaps for any other man, to say; but that he did do it is evident, and that is all I mean to assert. The rest I leave for wiser heads than mine." And turning from me with an indescribable look that to my reason, if not to my head, seemed to belie his words, he offered his arm to his bewildered sister and quietly led her towards the door.

The breath of relief I gave as the *portiere* closed behind them was, however, premature, for scarcely had he seen her on her way upstairs than he came back, and taking his stand directly before me, said:

"You and I do not agree on this question; I see it in your eyes. Now what explanation do you give of Mr. Barrows' death?"

The suddenness of the attack brought the blood to my cheeks, while the necessity of answering drove it as quickly away. He saw I was agitated, and a slight tremble—it could not be called a smile—disturbed the set contour of his lips. The sight of it gave me courage. I let my own curl as I replied:

"You do me too much honor to ask my opinion. But since you wish to know what I think, I consider it only justice to say that it would be easier for an unprejudiced mind to believe that Mr. Barrows had a secret enemy, or that his death was owing to some peculiar and perhaps unexplainable accident, than that he should seek it himself, having, as he did, every reason for living."

"He was very happy, then?" murmured my companion, looking for an instant away, as if he could not bear the intensity of my gaze.

"He loved deeply a noble woman; they were to have been married in a month; does that look like happiness?" I asked.

The roving eye came back, fixed itself upon me, and turned dangerously dark and deep.

"It *looks* like it," he emphasized, and a strange smile passed over his lips, the utter melancholy of which was all that was plain to me.

"And it *was!*" I persisted, determined not to yield an iota of my convictions to the persuasiveness of this man. "The woman who knew him best declared it to be so as she was dying; and I am forced to trust in her judgment, whatever the opinion of others may be."

"But happy men——" he began.

"Sometimes meet with accidents," I completed.

"And your credulity is sufficient to allow you to consider Mr. Barrows' death as the result of accident?"

Lightly as the question was put, I felt that nothing but a deep anxiety had prompted it, else why that earnest gaze from which my own could not falter, or that white line showing about the lip he essayed in vain to steady? Recoiling inwardly, though I scarcely knew why, I forced myself to answer with the calmness of an inquisitor:

"My credulity is not sufficient for me to commit myself to that belief. If investigation should show that Mr. Barrows had an enemy——"

"Mr. Barrows had no enemy!" flashed from Mr. Pollard's lips. "I mean," he explained, with instant composure, "that he was not a man to awaken jealousy or antagonism; that, according to all accounts, he had the blessing, and not the cursing, of each man in the community."

"Yes," I essayed.

"He never came to his death through the instrumentality of another person," broke in Mr. Pollard, with a stern insistence. "He fell into the vat intentionally or unintentionally, but no man put him there. Do you believe me, Miss Sterling?"

Did I believe him? Was he upon trial, then, and was he willing I should see he understood it? No, no, that could not be; yet why asseverate so emphatically a fact of which no man could be sure unless he had been present at the scene of death, or at least known more of the circumstances attending it than was compatible with the perfect ignorance which all men professed to have of them. Did he not see that such words were calculated to awaken suspicion, and that it would be harder, after such a question, to believe he spoke from simple conviction, than from a desire to lead captive the will of a woman whose intuitions, his troubled conscience told him, were to be feared? Rising, as an intimation that the conversation was fast becoming insupportable to me, I confronted him with my proudest look.

"You must excuse me," said I, "if I do not linger to discuss a matter whose consequences just now are more important to us than the fact itself. While your mother lies insensible I cannot rest comfortable away from her side. You will therefore allow me to return to her."

"In a moment," he replied. "There are one or two questions it would please me to have you answer first." And his manner took on a charm that robbed his words of all peremptoriness, and made it difficult, if not impossible, for me to move. "You have spoken of Miss Reynolds," he resumed; "have told me that she declared upon her dying bed that the relations between Mr. Barrows and herself were very happy. Were you with her then? Did you know her well?"

"She was my room-mate," I returned.

It was a blow; I saw it, though not a muscle of his face quivered. He had not expected to hear that I was upon terms of intimacy with her.

"I loved her," I went on, with a sense of cruel pleasure that must have sprung from the inward necessity I felt to struggle with this strong nature. "The proof that she loved me lies in the fact that she has made me heir to all her little savings. We were friends," I added, seeing he was not yet under sufficient control to speak.

"I see," he now said, moving involuntarily between me and the door. "And by friends you mean confidantes, I presume?"

"Perhaps," I answered, coolly, dropping my eyes.

His voice took a deeper tone; it was steel meeting steel, he saw.

"And she told you Mr. Barrows was happy?"

"That has been already discussed," said I.

"Miss Sterling"—I think I never heard such music in a human voice— "you think me inquisitive, presuming, ungentlemanly, persistent, perhaps. But I have a great wish to know the truth about this matter, if only to secure myself from forming false impressions and wrongfully influencing others by them. Bear with me, then, strangers though we are, and if you feel you can trust me"—here he forced me to look at him,—"let me hear, I pray, what reasons you have for declaring so emphatically that Mr. Barrows did not commit suicide?"

"My reasons, Mr. Pollard? Have I not already given them to you? Is it necessary for me to repeat them?"

"No," he earnestly rejoined, charming me, whether I would or not, by the subtle homage he infused into his look, "if you will assure me that you have no others—that the ones you have given form the sole foundation for your conclusions. Will you?" he entreated; and while his eyes demanded the truth, his lip took a curve which it would have been better for me not to have seen if I wished to preserve unmoved my position as grand inquisitor.

I was compelled, or so it seemed to me, to answer without reserve. I therefore returned a quiet affirmative, adding only in qualification of the avowal, "What other reasons were necessary?"

"None, none," was the quick reply, "for *you* to believe as you do. A woman but proves her claim to our respect when she attaches such significance to the master-passion as to make it the argument of a perfect happiness."

I do not think he spoke in sarcasm, though to most minds it might appear so. I think he spoke in relief, a joyous relief, that was less acceptable to me at that moment than the sarcasm would have been. I therefore did not blush, but rather grew pale, as with a bow I acknowledged his words, and took my first step towards the doorway.

"I have wounded you," he murmured, softly, following me.

"You do not know me well enough," I answered, turning with a sense of victory in the midst of my partial defeat.

"It is a misfortune that can be remedied," he smiled.

"Your brother waits for us," I suggested, and, lifting the *portiere* out of his hand, I passed through, steady as a dart, but quaking, oh, how fearfully quaking within! for this interview had not only confirmed me in my belief that something dark and unknown connected the life of this household with that which had suddenly gone out in the vat at the old mill, but deepened rather than effaced the fatal charm which, contrary to every instinct of my nature, held me in a bondage that more than all things else must make any investigation into this mystery a danger and a pain from which any woman might well recoil, even though she bore in her heart memories of a past like mine.

VI

MRS. POLLARD

My mind she has mated, and amazed my sight;
I think but dare not speak.

—MACBETH.

That day was a marked one in my life. It was not only the longest I have ever known, but it was by far the dreariest, and, if I may use the word in this connection, the most unearthly. Indeed, I cannot think of it to this day without a shudder; its effect being much the same upon my memory as that of a vigil in some underground tomb, where each moment was emphasized with horror lest the dead lying before me might stir beneath their cerements and wake. The continual presence of one or both of the brothers at my side did not tend to alleviate the dread which the silence, the constant suspense, the cold gloom of the ever dimly-lighted chamber were calculated to arouse; for the atmosphere of unreality and gloom was upon them too, and, saving the quick, short sigh that escaped from their lips now and then, neither of them spoke nor relaxed for an instant from that strain of painful attention which had for its focus their mother's stony face. Mrs. Harrington, who, in her youthful freshness and dimpled beauty, might have relieved the universal sombreness of the scene, was not in the room all day; but whether this was on account of her inability to confront sickness and trouble, or whether it was the result of the wishes of her brothers, I have never been able to decide; probably the latter, for, though she was a woman of frivolous mind, she had a due sense of the proprieties, and was never known to violate them except under the stress of another will more powerful than her own.

At last, as the day waned, and what light there was gradually vanished from the shadowy chamber, Guy made a movement of discouragement, and, rising from his place, approached his brother, dropped a word in his ear, and quietly left the room. The relief I felt was instantaneous. It was like having one coil of an oppressive nightmare released from my breast. Dwight, on the contrary, who had sat like a statue ever since the room began to darken, showed no evidence of being influenced by this change, and, convinced that any movement towards a more cheerful order of things must come from me, I rose, and, without consulting his wishes, dropped the curtains and lighted the lamp. The instant I had done so I saw why he was so silent and immovable. Overcome by fatigue, and possibly by a long strain of suppressed emotion, he had fallen asleep, and, ignorant of the fact that Guy had left the room, slumbered as peacefully as if no break had occurred in the mysterious watch they had hitherto so uninterruptedly maintained over their mother and me.

The peacefulness of his sleeping face made a deep impression upon me. Though I knew that with his waking the old look would come back, it was an indescribable pleasure to me to see him, if but for an instant, free from that shadowy something which dropped a vail of mistrust between us. It seemed to show me that evil was not innate in this man, and explained, if it did not justify, the weakness which had made me more lenient to what was doubtful in his appearance and character than I had been to that of his equally courteous but less attractive brother.

The glances I allowed myself to cast in his direction were fleeting enough, however. Even if womanly delicacy had not forbidden me to look too often and too long that way, the sense of the unfair advantage I was possibly taking of his weakness made the possibility of encountering his waking eye a matter of some apprehension. I knew that honor demanded I should rouse him, that he would not thank me for letting him sleep after his brother had left the room; and yet, whether from too much heart—he was in such sore need of rest—or from too little conscience—I was in such sore need of knowledge—I let him slumber on, and never made so much as a move after my first startled discovery of his condition.

And so five minutes, ten minutes, went by, and, imperceptibly to myself, the softening influence which his sleeping countenance exerted upon me deepened and strengthened till I began to ask if I had not given too much scope to my, imagination since I had been in this house, and foolishly attributed a meaning to expressions and events that in my calmer moments would show themselves to possess no special significance.

The probability was that I had, and once allowing myself to admit this idea, it is astonishing how rapidly it gained possession of my judgment, altering the whole tenor of my thoughts, and if not exactly transforming the situation into one of cheerfulness and ease, at least robbing it of much of that sepulchral character which had hitherto made it so nearly unbearable to me. The surroundings, too, seemed to partake of the new spirit of life which had seized me. The room looked less shadowy, and lost some of that element of mystery which had made its dimly seen corners the possible abode of supernatural visitants. Even the clock ticked less lugubriously, and that expressionless face on the pillow—

Great God! it is looking at me! With two wide open, stony eyes it is staring into my very soul like a spirit from the tomb, awakening there a horror infinitely deeper than any I had felt before, though I knew it was but the signal of returning life to the sufferer, and that I ought to rouse myself and welcome it with suitable ministrations, instead of sitting there like a statue of fear in the presence of an impending fate. But do what I would, say to myself what I would, I could not stir. A nightmare of terror was upon me, and not till I saw the stony lips move and the face take a look of life in the effort made to speak, did I burst the spell that held me and start to my feet. Even then I dared not look around nor raise my voice to warn the sleeper behind me that the moment so long waited for had come. A power behind myself seemed to hold me silent, waiting, watching for those words that struggled to life so painfully before me. At last they came, filling the room with echoes hollow as they were awful!

"Dwight! Guy! If you do not want me to haunt you, swear you will never divulge what took place between you and Mr. Barrows at the mill."

"*Mother!*" rang in horror through the room. And before I could turn my head, Dwight Pollard leaped by me, and hiding the face of the dying woman on his breast, turned on me a gaze that was half wild, half commanding, and said:

"Go for my brother! He is in the northwest room. Tell him our mother raves." Then, as I took a hurried, though by no means steady, step towards the door, he added: "I need not ask you to speak to no one else?"

"No," my cold lips essayed to utter, but an unmeaning murmur was all that left them. The reaction from hope and trust to a now really tangible fear had been too sudden and overwhelming.

But by the time I had reached the room to which I had been directed, I had regained in a measure my self-control. Guy Pollard at least should not see that I could be affected by any thing which could happen in this house. Yet when, in answer to my summons, he joined me in the hall, I found it difficult to preserve the air of respectful sympathy I had assumed, so searching was his look, and so direct the question with which he met his brother's message.

"My mother raves, you say; will you be kind enough to tell me what her words were?"

"Yes," returned I, scorning to prevaricate in a struggle I at least meant should be an honest one. "She called upon her sons, and said that she would haunt them if ever they divulged what took place between them and Mr. Barrows at the mill."

"Ah!" he coldly laughed; "she does indeed rave." And while I admired his self-control, I could not prevent myself from experiencing an increased dread of this nature that was so ready for all emergencies and so panoplied against all shock.

I might have felt a more vivid apprehension still, had I known what was passing in his mind as we traversed the hall back to the sick- chamber. But the instinct which had warned me of so much, did not warn me of that, and it was with no other feeling than one of surprise that I noted the extreme deference with which he opened his mother's door for me, and waited even in that moment of natural agitation and suspense for me to pass over the threshold before he presumed to enter himself.

Dwight Pollard, however, did not seem to be so blind, for a change passed over his face as he saw us, and he half rose from the crouching position he still held over his mother's form. He subsided back, however, as I drew to one side and let Guy pass unheeded to the bed, and it was in quite a natural tone he bade me seat myself in the alcove towards which he pointed, till his mother's condition required my services.

That there was really nothing to be done for her, I saw myself in the one glimpse I caught of her face as he started up. She was on the verge of death, and her last moments were certainly due to her children. So I passed into the alcove, which was really a small room opening out of the large one, and flinging myself on the lounge I saw there, asked myself whether I ought to shut the door between us, or whether my devotion to Ada's cause bade me listen to whatever came directly in my way to hear? The fact that I was in a measure prisoned there, there being no other outlet to the room than the one by which I had entered, determined me to ignore for once the natural instincts of my ladyhood; and pale and trembling to a degree I would not have wished seen by either of these two mysterious men, I sat in a dream of suspense, hearing and not hearing the low hum of their voices as they reasoned with or consoled the mother, now fast drifting away into an endless night.

Suddenly—shall I ever forget the thrill it gave me?—her voice rose again in those tones whose force and commanding power I have found it impossible to describe.

"The oath! the oath! Dwight, Guy, by my dying head—"

"Yes, mother," I heard one voice interpose; and by the solemn murmur that followed, I gathered that Guy had thought it best to humor her wishes.

The long-drawn sigh which issued from her lips testified to the relief he had given her, and the "Now Dwight!" which followed was uttered in tones more gentle and assured.

But to this appeal no solemn murmur ensued, for at that instant a scream arose from the bed, and to the sound of an opening door rang out the words: "Keep her away! What do you let her come in here for, to confound me and make me curse the day she was born! Away! I say, away!"

Horrified, and unable to restrain the impulse that moved me, I sprang to my feet and rushed upon the scene. The picture that met my eyes glares at me now from the black background of the past. On the bed, that roused figure, awful with the shadows of death, raised, in spite of the constraining hands of her two sons, into an attitude expressive of the most intense repulsion, terror, and dread; and at the door, the fainting form of the pretty, dimpled, care-shunning daughter, who, struck to the heart by this poisoned dart from the hand that should have been lifted in blessing, stood swaying in dismay, her wide blue eyes fixed on the terrible face before her, and her hands outstretched and clutching in vague fear after some support that would sustain her, and prevent her falling crushed to the floor.

To bound to her side, and lift her gently out of her mother's sight, was the work of a moment. But in that moment my eyes had time to see such a flash of infinite longing take the place of the fierce passions upon that mother's face, that my heart stood still, and I scarcely knew whether to bear my burden from the room, or to rush with it to that bedside and lay it, in all its childlike beauty, on that maddened mother's dying breast. A low, deep groan from the bed decided me. With that look of love on her face, otherwise distorted by every evil passion, Mrs. Pollard had fallen back into the arms of her two sons, and quietly breathed her last.

VII

ADVANCES

For they are actions that a man might play;
But I have that within which passeth show.

—HAMLET.

"Miss Sterling?"

I was sitting by the side of Mrs. Harrington in her own room.
By a feverish exertion of strength I had borne her thither from
her mother's chamber, and was now watching the returning
hues of life color her pale cheek. At the sound of my name,
uttered behind me, I arose. I had expected a speedy visit from
one of the brothers, but I had been in hopes that it would be
Dwight, and not Guy, who would make it.

"I must speak to you at once; will you follow me?" asked that
gentleman, bowing respectfully as I turned.

I glanced at Mrs. Harrington, but he impatiently shook his
head.

"Anice is at the door," he remarked. "She is accustomed to
Mrs. Harrington, and will see that she is properly looked
after." And, leading the way, he ushered me out, pausing only
to cast one hurried glance back at his sister, as if to assure

himself she was not yet sufficiently recovered to note his action.

In the hall he offered me his arm.

"The gas has not yet been lighted," he explained, "and I wish you to go with me to the parlor."

This sounded formidable, but I did not hesitate. I felt able to confront this man.

"I am at your service," I declared, with a comfortable sensation that my tone conveyed something of the uncompromising spirit I felt.

The room to which he conducted me was on the first floor, and was darkness itself when we entered. It was musty, too, and chill, as with the memory of a past funeral and the premonition of a new one.

Even the light which he soon made did not seem to be at home in the spot, but wavered and flickered with faint gasps, as if it longed to efface itself and leave the grand and solitary apartment to its wonted atmosphere of cold reserve. By its feeble flame I noted but two details: one was the portrait of Mrs. Pollard in her youth, and the other was my own reflection in some distant mirror. The first filled me with strange thoughts, the face was so wickedly powerful, if I may so speak; handsome, but with that will beneath its beauty which, when allied to selfishness, has produced the Lucretia Borgias and Catherine de Medicis of the world.

The reflection of which I speak, dimly seen as it was, had, on the contrary, a calming effect upon my mind. Weary as I undoubtedly was, and pale if not haggard with the emotions I had experienced, there was still something natural and alive in my image that recalled happier scenes to my eyes, and gave me the necessary strength to confront the possibilities of the present interview.

Anna Katherine Green

Mr. Pollard, who in his taciturn gloom seemed like the natural genius of the spot, appeared to be struck by this same sensation also, for his eyes wandered more than once to the mirror, before he summoned up courage, or, perhaps, I should say, before he took the determination to look me in the face and open the conversation. When he did, it was curious to note the strife of expression between his eye and lip: the one hard, cold, and unyielding; the other deprecating in its half-smile and falsely gentle, as if the mind that controlled it was even then divided between its wish to subdue and the necessity it felt to win.

"Miss Sterling," so he began, "it would be only folly for me to speak as if nothing had occurred but an ordinary and natural death. It would be doing your good sense and womanly judgment but little honor, and putting myself, or, rather, ourselves—for we children are but one in this matter—in a position which would make any after-explanations exceedingly difficult. For explanations can be given, and in a word; for what has doubtless struck you as strange and terrible in my mother's last hours,—explanations which I am sure you will be glad to accept, as it is not natural for one so blooming in her womanliness to wish to hamper her youth with dark thoughts, or to nurse suspicions contrary to her own candid and noble nature."

He paused, but meeting with no response beyond a rather cool bow, the strife between his eye and lip became more marked. He went on, however, as if perfectly satisfied, his voice retaining its confident tone, whatever the disturbance communicated to his inward nature.

"The explanation to which I allude is this," said he. "My mother for the past three months has been the victim of many unwholesome delusions. The sickness of my father, which was somewhat prolonged, made great inroads upon her strength; and his death, followed by the necessity of parting with Mrs. Harrington—whom you perhaps know was for family reasons married immediately upon my father's decease,—sowed the seed of a mental weakness which culminated on her deathbed into a positive delirium. She had a notion, and has had it for weeks, unknown to every one but my brother and myself, that Mrs. Harrington had been the occasion of some great misfortune to us; whereas the innocent girl had done nothing but follow out her mother's wishes, both in her marriage and in her settlement in a distant town. But the love my mother had felt for her was always the ruling passion of her life, and when she came to find herself robbed of a presence that was actually necessary to her well-being, her mind, by some strange subtlety of disease I do not profess to understand, confounded the source of her grief with its cause, attributing to this well-beloved daughter's will the suffering, which only sprang out of the circumstances of the case. As to her wild remarks in regard to Mr. Barrows," he added, with studied indifference, "and the oath she wished us to take, that was but an outgrowth of the shock she had received in hearing of the clergyman's death. For, of course, I need not assure you, Miss Sterling, that for all our readiness to take the oath she demanded, neither my brother nor myself ever were at the mill, or knew any more of the manner or cause of Mr. Barrows' death than you do."

This distinct denial, made in quiet but emphatic tones, caused me to look up at him with what was perhaps something of an expressive glance. For at its utterance the longing cry had risen in my heart, "Oh, that it were Dwight who had said that!" And the realization which it immediately brought of the glad credence which it would have received from me had it only fallen from *his* lips caused an inward tremble of self-consciousness which doubtless communicated itself to my glance. For Guy Pollard, without waiting for any words I might have to say, leaned towards me with a gratified air, and with what I would like to call a smile, exclaimed:

"You have been in the house scarce twenty-four hours, but I feel as if I could already give you the title of friend. Will you accept it from me, Miss Sterling, and with it my most cordial appreciation and esteem?"

"Ah, this is mere bait!" I thought, and was tempted to indignantly repel the hand he held out; but something restrained me which I am to proud to call fear, and which in reality I do not think was fear, so much as it was wonder and a desire to understand the full motive of a condescension I could not but feel was unprecedented in this arrogant nature. I therefore gave him my hand, but in a steady, mechanical way that I flattered myself committed me to nothing; though the slight but unmistakable pressure he returned seemed to show that he took it for a sign of amity, if not of absolute surrender.

"You relieve me of a great weight," he acknowledged. "Had you been of the commonplace type of woman, you might have made it very uncomfortable for us." "And what have I said and done," I could not help remarking, though neither so bitterly nor with so much irony as I might have done had that desire of which I have spoken been less keen than it was, "to lead you to think I shall not yet do so?"

"Your glance is your surety," was the response he made. "That and your honest hand, which does not lightly fall in that of a stranger." And with a real smile now, though it was by no means the reassuring and perhaps attractive one he doubtless meant it to be, he fixed me with his subtle glance, in which I began to read a meaning, if not a purpose, that made the blood leap indignantly to my heart, and caused me to feel as if I had somehow stumbled into a snare from which it would take more than ordinary skill and patience to escape.

A look down the shadowy room restored my equanimity, however. It was all so unreal, so ghostly, I could not help acknowledging to myself that I was moving in a dream which exaggerated every impression I received, even that which might be given by the bold gaze of an unscrupulous man. So I determined not to believe in it, or in any thing else I should see that night, unless it were in the stern soul of the woman who had just died; a qualification which my mind could not help making to itself as my eyes fell again upon her portrait, with its cruel, unrelenting expression.

"You do not feel at home!" exclaimed Guy, interpreting according to his needs my silence and the look I had thrown about me. "I do not wonder," he pursued. "Dreariness like this has little to do with youth and beauty. But I hope"—here he took a step nearer, while that meaning look—oh, my God! was I deceiving myself?—deepened in his eyes—"I hope the day will come when you will see the sunshine stream through the gloom of these dim recesses, and in the new cheer infused into the life of this old mansion forget the scenes of horror that encompassed the beginning of our friendship." And with a bow that seemed to intimate that necessity, and not his wishes, forced him to terminate this interview, he was stepping back, when the door opened quickly behind him, and the face of Dwight Pollard showed itself on the threshold.

The look he cast first at his brother and then at me caused a fresh tumult to take place in my breast. Was it displeasure he showed? I was pleased to think so. I could not be sure of his feeling, however, for almost on the instant his brow cleared, and advancing with an excuse for his interruption, he spoke a few low words to Guy. The latter gravely bowed, and with just a slight glance in my direction, immediately left the room. I was once more alone with Dwight Pollard.

He seemed to feel the situation as much as I did, for it was several moments before he spoke, and when he did, his voice had a subdued tremble in it which I had not noticed before.

"Miss Sterling," he remarked, "my brother has been talking to you, trying, I presume, to explain to you the distressing scene to which you have just been witness."

I bowed, for I seemed to have no words to say, though he evidently longed to hear me speak.

"My brother is not always considerate in his manner of address," he went on, after a moment's intent scrutiny of my face. "I hope he has not made you feel other than satisfied of our good-will towards you?"

"No," I faintly smiled, wishing I knew what feeling prompted this subtle attempt to learn the nature of the interview which had just passed. "Mr. Guy Pollard has never been any thing but polite to me."

He looked at me again as if he would read my very soul, but I gave him no help to its understanding, and he presently dropped his eyes.

"Did he tell you," he at last resumed, with some effort, "that it is our wish for you to remain in this house till our mother is buried?"

"No," I returned, "he said nothing about it."

"But you will do so?" he queried, in that rich and deep tone which thrilled so dangerously to my heart.

"I—I must have time to think," I faltered, taken by surprise, and not seeing my way as clearly as I could wish. "It is my desire to attend the funeral of Mr. Barrows and Miss Reynolds, and—Mr. Pollard!" I suddenly exclaimed, taking perhaps the most courageous resolution of my life, "I must be honest with you. It is useless for me to deny that the manner and circumstances of your mother's death have made a great impression upon me; that I cannot, in spite of all explanations, but connect some special significance to the oath you were requested to take; and that, weakened as your mother may have been, something more terrible than the mere shock of hearing of her pastor's sudden decease must have occasioned emotions so intense as to end in death and delirium. If, therefore, you are willing to assure me, as your brother has done, that it was entirely a fancy of hers that you ever held any communication with Mr. Barrows at the mill, I will gladly promise to disabuse my mind of all unfavorable impressions, and even promise to stay here, if such be your desire, till the days of your trouble are over, and the body of your mother is laid in her grave."

"And has my brother given you such an assurance as you speak of?"

"He has," I returned.

"Then why do you ask one from me?"

Was it possible for me to tell him?

"If it was not enough coming from his lips, how could it be coming from mine?" he continued.

Shame and confusion kept me silent.

"Would it be?" he persisted, this time with feeling and something like a hint of eagerness in his voice.

I dared not say "Yes," and yet I must have the assurance I demanded, if ever I was to know peace again.

"You no not answer; but I think, I feel confident you would believe my word, Miss Sterling."

"I have asked for it," I returned.

He turned frightfully pale; it seemed as if he would speak, but the words did not come. I felt, my heart growing sick, and as for him, he started violently away from my side, and took a turn or two up and down the room.

"I cannot deny what looks like an accusation," he declared at last, coming and standing before me with a sombre but determined air. "My pride alone is sufficient to deter me. Will you accept from me any thing less. I am not such a man as my brother."

"I will accept your assurance that as the true friend to Ada Reynolds I may remain in this house without stain to her memory or love."

"Then you think—"

"No," said I, with a burst I could not control, "I do not think; I do not want to think; do not make me, I entreat."

He smiled, a sad and fearful smile, and took another turn up and down the seemingly darkening room. When he came back I was cold as marble, and almost as insensible.

"Miss Sterling," were his words, "do you remember a conversation we had this morning?"

I bowed, with a sudden rush of hope that almost melted me again.

"In that conversation I made a solemn assertion; do you recollect what it was?"

"Yes," I looked, if I did not audibly reply.

"I make that assertion again—is it sufficient?" he asked.

At that moment it seemed to me that it was. I looked and felt as if a great weight had been lifted from my heart, and though he flushed deeply, as any man of spirit, let alone one of such a proud and aristocratic nature as his, would be apt to under the circumstances, I saw that he experienced a relief also, and giving way to an impulse I do not yet know whether to regret or not, I held out my hand, saying calmly:

"I will remain, Mr. Pollard."

VIII

A FLOWER FROM THE POLLARD CONSERVATORY

You may wear your rue with a difference.

—HAMLET.

Mrs. Harrington did not immediately recover from the shock she had received. I therefore found myself fully employed the next day. Towards evening, however, a respite came, and I took the opportunity for a stroll up-street, as much for the sake of hearing the gossip of the town as to escape from the atmosphere of sorrow and perplexity by which I was surrounded.

My walk down to the gate was full of a certain uneasy apprehension. I had made no secret of my intentions at the supper-table, and for the reason that neither of the brothers had ventured upon any reply to my remark, I expected one, if not both, of them to join me on the way. But I reached the last turn of the path without meeting any one, and I was congratulating myself upon the prospect of having an hour of perfect freedom, when I detected, leaning on the gate before me, the firm, well-knit figure of a man.

As the two Pollards were more or less alike in form, I could not distinguish at first glance which of the brothers it was. I therefore faltered back a step, and was indeed debating whether I should not give up my project and return to the house, when I saw the gentleman's head turn, and realized that it was too late to retreat. I therefore advanced with as much calmness as I could assume, determined not to vary my conduct, no matter which of the brothers it should turn out to be. But, to my great surprise, the gentleman before me gave me no opportunity to test my resolution. No sooner did he perceive me than he made a hurried gesture that I did not at that moment understand; and, just lifting his hat in courteous farewell, vanished from my sight in the thick bushes which at that place encumbered the grounds.

"It was Dwight; it was Guy," I alternately explained to myself, and knew not whether it would give me most relief to find myself shunned by the one or the other. My final conclusion, that I wished to have nothing further to do with either of them, received, notwithstanding, a rude shock when I arrived at the gate-post. For there, on its broad top, lay a magnificent blossom, the choicest fruit of the hot-house, and it was to beg my acceptance of this that the gentleman had made the peculiar gesture I had noticed—an act which, if it came from Dwight, certainly possessed a significance which I was not yet ready to ignore; while, if it proceeded from his cold and crafty brother—But I would not allow myself to dwell upon that possibility. The flower must be mine, and if afterwards I found that it was to Guy I owed its possession, it would be time enough then for me to determine what to do. So I took the gorgeous blossom off the post and was speeding away down the street, when I was suddenly stopped by the thought that only Guy would have the egotism to bestow a gift upon me in this way; that Dwight, if he had wished to present it at all, would have done so with his own hand, and not left it lying on a gate-post with the assurance it would be gathered up by the fortunate recipient of his favor.

Disgusted with myself, and instantly alive to the possible consequences of my act, I opened my fingers with the laudable intention of dropping the flower to the ground, when I saw standing in the road directly in front of me the beautiful idiot boy whose peculiarities of appearance and conduct had so attracted my attention in the summer-house the day before. He was looking at me with a strange gaze of mingled curiosity and imbecile good-nature, and his hands, white as milk, trembled in the air before him, as if he could scarcely restrain himself from snatching out of my grasp the superb flower I seemed so willing to throw away.

A happy impulse seized me.

"Here," said I, proffering him the blossom. "This will give you more pleasure than it will me."

But, to my great astonishment, he turned on his heel with a loud laugh, and then, shaking his head, and rolling it curiously from side to side, exclaimed, with his usual repetition:

"No, no, it is a lover's gift, a lover's gift; you will wear it in your hair." And he danced about me with grotesque gayety for a moment, then flitted away to a position from which he could still see me without being within reach of my hand.

Under these circumstances I was too proud to fling the flower away; so I dropped it into a basket I held, and walked swiftly down the street. The idiot boy followed me; now skipping a pace or two in advance, and now falling back till I had passed far beyond him. As he flashed back and forth, I saw that his eyes were always on my face, and once, as I confronted him with mine, he broke out into a series of chuckles, and cried: "Do they like you now? do they like you now?" and laughed and danced, and laughed again, till I began to find the situation somewhat embarrassing, and was glad enough when at the corner of a street he disappeared from my view, with the final cry of: "One day, two days; wait till you have been there ten; wait till you have been there twenty!"

Hot and trembling with apprehension lest his foolish speeches had been heard by some passer-by, I hurried on my way to the house where I lived. I reached it in a few minutes, and being so fortunate as to find my landlady in, succeeded before another half-hour had passed in learning all that was generally known about the serious occurrences in which I was just then so profoundly interested.

I heard first that the vat in the old mill had been examined for the purpose of ascertaining how it came to be full enough of water to drown a man; and it was found that, owing to a heavy storm which had lately devastated the country, a portion of the wall above the vat had been broken in by a falling tree, allowing the rain to enter in floods from a jutting portion of the roof. Next, that although an inquest had been held over Mr. Barrows' remains, and a verdict been given of accidental death, the common judgment of the community ascribed his end to suicide. This was mainly owing to the fact that the woman in whose house he had lived had testified to having observed a great change in his appearance during the last few weeks; a change which many were now ready to allow they had themselves perceived; though, from the fact of its having escaped the attention of Ada, I cannot but think they were greatly helped to this conclusion by their own imagination.

The last thing I made sure of was that the two deaths which had followed his so tragically had awakened on all sides the deepest interest and pity, but nothing more. That although the general features of Mrs. Pollard's end were well enough known, no whisper of suspicion had been breathed against her or hers, that showed in the faintest way that any doubt mingled with the general feeling of commiseration. And yet it was too evident she was no favorite with the world at large, and that the respect with which she was universally mentioned was rather the result of the pride felt in her commanding manners and position, than from any personal liking for the woman herself.

As for the sons, they were fine young men in their way, and had the sympathy of everybody in their bereavement; but gossip, if it busied itself with their names at all, was much more interested in wondering what disposition they would make of the property now coming to them, than in inquiring whether or not they could have had any secret relations with the man now dead, which were calculated to explain in any way his mysterious end.

Finally I learned that Ada and Mr. Barrows were to be buried the next day.

Satisfied with the information obtained, I started immediately for the Pollard mansion. It was my wish to re-enter it before dark. But the twilight fell fast, and by the time I reached the gate I could barely discern that a masculine figure was again leaning there, waiting, as it appeared, for my return. The discovery caused me a sensation of relief. Now I should at least learn which of the two brothers showed this interest in my movements, for this time the gentleman betrayed no disposition to leave at my approach; on the contrary, he advanced, and in the mellow accents I had learned in so short a time to listen for, observed:

"I knew you wished to go alone, Miss Sterling, or I should have offered you my protection in your dismal walk. I am glad to see you return before it is quite dark."

"Thank you," I responded, with almost a degree of joyousness in my tone, I was so glad to be rid of the perplexity that had weighed down my spirits for the last half-hour. "It is not pleasant to walk the streets at dusk alone, but necessity has accustomed me to it, and I scarcely think of its dangers now."

"You utter that in a proud tone," he declared, reaching out and taking the basket that hung on my arm.

"I have reason to," I replied, glad it was so dark he could not see the blush which his action had caused. "It was no slight struggle for me to overcome certain prejudices in which I have been reared. That I have been able to do so gives me whole-some satisfaction. I am no longer ashamed to own that I stand by myself, and work for every benefit I obtain."

"Nor need you be," he murmured. "In this age and in this country a woman like you forfeits nothing by maintaining her own independence. On the contrary, she gains something, and that is the respect of every true-hearted man that knows her." And his step lagged more and more in spite of my conscientious efforts to maintain the brisk pace in which I had indulged before I had encountered him at the gate.

"This is a grand old place," I remarked, vaguely anxious to change the drift of the conversation.

"Yes," he answered, moodily; "but it is shadowed." And with a sudden relapse into his most sombre self, he walked at my side in silence, till the sight of the high porch showing itself through the trees warned him that if he had any thing further to say to me, it must be said soon. He therefore paused, forcing me by the action to pause too, and earnestly observed: "I know, however you may address me, Miss Sterling, you cherish a doubt of me in your heart. I cannot resent this, much as my natural pride might prompt me to do so. During the short time in which I have known you, you have won so deeply upon my esteem, that the utmost which I feel able to ask of you under the circumstances is, that, in the two or three days you will yet remain with us, you will allow yourself but one thought concerning me, and that is, that I aspire to be an honest man, and to do not only what the world thinks right, but even what such a conscientious soul as yours must consider so. Are you willing to regard me in this light, and will my mere word be sufficient to cause you to do so?"

It was a searching question after his proffer, and my acceptance of the flower I held concealed, and I hesitated a moment before replying to it. I am so intensely proud; and then I could not but acknowledge to myself that, whatever my excuse, I was certainly running a risk of no ordinary nature in listening to the addresses of a man who could inspire me, or ever had inspired me, with the faintest element of distrust.

He noted my silence and drew back, uttering a sigh that was

half impatient and half sorrowful. I felt this sigh, nondescript as it was, re-echo painfully in my heart, and hung my head in remorse; but not before I had caught a glimpse of his face, and been struck by its expression of deep melancholy.

"You have no favor to show me, then?" he asked.

Instantly and without premeditation I seized upon the basket he held in his hand, and impetuously opened the lid.

"Have I not shown you one?" I inquired.

A sound—it never came from him or from me—made us both start. With a fierce expression he turned towards the bushes at our right, but not before I had seen, by the look of astonishment he had cast upon the flower, that, notwithstanding the coincidence of finding him at the gate, he had had nothing to do with its culling or presentation.

"Some one is presuming to play the spy upon us," said he, and drawing my hand through his arm, he led me swiftly towards the porch. "You need not tremble so," he whispered, as we halted an instant between the cedars before mounting the steep steps. "No one in this house wishes to annoy you—or if there should be any one who does," he corrected in a quick tone, while he cast a glance of quick suspicion at the basket in my hand, "that person and I will soon come to an understanding."

"I was only startled," was my quick rejoinder, glad to explain my tremulousness in this way. "Let us go in," I added, feeling that I must escape to some place of solitude, if only to hide my shame and chagrin from every eye.

He acquiesced in my wishes at once, and we were proceeding slowly up the steps, when suddenly a shrill, strange laugh broke from amid the bushes, and the weird voice of the idiot boy, whom I thought had been left behind me in the town, rose once more to my ear, uttering those same words which had so annoyed me earlier in the evening.

"Oh, do you think they like you now? Say, say, do you think they like you now?" But the tone with which he addressed me this time had a ring of menace in it, and I was not surprised to see Dwight Pollard start, though I was somewhat affected by the deep agitation he showed as I tried to explain:

"Oh, it is only the little idiot boy whom you must have seen running about the streets. He seems to have taken a fancy to me, for he followed me nearly all the while I was gone, with something of the same senseless remarks as now."

"The idiot boy!" repeated Mr. Pollard. "Well, we will leave the idiot boy outside." And he held the door open till I had hurried in, when he vehemently closed it, looking at the same time as if he had shut the door on a threatening evil, or, at the most, on a bitter and haunting memory.

That night I did an unworthy thing; I listened to conversation which was not intended for my ears. It happened in this wise: I had been down-stairs on an errand for Mrs. Harrington, and was coming back through the dimly lighted hall, when I saw Dwight Pollard step out of a room in front of me and accost a man that was locking and bolting the front door.

"Simon," I heard him say, "you remember that beautiful flower I noticed yesterday in the conservatory?"

"Yes, sir," the man replied, with some embarrassment in his voice.

"Well, I want it picked to-morrow for my mother's funeral. You will bring it to my room."

"Oh, sir," I heard the man hurriedly interpose, "I'm sure I'm very sorry, sir; but it has already been picked, and there won't be another out before next week."

I knew I ought not to stay there and listen, especially as I could easily have gone on my way without attracting attention; but having heard thus much, I found it impossible to go on till I had at least learned if Mr. Pollard had the motive I suspected in these inquiries of his. His next words satisfied me on this point.

"And who was the fortunate one to obtain this flower?" he asked, in an accent indifferent enough to deceive a merely casual listener.

"Mr. Guy, sir."

"Ah, so he noticed it too!" was the remark with which Mr. Pollard dropped the subject, and hurried away from the gardener's side.

The next instant I perceived him pass into Guy's room, and I saw that an explanation of some kind was about to take place between the brothers.

IX

AN UNEXPECTED DISCOVERY

Hold, hold my heart!
And you, my sinews, grow not instant old.
But bear me stiffly up!

Whether intentionally or unintentionally, I was saved the
embarrassment of meeting Guy Pollard at the breakfast-table
the next morning. I was, therefore, left in ignorance as to the
result of the conversation between the brothers, though from
the softened manner of Dwight, and the quiet assurance with
which he surrounded me with the delicate atmosphere of his
homage, I could not but argue that he had come out master of
the situation.

It was, therefore, with mingled feelings of pleasure and
apprehension that I left the house at the hour appointed for
the double funeral; feelings that would have been yet more
alive had I realized that I should not re-enter those gates again,
or see the interior of that fatal house, till I had passed through
many bitter experiences.

The ceremonies, in spite of the latent suspicion of the
community that Mr. Barrows' death had been one of his own
seeking, were of the most touching and impressive description.
I was overcome by them, and left the churchyard before the
final prayer was said, feeling as if the life of the last three days

had been a dream, and that here in the memory of my lovely Ada and her griefs lay my true existence and the beginning and ending of my most sacred duty.

Pursuant to this thought I did not turn immediately back to the gloomy mansion which claimed me for the present as its own, but wandered away in an opposite direction, soothing my conscience by the thought that it was many hours yet before the services would be held for Mrs. Pollard, and that neither the brothers nor Mrs. Harrington could have any use for me till that time.

The road I had taken was a sequestered one, and strange as it may seem to some, did not awaken special memories in my mind till I came to a point where an opening in the trees gave to my view the vision of two tall chimneys; when like a flash it came across me that I was on the mill road, and within a few short rods of the scene of Mr. Barrows' death.

The sensation that seized me at this discovery was of the strangest kind. I felt that I had been led there; and without a thought of what I was doing, pressed on with ever-increasing rapidity till I came to the open doorway with its dismantled entrance.

To pass over the now much-trodden grass and take my stand by the dismal walls was the work of an instant; but when I had done this and experienced in a rush the loneliness and ghostly influence of the place, I was fain to turn back and leave it to the dream of its own fearful memories. But the sight of a small piece of paper pinned or pasted on the board that had been nailed in futile precaution across the open doorway deterred me. It was doubtless nothing more important than a notice from the town authorities, or possibly from the proprietors of the place, but my curiosity was excited, and I desired to see it. So I hastened over to where it was, and with little apprehension of the shock that was destined to overwhelm me, read these words:

"Those who say Mr. Barrows committed suicide lie. He was murdered, and by parties whose position places them above suspicion, as their wealth and seeming prosperity rob them of even the appearance of motive for such a terrible deed."

No names mentioned; but O God! And that word *murdered*. It swam before my eyes; it burned itself into every thing upon which I looked, it settled like a weight of iron upon my heart, pressing me nearer and nearer and nearer to the ground, till finally—Ah! can it be that this is really I, and that I am standing here in a desolate place alone, with no human being in sight, and with a paper in my hand that seems to grow larger and larger as I gaze, and ask me what I mean to do now, and whether in tearing it from the wall where it hung, I allied myself to the accused, or by one stroke proclaimed myself that avenger which, if the words on this paper were true, I owed it to my Ada and the promise which I had given her to be? The cloud that enveloped my brain pressed upon me too closely for me to give an answer to questions so vital and terrific. I was in a maze,—a horrible dream; I could not think, I could only suffer, and at last creep away like a shadow of guiltiness to where a cluster of pine-trees made a sort of retreat into which I felt I could thrust my almost maddened head and be lost.

For great shocks reveal deep secrets, and in the light of this pitiless accusation, this fact had revealed itself without disguise to my eyes, that it was love I felt for Dwight Pollard; not admiration, not curiosity, not even the natural desire to understand one so seemingly impenetrable, but love, real, true, yearning, and despotic love, which if well founded might have made my bliss for a lifetime, and which now—I thrust the paper between my lips to keep down the cry that rose there, and hiding my face deep down in the turf, mourned the weakness that made me so ready a victim, while at the same time I prepared to sustain the struggle which I knew must there and then be waged and decided if I was ever to face the world again with the strength and calmness which my nature demanded, and the extraordinary circumstances of my position imposed.

The result was an hour of misery, with a sensation of triumph at the end; though I do not pretend to say that in this one effort I overcame the admiration and interest which attached my thoughts to this man. The accusation was as yet too vague, and its source too doubtful, to blot his image with ineffaceable stains; but I did succeed in gaining sufficient mastery over myself to make it possible to review the situation and give what I meant should be an unbiased judgment as to the duty it imposed upon me.

The result was a determination to hold myself neutral till I had at least discovered the author of the lines I held in my hand. If they came from a credible person—but how could they do so and be written and posted up in the manner they were? An honest man does not seek any such roundabout way to strike his blow. Only a coward or a villain would take this method to arouse public curiosity, and perhaps create public suspicion.

And yet who could say that a coward and a villain might not be speaking the truth even in an accusation of this nature? The very fact that it met and gave form and substance to my own dim and unrecognized fears, proved that something as yet unknown and unsounded connected the mysterious death of Mr. Barrows with the family towards which this accusation evidently pointed. While my own heart beat with dread, how could I ignore the possibility of these words being the work of an accomplice disgusted with his crime, or of a tool anxious to save himself, and at the same time to avenge some fancied slight? I could not. If peace and hope were lost in the effort, I must learn the truth and satisfy myself, once and for all, as to whose hatred and fear the Pollards were indebted for insinuations at once so tremendous and so veiled.

That I was the only person who had probably seen and read these fatal words, lent purpose to my resolution. If, as I madly hoped, they were but the expression of suspicion, rather than of knowledge, what a satisfaction it would be for me to discover the fact, and possibly unmask the cowardly author, before the public mind had been infected by his doubts.

But how could I, a woman and a stranger, with no other talisman than my will and patience, accomplish a purpose which would be, perhaps, no easy one for a trained detective to carry out to a successful issue? The characters in which the fatal insinuations had been conveyed offered no clue. They were printed, and in so rough and commonplace a manner that the keenest mind would have found itself baffled if it had attempted to trace its way to the writer through the mere medium of the lines he had transcribed. I must, therefore, choose some other means of attaining my end; but what one?

I had never, in spite of the many trials and embarrassments of my life, been what is called an intriguing woman. Nor had I ever amused myself with forming plots or devising plans for extricating imaginary characters out of fancied difficulties by the mere exercise of their wits. *Finesse* was almost an unknown word to me, and yet, as I sat there with this fatal bit of paper in my hand, I felt that a power hitherto unguessed was awakening within me, and that if I could but restrain the emotions which threatened to dissipate my thoughts, I should yet hit upon a plan by which my design could be attained with satisfaction to myself and safety to others.

For—and this was my first idea—the paper had not been on the wall long. It was too fresh to have hung there overnight, and had, moreover, been too poorly secured to have withstood even for an hour the assaults of a wind as keen as that which had been blowing all the morning. It had, therefore, been put up a few moments before I came, or, in other words, while the funeral services were being held; a fact which, to my mind, argued a deep calculation on the part of the writer, for the hour was one to attract all wanderers to the other end of the town, while the following one would, on the contrary, see this quarter overflow with human beings, anxious to complete the impression made by the funeral services, by a visit to the scene of the tragedy.

That the sky had clouded over very much in the last half-hour, and that the first drops of a heavy thunder-shower were even now sifting through the branches over my head, was doubtless the reason why no one besides myself had yet arrived upon the scene; and, should the storm continue, this evil might yet be averted, and the one person I was most anxious to see, have an opportunity to show himself at the place, without being confounded with a mass of disinterested people. For I felt he would return, and soon, to note the result of his daring action. In the crowd, if a crowd assembled, or alone, if it so chanced that no one came to the spot, he would draw near the mill, and, if he found the notice gone, would betray, must betray, an interest or an alarm that would reveal him to my watchful eye. For I intended to take up my stand within the doorway, using, if necessary, the storm as my excuse for desiring its shelter; while as a precaution against suspicions that might be dangerous to me, as well as a preventive against any one else ever reading these accusatory lines, I determined to dip the paper in the stream, and then drop it near the place where it had been tacked, that it might seem as if it had been beaten off by the rain, now happily falling faster and faster.

All this I did, not without some apprehension of being observed by a watchful eye. For what surety had I that the writer of these words was not even now in hiding, or had not been looking at me from some secret retreat at the very moment I tore the paper off the wall and fled with it into the bushes?

But this fear, if fear it was, was gradually dispelled as the moments sped by, and nothing beyond the wind and the fast driving rain penetrated to where I stood. Nor did it look as if any break in what seemed likely to become a somewhat dread monotony would ever occur. The fierce dash of the storm was like a barrier, shutting me off from the rest of the world, and had my purpose been less serious, my will less nerved, I might have succumbed to the dreariness of the outlook and taken myself away while yet the gruesome influences that lay crouched in the darkness at my back remained in abeyance, and neither ghost's step nor man's step had come to shake the foundations of my courage and make of my silent watch a struggle and a fear.

But an intent like mine was not to be relinquished at the first call of impatience or dread. Honor, love, and duty were at stake, and I held to my resolution, though each passing moment made it more difficult to maintain my hope as well as to sustain my composure.

At last—oh, why did that hollow of darkness behind me reverberate so continually in my fancy?—there seemed, there was, a movement in the bushes by the road, and a form crept gradually into sight that, when half seen, made the blood cease coursing through my veins; and, when fully in view, sent it in torrents to heart and brain; so deep, so vivid, so peculiar was the relief I felt. For—realize the effect upon me if you can— the figure that now stole towards me through the dank grass, looking and peering for the notice I had torn from the wall, was no other than my friend—or was it my enemy?—the idiot boy.

He was soaked with the rain, but he seemed oblivious of the fact. For him the wind had evidently no fierceness, the wet no chill. All his energies—and he seemed, as in that first moment when I saw him in the summer-house, to be alive with them— were concentrated in the gaze of his large eyes, as, coming nearer and nearer, he searched the wall, then the ground, and finally, with a leap, picked up the soaked and useless paper which I had dropped there.

His expression as he raised himself and looked fiercely about almost made me reveal myself. This an idiot, this trembling, wrathful, denunciatory figure, with its rings of hair clinging to a forehead pale with passion and corrugated with thought! Were these gestures, sudden, determined, and full of subdued threatening, the offspring of an erratic brain or the expression of a fool's hatred? I could not believe it, and stood as if fascinated before this vision, that not only upset every past theory which my restless mind had been able to form of the character and motives of the secret denunciator of the Pollards, but awakened new thoughts and new inquiries of a nature which I vaguely felt to be as mysterious as any which had hitherto engaged my attention.

Meantime the boy had crushed the useless paper in his hand, and, flinging it aside, turned softly about as if to go. I had no wish to detain him. I wished to make inquiries first, and learn if possible all that was known of his history and circumstances before I committed myself to an interview. If he were an idiot—well, that would simplify matters much; but, if he were not, or, being one, had moments of reason, then a mystery appeared that would require all the ingenuity and tact of a Machiavelli to elucidate. The laugh which had risen from the shrubbery the night before, and the look which Dwight Pollard had given when he heard it, proved that a mystery did exist, and gave me strength to let the boy vanish from my sight with his secret unsolved and his purposes unguessed.

Anna Katherine Green

X

RHODA COLWELL

I spare you common curses.

—MRS. BROWNING.

It was not long after this that the storm began to abate. Sunshine took the place of clouds, and I was enabled to make my way back to the town at the risk of nothing worse than wet feet. I went at once to my boarding-house. Though I was expected back at the Pollards', though my presence seemed almost necessary there, I felt that it would be impossible for me to enter their door till something of the shadow that now enveloped their name had fallen away. I therefore sent them word that unlooked-for circumstances compelled me to remain at home for the present; and having thus dismissed one anxiety from my mind, set myself to the task of gleaning what knowledge I could of the idiot boy.

The result was startling. He was, it seemed, a real idiot—or so had always been regarded by those who had known him from his birth. Not one of the ugly, mischievous sort, but a gentle, chuckling vacant- brained boy, who loved to run the streets and mingle his harmless laughter with the shouts of playing children and the noise of mills and manufactories.

He was an orphan, but was neither poor nor dependent,

for—and here was where the fact came in that astonished me—he had for protector a twin sister whose wits were as acute as his were dull; a sister who through years of orphanage had cherished and supported him, working sometimes for that purpose in the factories, and sometimes simply with her needle at home. They lived in a nest of a cottage on the edge of the town, and had the sympathy of all, though not perhaps the full liking of any. For Rhoda, the sister, was a being of an unique order, who, while arousing the interest of a few, baffled the comprehension of the many. She was a problem; a creature out of keeping with her belongings and the circumstances in which she was placed. An airy, lissom, subtle specimen of woman, whose very beauty was of an unknown order, causing as much inquiry as admiration. A perfect blonde like her brother, she had none of the sweetness and fragility that usually accompanies this complexion. On the contrary, there was something bizarre in her whole appearance, and especially in the peculiar expression of her eye, that awakened the strangest feelings and produced even in the minds of those who saw her engaged in the most ordinary occupations of life an impression of remoteness that almost amounted to the uncanny. The fact that she affected brilliant colors and clothed both herself and brother in garments of a wellnigh fantastic make, added to this impression, and gave perhaps some excuse to those persons who regarded her as being as abnormally constituted as her brother, finding it impossible, I suppose, to reconcile waywardness with industry, and a taste for the rich and beautiful with a poverty so respectable, it scarcely made itself known for the reality it was. A blonde gypsy some called her, a dangerous woman some others; and the latter would undoubtedly have been correct had the girl possessed less pride of independence or been unhampered, as she was untrammelled, by the sense of responsibility towards her imbecile brother. As it was, more than one mother had had reason to ask why her son wore such a moody brow after returning from a certain quarter of the town, and at one time gossip had not hesitated to declare that Dwight Pollard—the haughty Dwight Pollard—had not been ashamed to be seen entering her door, though every one knew that no one stepped under its wreath of vines except their intentions were as honorable as the beauty, if not the poverty, of its owner demanded.

When I heard this, and heard also that he visited her no more, I seemed to have gained some enlightenment as to the odd and contradictory actions of my famous idiot boy. He loved his sister, and was in some way imbued with a sense that she had been wronged. He was, therefore, jealous of any one who had, or seemed to have, gained the attention of the man who had possibly forsaken her. Yet even with this explanation of his conduct, there was much for which I could not account, making my intended interview with the sister a matter to be more or less apprehended.

It was therefore with a composure altogether outward and superficial that I started for the quaint and tiny cottage which had been pointed out to me as the abode of these remarkable twins. I reached it just as the clock struck three, and was immediately impressed, as my informants evidently expected me to be, by the air of poetry and refinement that characterized even its humble exterior. But it was not till I had knocked at the door and been ushered into the house by the idiot brother, that my real astonishment began. For though the room in which I found myself did not, as I was afterwards assured, contain a single rich article, it certainly had the effect of luxuriousness upon the eye; and had it not been for my inward agitation and suspense, would have produced a sense of languid pleasure, scarcely to be looked for in the abode of a simple working-girl. As it was, I was dimly conscious of a slight relief in the keen tension of my feelings, and turned with almost a sensation of hope to the boy who was smiling and grimacing beside me. But here another shock awaited me, for this boy was not the one I had seen at the mill barely two hours ago, or, rather, if it were the same—and the identity of his features, figure, and dress with those I knew so well, seemed to proclaim him to be—he was in such a different mood now as to appear like another being. Laughing, merry, and inane, he bore on his brow no sign nor suggestion of the fierce passion I had seen there, nor did his countenance change, though I looked at him steadily and long with a gaze that was any thing but in keeping with his seemingly innocent mirth.

"It is not the boy I have known," I suddenly decided in my mind; and I cannot say in what wild surmises I might have indulged, if at that moment the door at my back had not opened and a figure stepped in which at the first glance attracted my whole attention and absorbed all my thought.

Imagine a woman, lithe, blonde, beautiful, intense; with features regular as the carver's hand could make them, but informed with a spirit so venomous, passionate, and perverse, that you lost sight of her beauty in your wonder at the formidable nature of the character she betrayed. Then see her dressed as no other woman ever dressed before, in a robe of scarlet of a cut and make quite its own, and conceive, if you can, the agitation I felt as I realized that in her I beheld my rival, my antagonist, the enemy of Dwight Pollard's peace and mine.

That her face, even the hatred that visibly contracted it as her eyes met mine, were familiar to me in the countenance and expression of the boy I had met, went for nothing. The beauty and malice of a seeming imbecile, and the same characteristics in a woman subtle and decided as this, awaken very different emotions in the mind. Though I had seen that same brow corrugated before, it was like a revelation to behold it now, and watch how the rosy lips took a straight line and the half-shut, mysterious eyes burned like a thread of light, as she stretched out one white hand and asked half imperiously, half threateningly:

"Who are you, and for what do you come to *me?*"

"I am Constance Sterling," I retorted, satisfied that nothing short of the heroic treatment would avail with this woman; "and if I do not mistake, I think you know very well why I come here."

"Indeed!" came in something like a hiss from between her set lips. And in one short instant all that was best in her and all that was worst became suddenly visible, as turning to her softly chuckling brother, she motioned him gently out of the room, and then turning to me, advanced a step and said: "Will you explain yourself, Miss—or is it Mrs. Constance Sterling?"

"I will explain myself," I returned, wondering, as I saw her cheeks pale and her eyes emit strange and fitful sparks, if I exerted any such influence over her as she did over me. "I said I thought you knew why I came here. I said this, because this is not the first time we have met, nor am I the first one who has presumed to address the other in a tone that to a sensitive ear sounded like menace. The idiot boy—"

"We will leave my brother out of the discussion," she broke in, in a voice so distinct I scarcely noticed that it was nothing but a whisper.

"I am not alluding to your brother," I declared, meeting her eyes with a look steady as her own, and I hope more open.

"Oh, I see," she murmured; and she took another step, while the flash of her glance cut like a knife. "You accuse me then—"

"Of assuming a disguise to spy upon Dwight Pollard."

It was a well-sped shaft, and quivered alive and burning in her heart of hearts. She gave a spring like the panther she seemed at that minute, but instantly recovered herself, and launching, upon me the strangest smile, mockingly exclaimed:

"You are a brave woman." Then as I did not quail before her passion, drew up her slight figure to its height and said: "We are worthy of each other, you and I. Tell me what you want."

Then I felt my own cheek turn pale, and I was fain to sit upon the pile of cushions that were arranged in one corner for a seat.

"What I want?" I repeated. "I want to know how you dared put in language the insinuations which you hung up on the door of the old mill this morning?"

Her eyes, narrowed, as I have said, in her seemingly habitual desire to keep their secrets to herself, flashed wide open at this, while a low and mirthless laugh escaped her lips.

"So my labor was not entirely wasted!" she cried. "You saw—"

"Both the lines and the writer," I completed, relentlessly preserving the advantage I felt myself to have gained—"the lines before they were defaced by the storm, the writer as she picked up the useless paper and went away."

"So!" she commented, with another echo of that joyless laughter; "there are two spies instead of one in this game!"

"There are two women instead of one who know your enmity and purpose," I retorted.

"How came you at the mill?" she suddenly asked, after a moment of silent communion with her own repressed soul.

"By accident," was all my reply.

"Were you alone?"

"I was."

"Then no one but yourself saw the paper?"

"No one but myself."

She gave me a look I made no sign of understanding.

"Have you told any one of what you saw and read?" she inquired at last, as she perceived I meant to volunteer nothing.

"That I am not called upon to state," I returned.

"Oh, you would play the lawyer!" was her icy and quiet remark.

"I would *play* nothing," was the answer that came from my lips.

She drew back, and a change passed over her.

Slowly as a fire is kindled, the passion grew and grew on her face. When it was at its height she leaned her two hands on a table that stood between us, and, bending forward, whispered:

"Do you love him? Are you going to fight to keep his name free from stain and his position unassailed before the world?"

Believe me if you can, but I could not answer; possibly because I had as yet no answer to the question in my soul.

She took advantage of my hesitation.

"Perhaps you think it is not worth while to fight me; that I have no real weapons at my command?" and her eyes shot forth a flame that devoured my rising hopes and seared my heart as with a fiery steel.

"I think you are a cruel woman," I declared, "anxious to destroy what no longer gives you pleasure."

"You know my story then?" she whispered. "He has talked about me, and to you?"

"No," I replied, in quiet disdain. "I know nothing save what your own eyes and your conduct tell me."

"Then you shall," she murmured, after a moment's scrutiny of my face. "You shall hear how I have been loved, and how I have been forsaken. Perhaps it will help you to appreciate the man who is likely to wreck both our lives."

I must have lifted my head at this, for she paused and gave me a curious look.

"You don't love him?" she cried.

"I shall not let him wreck my life," I responded.

Her lip curled and her two hands closed violently at her sides.

"You have not known him long," she declared. "You have not seen him at your feet, or heard his voice, as day by day he pleaded more and more passionately for a word or smile? You have not known his touch!"

"No," I impetuously cried, fascinated by her glance and tone.

I thought she looked relieved, and realized that her words might have been as much an inquiry as an assertion.

"Then do not boast," she said.

The blood that was in my cheeks went out of them. I felt my eyes close spasmodically, and hurriedly turned away my head. She watched me curiously.

"Do you think I succumbed without a struggle?" she vehemently asked, after a moment or two of this silent torture "Look at me. Am I a woman to listen to the passionate avowals of the first man that happens to glance my way and imagine he would like to have me for his wife? Is a handsome face and honeyed tongue sufficient to gain my good graces, even when it is backed by the wealth. I love and the position to which I feel myself equal? I tell you you do not know Rhoda Colwell, if you think she could be won easily. Days and days he haunted this room before I let his words creep much beyond my ears. I had a brother who needed all my care and all my affection, and I did not mean to marry, much less to love. But slowly and by degrees he got a hold upon my heart, and then, like the wretch who trusts himself to the maelstrom, I was swept round and round into the whirlpool of passion till not earth nor heaven could save me or make me again the free and light-hearted girl I was. This was two years ago, and today—"

She stopped, choked. I had never seen greater passion, as I had never seen a more fiery nature.

"It is his persistency I complain of," she murmured at last. "He forced me to love him. Had he left me when I first said 'No,' I could have looked down on his face to-day with contempt. But, no, he had a fancy that I was his destiny, and that he must possess me or die. Die? He would not even let *me* die when I found that my long-sought 'Yes' turned his worship into indifference, and his passion into constraint. But—" she suddenly cried, with a repetition of that laugh which now sounded so fearful in my ears—"all this does not answer your question as to how I dared publish the insinuations I tacked up on the mill-door this morning."

"No," I shudderingly cried.

"Ah! I have waited long," she passionately asserted. "Wrongs like mine are very patient, and are very still, but the time comes at last when even a woman weak and frail as I am can lift her hand in power; and when she does lift it—"

"Hush!" I exclaimed, bounding from my seat and seizing her upraised arm; for her vivid figure seemed to emit a flame like death. "Hush! we want no tirades, you nor I; only let me hear what Dwight Pollard has done, and whether you knew what you were saying when you called him and his family—"

"Murderers!" she completed.

I shook, but bowed my head. She loosed her arm from my grasp and stood for one moment contemplating me.

"You are a powerful rival," she murmured. "He will love you just six months longer than he did me."

I summoned up at once my pride and my composure.

"And that would be just six months too long," I averred, "if he is what you declare him to be."

"What?" came from between her set teeth, and she gave a spring that brought her close to my side. "You would hate him, if I proved to you that he and his brother and his mother were the planners, if not the executors, of Mr. Barrows' death."

"Hate him?" I repeated, recoiling, all my womanhood up in arms before the fearful joy expressed in her voice and attitude. "I should try and forget such a man ever existed. But I shall not be easily convinced," I continued, as I saw her lips open with a sort of eager hope terrible to witness. "You are too anxious to kill my love."

"Oh, you will be convinced," she asserted. "Ask Dwight Pollard what sort of garments those are which lie under the boards of the old mill, and see if he can answer you without trembling."

"Garments?" I repeated, in astonishment; "garments?"

"Yes," said she. "If he can hear you ask that question and not turn pale, stop me in my mad assertions, and fear his doom no more. But if he flinches—"

A frightful smile closed up the gap, and she seemed by a look to motion me towards the door.

"But is that all you are going to tell me?" I queried, dismayed at the prospect of our interview terminating thus.

"Is it not enough?" she asked. "When you have seen *him*, I will see *you* again. Can you not wait for that hour?"

I might have answered No. I was tempted to do so, as I had been tempted more than once to exert the full force of my spirit and crush her. But I had an indomitable pride of my own, and did not wish to risk even the semblance of defeat. So I controlled myself and merely replied:

"I do not desire to see Dwight Pollard again. I am not intending to return to his house."

"And yet you will see him," she averred. "I can easily be patient till then." And she cast another look of dismissal towards the door.

"You are a demon!" I felt tempted to respond, but my own dignity restrained me as well as her beauty, which was something absolutely dazzling in its intensity and fire. "I will have the truth from you yet," was what I did say, as I moved, heart-sick and desponding, from her side.

And her slow "No doubt," seemed to fill up the silence like a knell, and give to my homeward journey a terror and a pang which proved that however I had deceived myself, hope had not quite given up its secret hold upon my heart.

And I dreamed of her that night, and in my dream her evil beauty shone so triumphantly that my greatest wonder was not that Dwight Pollard had succumbed to her fascinations, but that having once seen the glint of that subtle soul shine from between those half-shut lids, he could ever have found strength to turn aside and let the fire he had roused burn itself away.

XI

UNDER THE MILL FLOOR

I know, this act shows terrible and grim.

—OTHELLO.

I had never considered myself a courageous person. I was therefore surprised at my own temerity when, with the morning light, came an impulse to revisit the old mill, and by an examination of its flooring, satisfy myself to whether it held in hiding any such articles as had been alluded to by Rhoda Colwell in the remarkable interview just cited. Not that I intended to put any such question to Dwight Pollard as she had suggested, or, indeed, had any intentions at all beyond the present. The outlook was too vague, my own mind too troubled, for me to concoct plans or to make any elaborate determinations. I could only perform the duty of the moment, and this visit seemed to me to be a duty, though not one of the pleasantest or even of the most promising character.

I had therefore risen and was preparing myself in an abstracted way for breakfast, when I was violently interrupted by a resounding knock at the door. Alarmed, I scarcely knew why, I hastened to open it, and fell back in very visible astonishment when I beheld standing before me no less a person than Anice, the late Mrs. Pollard's maid.

Anna Katherine Green

"I wanted to see you, miss," she said, coming in without an invitation, and carefully closing the door behind her. "So, as I had leave to attend early mass this morning, I just slipped over here, which, if it is a liberty, I hope you will pardon, seeing it is for your own good."

Not much encouraged by this preamble, I motioned her to take a seat, and then, turning my back to her, went on arranging my hair.

"I cannot imagine what errand you have with me, Anice," said I; "but if it is any thing important, let me hear it at once, as I have an engagement this morning, and am in haste."

A smile, which I could plainly see in the mirror before which I stood, passed slyly over her face. She took up her parasol from her lap, then laid it down again, and altogether showed considerable embarrassment. But it did not last long, and in another moment she was saying, in quite a bold way:

"You took my place beside the mistress I loved, but *I* don't bear you no grudge, miss. On the contrary, I would do you a good turn; for what are we here for, miss, if it's not to help one another?"

As I had no answer for this worthy sentiment, she lapsed again into her former embarrassed state and as speedily recovered from it. Simpering in a manner that unconsciously put me on my guard, she remarked:

"You left us very suddenly yesterday, miss. Of course that is your own business, and I have nothing to say against it. But I thought if you knew what might be gained by staying—" She paused and gave me a look that was almost like an appeal.

But I would not help her out.

"Why," she went on desperately, with a backward toss of her head, "you might think as how we was not such very bad folks after all. I am sure you would make a very nice mistress to work for, Miss Sterling," she simpered; "and if you would just let me help you with your hair as I did old Mrs. Pollard—"

Angry, mortified, and ashamed of myself that I had listened to her so far, I turned on her with a look that seemed to make some impression even upon her.

"How dare you—" I began, then paused, shocked at my own imprudence in thus betraying the depth of the feelings she had aroused. "I beg your pardon," I immediately added, recovering my composure by a determined effort; "you doubtless did not consider that you are not in a position to speak such words to me. Even if your insinuations meant any thing serious, which I will not believe, our acquaintance"—I am afraid I threw some sarcasm into that word—"has scarcely been long enough to warrant you in approaching me on any subject of a personal nature, least of all one that involves the names of those you live with and have served so long. If you have nothing better to say—"

She rose with a jerk that seemed to my eyes as much an expression of disappointment as anger, and took a reluctant step or two towards the door.

"I am sure I meant no offence, miss," she stammered, and took another step still more reluctantly than before.

I trembled. Outrageous as it may seem, I wished at this moment that honor and dignity would allow me to call her back and question her as to the motive and meaning of her extraordinary conduct. For the thought had suddenly struck me that she might be a messenger—a most unworthy and humiliating one it is true,—and yet in some sort of a way a messenger, and my curiosity rose just in proportion as my pride rebelled.

Anice, who was not lacking in wit, evidently felt, if she could not see, the struggle she had awakened in my mind, for she

Anna Katherine Green

turned and gave me a look I no longer had the courage to resent.

"It is only something I overheard Mr. Guy say to his brother," she faltered, opening and shutting her parasol with a nervous hand; then, as I let my hair suddenly fall from my grasp, in the rush of relief I felt, blurted out: "You have beautiful hair, miss; I don't wonder Mr. Guy should say, 'One of us two must marry that girl,'" and was gone like a flash from the room, leaving me in a state that bordered on stupefaction.

This incident, so suggestive, and, alas! so degrading to my self-esteem, produced a deep and painful effect on my mind. For hours I could not rid my ears of that final sentence: "One of us two must marry that girl." Nor could the events that speedily followed quite remove from my mind and heart the sting which this knowledge of the Pollards' base calculation and diplomacy had implanted. It had one favorable consequence, however. It nerved me to carry out the expedition I had planned, and gave to my somewhat failing purpose a heart of steel.

The old mill to which I have twice carried you, and to which I must carry you again, was, as I have already said, a dilapidated and much-dismantled structure. Though its walls were intact, many of its staircases were rotten, while its flooring was, as I knew, heavily broken away in spots, making it a dangerous task to walk about its passage-ways, or even to enter the large and solitary rooms which once shook to the whirr and hum of machinery.

But it was not from such dangers as these I recoiled. If Heaven would but protect me from discovery and the possible intrusion of unwelcome visitants, I would willingly face the peril of a fall even in a place so lonesome and remote. Indeed, my one source of gratitude as I sped through the streets that morning lay in the fact, I was so little known in S——, I could pass and re-pass without awakening too much comment, especially when I wore a close veil, as I did on this occasion.

Rhoda Colwell's house lay in my way. I took especial pains not to go by it, great as the relief would have been to know she was at home and not wandering the streets in the garb and character of the idiot boy. Though I felt I could not be deceived as to her identity, the mere thought of meeting her, with that mock smile of imbecility upon her lip, filled me with a dismay that made my walk any thing but agreeable. It was consequently a positive relief when the entrance to the mill broke upon my view, and I found myself at my journey's end unwatched and unfollowed; nor could the unpromising nature of my task quite dash the spirit with which I began my search.

My first efforts were in a room which had undoubtedly been used as an office. But upon inspecting the floor I found it firm, and, convinced I should have to go farther for what I was seeking, I hastily passed into the next room. This was of much larger dimensions, and here I paused longer, for more than one board tilted as I passed over it, and not a few of them were loose and could be shifted aside by a little extra exertion of strength. But, though I investigated every board that rocked under my step, I discovered nothing beneath them but the dust and *debris* of years, and so was forced to leave this room as I had the other, without gaining any thing beyond a sense of hopelessness and the prospect of a weary back. And so on and on I went for an hour, and was beginning to realize the giant nature of my undertaking, when a sudden low sound of running water broke upon my ears, and going to one of the many windows that opened before me, I looked out and found I was at the very back of the mill, and in full sight of the dark and sullen stream that in times of yore used to feed the great wheel and run the machinery. Consequently I was in the last room upon the ground- floor, and, what struck me still more forcibly, near, if not directly over, that huge vat in the cellar which had served so fatal a purpose only a few short days before.

The sight of a flight of stairs descending at my right into the hollow darkness beneath intensified my emotion. I seemed to be in direct communication with that scene of death; and the thought struck me that here, if anywhere in the whole building, must be found the mysterious hiding-place for which I was in search.

It was therefore with extra care that I directed my glances along the uneven flooring, and I was scarcely surprised when, after a short examination of the various loose boards that rattled beneath me, I discovered one that could be shifted without difficulty. But scarcely had I stooped to raise it when an emotion of fear seized me, and I started back alert and listening, though I was unconscious of having heard any thing more than the ordinary swash of the water beneath the windows and the beating of my own overtaxed heart. An instant's hearkening gave me the reassurance I needed, and convinced that I had alarmed myself unnecessarily, I bent again over the board, and this time succeeded in moving it aside. A long, black garment, smoothly spread out to its full extent, instantly met my eye. The words of Rhoda Colwell were true; the mill did contain certain articles of clothing concealed within it.

I do not know what I expected when, a few minutes later, I pulled the garment out of the hole in which it lay buried, and spread it out before me. Not what I discovered, I am sure; for when I had given it a glance, and found it was nothing more nor less than a domino, such as is worn by masqueraders, I experienced a shock that the mask, which fell out of its folds, scarcely served to allay. It was like the introduction of farce into a terrible tragedy; and as I stood in a maze and surveyed the garment before me till its black outline swam before my eyes, I remember thinking of the effect which had been produced, at a certain trial I had heard of, by the prisoner suddenly bursting into a laugh when the sentence of death was pronounced. But presently this feeling of incongruity gave way to one of hideous dread. If Dwight Pollard could explain the presence of a domino and mask in this spot, then what sort of a man was Dwight Pollard, and what sort of a crime could it have been that needed for its perpetration such adjuncts as these? The highwaymen of olden time, with their "Stand and deliver!" seemed out of place in this quiet New England town; nor was the character of any of the parties involved, of a nature to make the association of this masquerade gear with the tragedy gone by seem either possible or even probable. And yet, there they lay; and not all my wonder, nor all the speculations which their presence evoked, would serve to blot them from the floor or explain the mystery of which they were the sign and seal.

So impressed was I at last by this thought that I broke the spell which bound me, and began to restore the articles to their place. I was just engaged in throwing the mask into the hole, when the low but unmistakable sound of an approaching foot-fall broke upon my ears, startling me more than a thunder-clap would have done, and filling me with a fear that almost paralyzed my movements. I controlled myself, however, and hastily pulled the board back to its place, after which I frantically looked about me for some means of concealment or escape. I found but one. The staircase which ran down to the cellar was but a few feet off, and if I could summon courage to make use of it, would lead to a place of comparative safety. But the darkness of that spot seemed worse than the light of this, and I stood hesitating on the brink of the staircase till the footsteps drew so near I dared not linger longer, and plunged below with such desperate haste, I wonder I did not trip and fall headlong to the cellar-floor. I did not, however, nor do I seem to have made any special noise, for the footsteps above did not hasten. I had, therefore, the satisfaction of feeling myself saved from what might have been a very special danger, and was moving slowly away, when the fascination which all horrible objects exert upon the human soul seized me with a power I could not resist, and I turned slowly but irresistibly towards the corner where I knew the fatal vat to be.

One glimpse and I would have fled; but just at the instant I turned I heard a sound overhead that sent the current of my thoughts in a fresh direction, and lent to my failing courage a renewed strength which made flight at that moment seem nothing more nor less than an impulse of cowardice. This was

nothing more nor less than a faint creaking, such as had
followed my own lifting of the board which hid the domino
and mask; a noise that was speedily followed by one yet more
distinct and of a nature to convince me beyond a doubt that
my own action was being repeated by some unknown hand.
Whose? Curiosity, love, honor, every impulse of my being
impelled me to find out. I moved like a spirit towards the
stairs. I placed my foot on one step, and then on another,
mounting in silence and without a fear, so intent was I upon
the discovery which now absorbed me. But just as I reached
the top, just when another movement would lift my head
above the level of the floor, I paused, realizing as in a flash
what the consequences might be if the intruder should prove
to be another than Rhoda Colwell, and should have not his
back but his face turned towards the place where I stood. The
sounds I heard, feeble as they were, did not seem to indicate
the presence of a woman, and in another instant a low
exclamation, smothered in the throat almost before it was
uttered, assured me that it was a man who stood not six feet
from me, handling the objects which I had been told were in
some way connected with a murder which I was by every
instinct of honor bound to discover, if not avenge.

A man! and ah, he was so quiet, so careful! I could not even
guess what he was doing, much less determine his identity, by
listening. I had a conviction that he was taking the articles out
of their place of concealment, but I could not be sure; and in a
matter like this, certainty was indispensable. I resolved to risk
all, and took another step, clinging dizzily to the first support
that offered. It was well I had the presence of mind to do this,
or I might have had a serious fall. For no sooner had I raised
my head above the level of the floor than my eyes fell upon the
well-known form of him I desired least of all men to see in this
place—my lover, if you may call him so—Dwight Pollard.

XII

DWIGHT POLLARD

Oh, 'tis too true! how smart
A lash that speech doth give my conscience!

—HAMLET.

He was standing with his back to me, and to all appearance was unconscious that he was under the surveillance of any eye. I had thus a moment in which to collect my energies and subdue my emotions; and I availed myself of it to such good purpose that by the time he had put the board back into its place I was ready to face him. He did not turn round, however; so, after a moment of silent suspense, I mounted the last stair, and thinking of nothing, hoping for nothing, wishing for nothing, stood waiting, with my eyes fixed on the domino he was now rapidly folding into smaller compass.

And thus I stood, like a pallid automaton, when the instant came for him to change his position, and he saw me. The cry that rose to his lips but did not escape them, the reel which his figure gave before it stiffened into marble, testified to the shock he had received, and also to the sense of unreality with which my appearance in this wise must have impressed him. His look, his attitude were those of a man gazing upon a spectre, and as I met his glance with mine, I was conscious of a feeling of unreality myself, as if the whole occurrence were a dream, and he and I but shadows which another moment would dissolve.

But alas! this was no more a dream than were the other strange and tragic events which had gone before; and in an instant we both knew it, and were standing face to face with wretched inquiry in the looks we fixed upon each other across the domino which had fallen from his hands. He was the first to speak.

"Miss Sterling!" he exclaimed, in a light tone, cruelly belied by the trembling lips from which it issued, "by what fortunate chance do I see you again, and in a place I should have thought to be the last you would be likely to visit?"

"By the same chance," I rejoined, "which appears to have brought you here. The desire to make sure if what I heard about the mill having been used as a secreting place for certain mysterious articles, was true." And I pointed to the mask and domino lying at my feet.

His eye, which had followed the direction of my finger, grew dark and troubled.

"Then it was your hand—" he impetuously began.

"Which disturbed these garments before you? Yes. And I shall make no apology for the action," I continued, "since it was done in the hope of proving false certain insinuations which had been made to me in your regard."

"Insinuations?" he repeated.

"Yes," I declared, in an agony between my longing to hear him vindicate himself and the desire to be true to the obligations I was under to Ada Reynolds. "Insinuations of the worst, the most terrible, character." Then, as I saw him fall back, stricken in something more than his pride, I hastened to inquire: "Have you an enemy in town, Mr. Pollard?"

He composed himself with a start, looked at me fixedly, and replied in what struck me as a strange tone even for such an occasion as this:

"Perhaps."

"One who out of revenge," I proceeded, "might be induced to attach your name to suspicions calculated to rob you of honor, if not life?"

"Perhaps," he again returned; but this time with a fierceness that almost made me recoil, though I knew it was directed against some one besides myself.

"Then it may be," I said, "that you have but to speak to relieve my mind of the heaviest weight which has ever fallen upon it. These articles," I pursued, "have they, or have they not, any connection with the tragedy which makes the place in which we stand memorable?"

"I cannot answer you, Miss Sterling."

"Cannot answer me?"

"Cannot answer you," he reiterated, turning haggard about the eyes and lips.

"Then," I brokenly rejoined, "I had better leave this place; I do not see what more I have to do or say here."

"O God!" he cried, detaining me with a gesture full of agony and doubt. "Do not leave me so; let me think. Let me weigh the situation and see where I stand, in your eyes at least. Tell me what my enemy has said!" he demanded, his face, his very form, flashing with a terrible rage that seemed to have as much indignation as fear in it.

"Your enemy," I replied, in the steady voice of despair, "accuses you in so many words—of murder."

I expected to see him recoil, burst forth into cursing or frenzied declamation, by which men betray their inward consternation and remorse; but he did none of these things. Instead of that he laughed; a hideous laugh that seemed to shake the rafters above us and echoed in and out of the caverned recesses beneath.

"Accuses *me*?" he muttered; and it is not in language to express the scorn he infused into the words.

Stunned, and scarcely knowing what to think, I gazed at him helplessly. He seemed to feel my glance, for, after a moment's contemplation of my face, his manner suddenly changed, and bowing with a grim politeness full of sarcasm, he asked:

"And when did you see my enemy and hold this precious conversation in which *I* was accused of murder?"

"Yesterday afternoon," I answered. "During the time of your mother's funeral," I subjoined, startled by the look of stupefaction which crossed his face at my words.

"I don't understand you," he murmured, sweeping his hand in a dazed way over his brow. "You saw him then? Spoke to him? Impossible!"

"It is not a man to whom I allude," I returned, almost as much agitated as himself. "It is a woman who is your accuser, a woman who seems to feel she has a right to make you suffer, possibly because she has suffered so much herself."

"A woman!" was all he said; "a woman!" turning pale enough now, God knows.

"Have you no enemies among the women?" I asked, wearied to the soul with the position in which my cruel fate had forced me.

"I begin to think I have," he answered, giving me a look that somehow broke down the barriers of ice between us and made my next words come in a faltering tone:

"And could you stop to bestow a thought upon a man while a woman held your secret? Did you think our sex was so long-suffering, or this special woman so generous—"

I did not go on, for he had leaped the gap which separated us and had me gently but firmly by the arm.

"Of whom are you speaking?" he demanded. "What woman has my secret— if secret I have? Let me hear her name, now, at once."

"Is it possible," I murmured, "that you do not know?"

"The name! the name!" he reiterated, his eyes ablaze, his hand shaking where it grasped my arm.

"Rhoda Colwell," I returned, looking him steadily in the eye.

"Impossible!" his lips seemed to breathe, and his clasp slowly unloosed from my arm like a ring of ice which melts away. "Rhoda Colwell! Good God!" he exclaimed, and staggered back with ever- growing wonder and alarm till half the room lay between us.

"I am not surprised at your emotion," I said; "she is a dangerous woman."

He looked at me with dull eyes; he did not seem to hear what I said.

"How can it be?" he muttered; and his glance took a furtive aspect as it travelled slowly round the room and finally settled upon the mask and domino at my feet. "Was it she who told you where to look for those?" he suddenly queried in an almost violent tone.

Anna Katherine Green

I bowed; I had no wish to speak.

"She is an imp, a witch, an emissary of the Evil One," he vehemently declared; and turned away, murmuring, as it seemed to me, those sacred words of Scripture, "Be sure your sin find you out."

I felt the sobs rise in my throat. I could bear but little more. To recover myself, I looked away from him, even passed to a window and gazed out. Any thing but the sight of this humiliation in one who could easily have been my idol. I was therefore standing with my back to him when he finally approached, and touching me with the tip of his finger, calmly remarked;

"I did not know you were acquainted with Miss Colwell."

"Nor was I till yesterday," I rejoined. "Fate made us know each other at one interview, if could be said to ever know such a woman as she is."

"Fate is to blame for much; is it also to blame for the fact that you sought her? Or did she seek you?"

"I sought her," I said; and, not seeing any better road to a proper explanation of my conduct than the truth, I told him in a few words of the notice I had seen posted upon the mill, and of how I had afterwards surprised Rhoda Colwell there, and what the conclusions were which I had thereby drawn; though, from some motive of delicacy I do not yet understand, I refrained from saying any thing about her disguise, and left him to infer that it was in her own proper person I had seen her.

He seemed to be both wonder-stricken and moved by the recital, and did not rest till he had won from me the double fact that Rhoda Colwell evidently knew much more than she revealed, while I, on the contrary, knew much less. The latter discovery seemed to greatly gratify him, and while his brow lost none of the look of heavy anxiety which had settled upon it with the introduction of this woman's name into our colloquy, I noticed that his voice was lighter, and that he surveyed me with less distrust and possibly with less fear. His next words showed the direction his thoughts were taking.

"You have shown an interest in my fate, Miss Sterling, in spite of the many reasons you had for thinking it a degraded one, and for this I thank you with all my heart. Will you prove your womanliness still further by clinging to the belief which I have endeavored to force upon you, that notwithstanding all you have heard and seen, I stand in no wise amenable to the law, neither have I uttered, in your hearing at least, aught but the truth in regard to this whole matter?"

"And you can swear this to me?" I uttered, joyfully.

"By my father's grave, if you desire it," he returned.

A flood of hope rushed through my heart. I was but a weak woman, and his voice and look at that moment would have affected the coldest nature.

"I am bound to believe you," I said; "though there is much I do not understand—much which you ought to explain if you wish to disabuse my mind of all doubt in your regard. I would be laying claim to a cynicism I do not possess, if I did not trust your words just so far as you will allow me. But—" And I must have assumed an air of severity, for I saw his head droop lower and lower as I gazed at him and forbore to finish my sentence.

"But you believe I am a villain," he stammered.

"I would fain believe you to be the best and noblest of men," I answered, pointedly.

He lifted his head, and the flush of a new emotion swept over his face.

"Why did I not meet you two years ago?" he cried.

The tone was so bitter, the regret expressed so unutterable, I could not help my heart sinking again with the weight of fresh doubt which it brought.

"Would it have been better for me if you had?" I inquired. "Is the integrity which is dependent upon one's happiness, or the sympathy of friends, one that a woman can trust to under all circumstances of temptation or trial?"

"I do not know," he muttered. "I think it would stand firm with you for its safeguard and shield." Then, as he saw me draw back with an assumption of coldness I was far from feeling, added gently: "But it was not you, but Rhoda Colwell, I met two years ago, and I know you too well, appreciate you too well, to lay aught but my sincerest homage at your feet, in the hope that, whatever I may have been in the past, the future shall prove me to be not unworthy of your sympathy, and possibly of your regard."

And, as if he felt the stress of the interview becoming almost too great for even his strength, he turned away from me and began gathering up the toggery that lay upon the floor.

"These must not remain here," he observed, bitterly.

But I, drawn this way and that by the most contradictory emotions, felt that all had not been said which should be in this important and possibly final interview. Accordingly, smothering personal feeling and steeling myself to look only at my duty, I advanced to his side, and, indicating with a gesture the garments he was now rolling up into a compact mass, remarked:

"This may or may not involve you in some unpleasantness. Rhoda Colwell, who evidently attaches much importance to her discoveries, is not the woman to keep silent in their regard. If she speaks and forces me to speak, I must own the truth,

Mr. Pollard. Neither sympathy nor regard could hold me back; for my honor is pledged to the cause of Mr. Barrows, and not even the wreck of my own happiness could deter me from revealing any thing that would explain his death or exonerate his memory. I wish you to understand this. God grant I may never be called upon to speak!"

It was a threat, a warning, or a danger for which he was wholly unprepared. He stared at me for a moment from his lowly position on the floor, then slowly rose and mechanically put his hand to his throat, as if he felt himself choking.

"I thank you for your frankness," he murmured, in almost inaudible tones. "It is no more than I ought to have expected; and yet—" He turned abruptly away. "I am evidently in a worse situation than I imagined," he continued, after a momentary pacing of the floor. "I thought only my position in your eyes was assailed; I see now that I may have to defend myself before the world." And, with a sudden change that was almost alarming, he asked if Rhoda Colwell had intimated in any way the source of whatever information she professed to have.

I told him no, and felt my heart grow cold with new and undefined fears as he turned his face toward the front of the building, and cried, in a suppressed tone, full of ire and menace:

"It could have come but in one way; I am to be made a victim if—" He turned upon me with a wild look in which there was something personal. "Are you worth the penalty which my good name must suffer?" he violently cried. "For I swear that to you and you only I owe the position in which I now stand!"

"God help me then!" I murmured, dazed and confounded by this unexpected reproach.

"Had you been less beautiful, less alluring in your dignity and grace, my brother—" He paused and bit his lip. "Enough!" he cried. "I had wellnigh forgotten that generosity and forbearance are to actuate my movements in the future. I beg your pardon—and his!" he added, with deep and bitter sarcasm, under his breath.

This allusion to Guy, unpleasant and shocking as it was, gave me a peculiar sensation that was not unlike that of relief, while at the same moment the glimpse of something, which I was fain to call a revelation, visited my mind and led me impetuously to say:

"I hope you are not thinking of sacrificing yourself for another less noble and less generous than yourself. If such is the clew to actions which certainly have looked dubious till now, I pray that you will reconsider your duty and not play the Don Quixote too far."

But Dwight Pollard, instead of accepting this explanation of his conduct with the eagerness of a great relief, only shook his head and declared:

"My brother—for I know who you mean, Miss Sterling—is no more amenable to the law than myself. Neither of us were guilty of the action that terminated Mr. Barrows' life."

"And yet," came in the strange and unexpected tones of a third person, "can you say, in the presence of her you profess to respect and of me whom you once professed to love, that either you or your brother are guiltless of his death?" and turning simultaneously toward the doorway, we saw gleaming in its heavy frame the vivid form and glittering eyes of his most redoubtable enemy and mine— Rhoda Colwell.

He fell back before this apparition and appeared to lose his power of speech. She advanced like an avenging Nemesis between us.

"Speak!" she vehemently exclaimed. "Are you—I say nothing of your brother, who is nothing to me or to her—are *you* guiltless, in the sense in which she would regard guilt, of David Barrows' death?" And her fierce eyes, shining through her half-closed lashes like lurid fires partly veiled, burned upon his face, which, turning paler and paler, drooped before her gaze till his chin settled upon his breast and we could barely hear the words that fell from his lips:

"God knows I would not dare to say I am."

Anna Katherine Green

XIII

GUY POLLARD

I will tell you why.

—HAMLET.

There was a silence, then Dwight Pollard spoke again. "I have made a confession which I never expected to hear pass my lips. She who has forced it from me doubtless knows how much and how little it means. Let her explain herself, then. I have no further business in this place." And, without lifting his head or meeting the eye of either of us, he strode past us towards the door.

But there he paused, for Rhoda Colwell's voice had risen in words that must be answered.

"And where, then, have you business if not here? Do you not know I hold your good name, if not your life, in my hands?"

"My good name," he slowly rejoined, without turning his head, "is already lost in the eyes I most valued. As for my life, it stands in no jeopardy. Would I could say the same for his!" was his fierce addition.

"His?" came from Rhoda Colwell's lips, in surprise. "His?" and with a quick and subtle movement she glided to his side and seized him imperatively by the arm. "Whom do you mean?" she asked.

He turned on her with a dark look.

"Whom do I mean?" he retorted. "Whom should I mean but the base and unnatural wretch who, for purposes of his own, has made you the arbitrator of my destiny and the avenger of my sin—my brother, my vile, wicked brother, whom may Heaven—"

"Stop! Your brother has had nothing to do with this. Do you suppose I would stoop to take information from him? What I know I know because my eyes have seen it, Dwight Pollard! And now, what do you think of the clutch I hold upon your life?" and she held out those two milk-white hands of hers with a smile such as I hope never to see on mortal face again.

He looked at them, then at her, and drew back speechless. She burst into a low but ringing laugh of immeasurable triumph.

"And you thought such a blow as this could come *from a man*! Dullard and fool you must be, Dwight Pollard, or else you have never known *me*. Why should he risk his honor and his safety in an action as dangerous to him as ungrateful to you? Because he admires *her*? Guy Pollard is not so loving. But I—I whom you taught to be a woman, only to fling aside like a weed—Ah, that is another thing! Reason for waiting and watching here; reason for denouncing, when the time came, the man who could take advantage of another man's fears! Ah, you see I know what I am talking about."'

"Speak!" he gasped. "How do you know? You say you saw. How could you see? Where were you, demon and witch in one?"

She smiled, not as before, but yet with a sense of power that only the evil glitter of her sidelong eye kept from making her wholly adorable.

"Will you come into the cellar below?" said she. "Or stay; that may be asking too much. A glance from one of these windows will do." And moving rapidly across the room, she threw up one of the broken sashes before her, and pointed to a stunted tree that grew up close against the wall. "Do you see that limb?" she inquired, indicating one that branched put towards a window we could faintly see defined beneath. "A demon or a witch might sit there for a half-hour and see, without so much as craning her neck, all that went on in the cellar below. That the leaves are thick, and, to those within, apparently hang like a curtain between them and the outer world, would make no difference to a demon's eyes, you know. Such folk can see where black walls intervene; how much more when only a fluttering screen like that shuts off the view." And, drawing back, she looked into his dazed face, and then into mine, as though she would ask: "Have I convinced you that I am a woman to be feared?"

His white cheek seemed to answer Yes, but his eyes, when he raised them, did not quail before her mocking glance, though I thought they drooped a little when, in another moment, they flashed in my direction.

"Miss Sterling," he inquired, "do you understand what Miss Colwell has been saying?"

I shook my head and faltered back. I had only one wish, and that was to be effaced from this spot of misery.

He turned again to her.

"Do you intend to explain yourself further?" he demanded.

She did not answer; her look and her attention were fixed upon me.

"You are not quite convinced he is all that I have declared him to be?" she said, moving towards me. "You want to know what I saw and whether there is not some loophole by which you can escape from utterly condemning him. Well, you shall have my story. I ask nothing more of you than that." And with a quiet ignoring of his presence that was full of contempt, she drew up to my side and calmly began: "You have seen me in the streets in the garb of my brother?"

"Your brother?" cried a startled voice.

It was Dwight Pollard who spoke. He had sprung to her side and grasped her fiercely by the wrist. It was a picture; all the more that neither of them said any thing further, but stood so, surveying each other, till he thought fit to drop her arm and draw back, when she quietly went on as though no interruption had occurred.

"It was a convenient disguise, enabling me to do and learn many things. It also made it possible for me to be out in the evening alone, and allowed me to visit certain places where otherwise I should have been any thing but welcome. It also satisfied a spirit of adventure which I possess, and led to the experience which I am now about to relate. Miss Sterling, my brother has one peculiarity. He can be intrusted to carry a message, and forget it ten minutes after it is delivered. This being generally known in town, I was not at all surprised when one evening, as I was traversing a very dark street, I was met and accosted by a muffled figure, who asked me if I would run to Mr. Barrows' house for him. I was about to say No, when something in his general air and manner deterred me, and I changed it into the half-laughing, half-eager assent which my brother uses on such occasions. The man immediately stooped to my ear and whispered:

"'Tell Mr. Barrows to come with all speed to the old mill. A man has been thrown from his carriage and is dying there. He wants Mr. Barrows' prayers and consolation. Can you remember?'"

"I nodded my head and ran off. I was fearful, if I stayed, I would betray myself; for the voice, with all its attempted disguise, was that of Guy Pollard, and the man injured might for all I knew be his brother. Before I reached Mr. Barrows' door, however, I began to have my doubts. Something in the man's manner betrayed mystery, and as Guy Pollard had never been a favorite of mine, I naturally gave to this any thing but a favorable interpretation. I did not stop, though, because I doubted. On the contrary, I pushed forward, for if there was a secret, I must know it; and how could I learn it so readily or so well as by following Mr. Barrows on his errand of mercy?

"The person who came to the door in answer to my summons was fortunately Mr. Barrows himself; fortunately for me, that is; I cannot say it was altogether fortunately for him. He had a little book in his hand, and seemed disturbed when I gave him my message. He did not hesitate, however. Being of an unsuspicious nature, he never dreamed that all was not as I said, especially as he knew my brother well, and was thoroughly acquainted with the exactness with which he always executed an errand. But he did not want to go; that I saw clearly, and laid it all to the little book; for he was the kindest man who ever lived, and never was known to shirk a duty because it was unpleasant or hard.

"I have said he knew my brother well. Remembering this when he came down stairs again ready to accompany me, I assumed the wildest manner in which my brother ever indulged, that I might have some excuse for not remaining at his side while still accompanying him in his walk. The consequence was that not a dozen words passed between us, and I had the satisfaction of seeing him draw near the old mill in almost complete forgetfulness of my proximity. This was what I wanted, for in the few minutes I had to think, many curious surmises had risen in my mind, and I wished to perform my little part in this adventure without hindrance from his watchfulness or care.

"It was a very dark night, as you remember, Dwight Pollard, and it is no wonder that neither he nor the man who came out of the doorway to meet him saw the slight figure that crouched against the wall close by the door they had to enter. And if they had seen it, what would they have thought? That the idiot boy was only more freakish than usual, or was waiting about for the dime which was the usual pay for his services. Neither the clouds, nor the trees, nor the surrounding darkness would have whispered that an eager woman's heart beat under that boy's jacket, and that they had better trust the wind in its sweep, the water in its rush, or the fire in its ravaging, than the will that lay coiled behind the feebly moving lip and wandering, restless eye of the seeming idiot who knelt there.

"So I was safe and for the moment could hear and see. And this was what I saw: A tall and gentlemanly form, carrying a lantern which he took pains should shine on Mr. Barrows' face and not on his own. The expression of the former was, therefore, plain to me, and in it I read something more than reluctance, something which I dimly felt to be fear. His anxiety, however, did not seem to spring from his companion, but from the building he was about to enter, for it was when he looked up at its frowning walls and shadowy portal that I saw him shudder and turn pale. They went in, however. Not without a question or two from Mr. Barrows as to whom his guide was and where the sick man lay, to all of which the other responded shortly or failed to respond at all, facts which went far to convince me that a deception of some kind was being practised upon the confiding clergyman.

"I was consequently in a fever of impatience to follow them in, and had at last made up my mind to do so, when I heard a deep sigh, and glancing up towards the doorway, saw that it was again occupied by the dark figure which I had so lately seen pass in with Mr. Barrows. He had no lantern now, and I could not even discern the full outlines of his form, but his sigh being repeated, I knew who he was as certainly as if I had seen him, for it was one which had often been breathed in my ears, and was as well known to me as the beatings of my own heart. This discovery, as you may believe, Miss Sterling, did not tend to allay either my curiosity or my impatience, and when in a few minutes the watcher drew back, I stole from my hiding-place, and creeping up to the open doorway, listened. A sound of pacing steps came to my ears. The entrance was guarded.

"For a moment I stood baffled, then remembering the lantern which had been carried into the building, I withdrew quietly from the door, and began a tour of inspection round about the mill in the hope of spying some glimmer of light from one or more of the many windows, and in this way learn the exact spot to which Mr. Barrows had been taken. It was a task of no mean difficulty, Miss Sterling, for the bushes cluster thick about those walls, and I had no light to warn me of their whereabouts or of the many loose stones that lay in heaps here and there along the way. But I would not have stopped if firebrands had been under my feet, nor did I cease my exertions or lose my hope till I reached the back of the mill and found it as dark as the side and front. Then indeed I did begin to despair, for the place was so solitary and remote from observation, I could not conceive of any better being found for purposes that required secrecy or concealment. Yet the sombre walls rose before me, dark and unrelieved against the sky; and nothing remained for me but to press on to the broad west end and see if that presented as unpromising an aspect as the rest.

"I accordingly recommenced my toilsome journey, rendered positively dangerous now by the vicinity of the water and the steepness of the banks that led down to it. But I did not go far, for as, in my avoidance of the stream, I drew nearer and nearer the walls, I caught glimpses of what I at first thought to be the flash of a fire-fly in the bushes, but in another moment discovered to be the fitful glimmer of a light through a window heavily masked with leaves. You can imagine what followed from what I told you. How I climbed the tree, and seated myself on the limb that ran along by the window, and pushing aside the leaves, looked in upon the scene believed by those engaged in it to be as absolutely unwitnessed as if it had taken place in the bowels of the earth.

"And what did I see there, Miss Sterling? At first little. The light within was so dim and the window itself so high from the floor, that nothing save a moving shadow or two met my eye. But presently becoming accustomed to the position, I discovered first that I was looking in on a portion of the cellar, and next that three figures stood before me, two of which I immediately recognized as those of Mr. Barrows and Guy Pollard. But the third stood in shadow, and I did not know then, nor do I know now, who it was, though I have my suspicions, incredible as they may seem even to myself. Mr. Barrows, whose face was a study of perplexity, if not horror, seemed to be talking. He was looking Guy Pollard straight in the face when I first saw him, but presently I perceived him turn and fix his eyes on that mysterious third figure which he seemed to study for some signs of relenting. But evidently without success, for I saw his eyes droop and his hands fall helplessly to his side as if he felt that he had exhausted every argument, and that nothing was left to him but silence.

"All this, considering the circumstances and the scene, was certainly startling enough even to one of my nature and history, but when in a few minutes later I saw Guy Pollard step forward, and seizing Mr. Barrows by the hand, draw him forward to what seemed to be the verge of a pit, I own that I felt as if I were seized by some deadly nightmare, and had to turn myself away and look at the skies and trees for a moment to make sure I was not the victim of a hallucination. When I looked back they were still standing there, but a change had come over Mr. Barrows' face. From being pale it had become ghastly, and his eyes, fixed and fascinated, were gazing into those horrid depths, as if he saw there the horrible fate which afterwards befell him. Suddenly he drew back, covering his face with his hands, and I saw a look pass from Guy Pollard to that watchful third figure, which, if it had not been on the face of a gentleman, I should certainly call demoniacal. The next instant the third figure stepped forward, and before I could move or utter the scream that rose to my lips, Mr. Barrows had disappeared from view in the horrid recesses of that black hole, and only Guy Pollard and that other mysterious one, who I now saw wore a heavy black domino and mask, remained standing on its dark verge.

"A cry, so smothered that it scarcely came to my ears, rose for an instant from the pit, then I saw Guy Pollard stoop forward and put what seemed to be a question to the victim below. From the nature of the smile that crossed his lip as he drew back, I judged it had not been answered satisfactorily; and was made yet more sure of this when the third person, stooping, took up the light, and beckoning to Guy Pollard, began to walk away. Yes, Miss Sterling, I am telling no goblin tale, as you can see if you will cast your eyes on our companion over there. They walked away, and the light grew dimmer and dimmer and the sense of horror deeper and deeper, till a sudden cry, rising shrill enough now from that deadly hole, drew the two conspirators slowly back to stand again upon its fatal brink, and, as it seemed to me, propound again that question, for answer to which they appeared ready to barter their honor, if not their souls.

"And this time they got it. The decisive gesture of the masked figure, and the speed with which Guy Pollard disappeared from the spot, testified that the knowledge they wanted was theirs, and that only some sort of action remained to be performed. What that action was I could not imagine, for, though Mr. Pollard carried away the lantern, the masked figure had remained.

"Meantime darkness was ours; a terrible darkness, as you may imagine, Miss Sterling, in which it was impossible not to wait for a repetition of that smothered cry from the depths of this unknown horror. But it did not come; and amid a silence awful as the grave, the minutes went by till at last, to my great relief, the light appeared once more in the far recesses of the cellar, and came twinkling on till it reached the masked figure, which, to all appearance, had not moved hand or foot since it went away.

"Miss Sterling, you have doubtless consoled yourself during this narration with the thought that the evil which I had seen done had been the work of Guy and a person who need not necessarily have been our friend here. But I must shatter whatever satisfaction you may have derived from the possible absence of Dwight Pollard from this scene, by saying that when the lantern paused and I had the opportunity to see who carried it, I found that it was no longer in the hand of the younger brother, but had been transferred to that of Dwight, and that he, not Guy, now stood in the cellar before me.

"As I realize that we are not alone, I will not dilate upon his appearance, much as it struck me at the time. I will merely say he offered a contrast to Guy, who, if I may speak so plainly in this presence, had seemed much at home in the task he had set himself, uncongenial as one might consider it to the usual instincts and habits of a gentleman. But Dwight—you see I can be just, Miss Sterling—looked anxious and out of place; and, instead of seeming to be prepared for the situation, turned and peered anxiously about him, as if in search of the clergyman he expected to find standing somewhere on this spot. His surprise and horror when the masked figure pointed to the pit were evident, Miss Sterling; but it was a surprise and a horror that immediately settled into resignation, if not apathy; and after his first glance and shuddering start in that direction he did not stir again, but stood quite like a statue while the masked figure spoke, and when he did move it was to return the way he had come, without a look or a gesture toward the sombre hole where so much that was manly and kind lay sunk in a darkness that must have seemed to that sensitive nature the prototype of his grave."

"And is that all, Miss Colwell?" came with a strange intonation from Dwight Pollard's lips, as she paused, with a triumphant look in my direction.

"It is all I have to tell," was the reply; and it struck me that her tone was as peculiar as his. "Minutes, seconds even, spent under such circumstances, seem like hours; and after a spell of what appeared an interminable waiting, I allowed myself to be overcome by the disquiet and terror of my situation, and dropping from my perch, crept home."

"You should have stayed another hour," he dryly observed. "I wonder at an impatience you had never manifested till then."

"Do you?"

The meaning with which she said this, the gesture with which she gave it weight, struck us both aback.

"Woman!" he thundered, coming near to her with the mingled daring and repugnance with which one advances to crush a snake, "do you mean to say that you are going to publish this much of your story and publish no more? That you will tell the world this and not tell—"

"What I did not see?" she interpolated, looking him straight in the eye as might the serpent to which I have compared her.

"Good God!" was his horrified exclamation; "and yet you know—"

"Pardon me," her voice broke in again. "You have heard what I know," and she bowed with such an inimitable and mocking grace, and yet with such an air of sinister resolve, that he stood like one fascinated, and let her move away towards the door without seeking by word or look to stop her. "I hold you tight, you see," were her parting words to him as she paused just upon the threshold to give us a last and scornful look. "So tight," she added, shaking her close-shut hand, "that I doubt if even your life could escape should I choose to remember in court what I have remembered before you two here to-day."

"And forget—" he began.

"And forget," she repeated, "what might defeat the ends of that justice which demands a life for the one so wantonly sacrificed in the vat whose hideous depths now open almost under your feet." And, having said these words, she turned to go, when, looking up, she found her passage barred by the dark form of Guy Pollard, who, standing in the doorway with his hands upon either lintel, surveyed her with his saturnine smile, in which for this once I saw something that did not make me recoil, certain as I now was of his innate villainy and absolute connection with Mr. Barrows' death.

She herself seemed to feel that she had met her master; for, with a hurried look in his face, she drew slowly back, and, folding her arms, waited for him to move with a patience too nonchalant not to be forced.

But he did not seem inclined to move, and I beheld a faint blush as of anger break out on her cheek, though her attitude retained its air of superb indifference, and her lips, where they closed upon each other, did not so much as break their lines for an instant.

"You are not going, Miss Colwell," were the words with which he at last broke the almost intolerable suspense of the moment; "at least, not till you have given us the date of this remarkable experience of yours."

"The date?" she repeated, icily. "What day was it that Mr. Barrows was found in the vat?" she inquired, turning to me with an indifferent look.

His hand fell like iron on her arm.

"You need not appeal to Miss Sterling," he remarked. "*I* am asking you this question, and I am not a man to be balked nor frightened by you when my life itself is at stake. What night was it on which you saw me place Mr. Barrows in the vat? I command you to tell me, or—"

His hands closed on her arm, and—she did not scream, but I did; for the look of the inquisitor was in his face, and I saw that she must succumb, or be broken like a reed before our eyes.

She chose to succumb. Deadly pale and shaking with the terror with which he evidently inspired her, she turned like a wild creature caught in the toils, and gasped out:

"It was a night in August—the seventeenth, I think. I wish you and your brother much joy of the acknowledgment."

He did not answer, only dropped her arm, and, looking at me, remarked:

"I think that puts a different face upon the matter."

It did indeed. For Mr. Barrows had only been dead four days, and to-day was the twenty-eight of September.

* * * * *

I do not know how long it was before I allowed the wonder and perplexity which this extraordinary disclosure aroused in me to express itself in words. The shock which had been communicated to me was so great, I had neither thought nor feeling left, and it was not till I perceived every eye fixed upon me that I found the power to say:

"Then Mr. Barrows' death was not the result of that night's work. The hand that plunged him into the vat drew him out again. But—but—" Here my tongue failed me. I could only look the question with which my mind was full.

Dwight Pollard immediately stepped forward.

"But whose were the hands that thrust him back four days ago? That is what you would ask, is it not, Miss Sterling?" he inquired, with a force and firmness he had not before displayed.

"Yes," I endeavored to say, though I doubt if a sound passed my lips.

His face took a more earnest cast, his voice a still deeper tone.

"Miss Sterling," he began, meeting my eye with what might have been the bravado of despair, but which I was fain to believe the courage of truth, "after what you have just heard, it would be strange, perhaps, if you should place much belief in any thing we may say upon this subject. And yet it is my business to declare, and that with all the force and assurance of which I am capable, that we know no more than you, how Mr. Barrows came to find himself again in that place; that we had nothing to do with it, and that his death, occurring in the manner and at the spot it did, was a surprise to us which cost my mother her life, and me—well, almost my reason," he added, in a lower tone, turning away his face.

"Can this be true?" I asked myself, unconsciously taking on an air of determination, as I remembered I was prejudiced in his favor, and wished to believe him innocent of this crime.

This movement on my part, slight as it was, was evidently seen and misinterpreted by them all. For a look of disappointment came into Dwight Pollard's face, while from his brother's eye flashed a dangerous gleam that almost made me oblivious to the fact that Rhoda. Colwell was speaking words full of meaning and venom.

"A specious declaration!" she exclaimed. "A jury would believe such assertions, of course; so would the world at large, It is so easy to credit that this simple and ordinary method of disposing of a valuable life should enter the mind of another person!"

"It is as easy to credit that," answered Dwight Pollard, with an emphasis which showed that he, if not I, felt the force of this sarcasm, "as it would be to believe that Mr. Barrows would return to a spot so fraught with hideous memories, except under the influence of a purpose which made him blind to all but its accomplishment. The fact that he died *there*, proves to my mind that no other will than his own plunged him anew into that dreadful vat."

"Ah! and so you are going to ascribe his death to suicide?" she inquired, with a curl of her lip that was full of disdain.

"Yes," he sternly responded with no signs of wavering now, though her looks might well have stung the stoutest soul into some show of weakness.

"It is a wise stroke," she laughed, with indescribable emphasis. "It has so much in Mr. Barrows' life and character to back it. And may I ask," she went on, with a look that included Guy Pollard's silent and contemptuous figure in its scope, "whether you have anything but words wherewith to impress your belief upon the public? I have heard that judge and jury like facts, or, at the least, circumstantial proof that a man's denial is a true one."

"And proofs we have!"

It was Guy Pollard who spoke this time, and with an icy self-possession that made her shiver in spite of herself.

"Proofs?" she repeated.

"That we were not near the mill the night before Mr. Barrows was found. We were both out of town, and did not return till about the time the accident was discovered."

"Ah!" was her single sarcastic rejoinder; but I saw—we all saw—that the blow had told, bravely as she tried to hide it.

"You, can make nothing by accusing us of this crime," he continued; "and if I might play the part of a friend to you, I would advise you not to attempt it." And his cold eye rested for a moment on hers before he turned and walked away to the other end of the room.

The look, the action, was full of contempt, but she did not seem to feel it. Following him with her gaze for a minute, she murmured, quietly: "We will see"; then turning her look upon

Dwight and myself, added slowly: "I think *you* are effect-ually separated at all events," and was gone almost without our realizing how or where.

I did not linger long behind. What I said or what they said I cannot remember. I only know that in a few minutes I too was flying along the highway, eager for the refuge which my solitary home offered me. Events had rushed upon me too thickly and too fast. I felt ill as I passed the threshold of my room, and was barely conscious when a few hours later the landlady came in to see why I had not made my appearance at the supper-table.

XIV

CORRESPONDENCE

Letters, my Lord.

—HAMLET.

My illness, though severe, was not of long continuance. In a week I was able to be about my room; and in a fortnight I was allowed to read the letters that had come to me. There were two, either of them calculated to awaken dangerous emotions; and, taken together, making a draft on my powers which my newly gained health found it hard to sustain. The one was signed Rhoda Colwell, and the other Dwight Pollard. I read Rhoda Colwell's first.

It opened without preamble:

I sought revenge and I have found it. Not in the way I anticipated, perhaps, but still in a way good enough to satisfy both myself and the spirit of justice. You will never trust Dwight Pollard again. You will never come any nearer to him than you have to-day. You have an upright soul, and whether you believe his declarations or not, can be safely relied upon to hold yourself aloof from a man who could lend his countenance to such a cowardly deed as I saw perpetrated in the old cellar a month or so ago. Honor does not wed with dishonor, nor truth with treachery. Constance Sterling may marry whom she may; it will never be Dwight Pollard.

Convinced of this, I have decided to push my vengeance no further. Not that I believe Mr. Barrows committed suicide, any more than I believe that Dwight and Guy Pollard could be saved by any mere alibi, if I chose to speak. Men like them can find ready tools to do their work, and if they had been an hundred miles away instead of some six, I should still think that the will which plunged Mr. Barrows into his dreadful grave was the same which once before had made him taste the horrors of his threatened doom. But public disgrace and execration are not what I seek for my recreant lover. The inner anguish which no eye can see is what I have been forced to endure and what he shall be made to suffer. Guilty or not he can never escape that now; and it is a future which I gloat upon and from which I would not have him escape, no, not at the cost of his life, if that life were mine, and I could shorten it at a stroke.

And yet since human nature is human nature, and good hearts as well as bad yield sometimes to a fatal weakness, I would add that the facts which I suppress are always facts, and that if I see in you or him any forgetfulness of the gulf that separates you, I shall not think it too late to speak, though months have been added to months, and years to years, and I am no longer any thing but old

RHODA COLWELL.

Close upon these words I read these others:

MISS STERLING:—Pardon me that I presume to address you. Pardon the folly, the weakness of a man who, having known you for less than a week, finds the loss of your esteem the hardest of the many miseries he is called upon to bear.

I know that I can never recover this esteem—if, indeed, I ever possessed it. The revelation of the secret which disgraced our family has been fatal; the secret which our mother commanded us on her death-bed to preserve, foreseeing that, if it should become known that we had been guilty of the occurrence of the seventeenth of August, nothing could save us from the suspicion that we were guilty of the real catastrophe of the twenty-fourth of September. Alas! my mother was a keen woman, but she did not reckon upon Rhoda Colwell; she did not reckon upon you. She thought if we kept silence, hell and heaven would find no tongue. But hell and heaven have both spoken, and we stand suspected of crime, if not absolutely accused of it.

Hard as this is to bear—and it is harder than you might think for one in whom the base and cowardly action into which he was betrayed a month ago has not entirely obliterated the sense of honor—I neither dare to complain of it nor of the possible consequences which may follow if Rhoda Colwell slights my brother's warning and carries out her revenge to the full. Deeds of treachery and shame must bear their natural fruit, and we are but reaping what we sowed on that dreadful night when we allowed David Barrows to taste the horrors of his future grave. But though I do not complain, I would fain say a final word to one whose truth and candor have stood in such conspicuous relief to my own secrecy and repression. Not in way of hope, not in way of explanation even. What we have done we have done, and it would little become me to assign motives and reasons for what in your eyes—and, I must now allow, in my own—no motive or reason can justify or even excuse. I can only place myself before you as one who abhors his own past; regarding it, indeed, with such remorse and detestation that I would esteem myself blessed if it had been my body, instead of that of Mr. Barrows, which had been drawn from the fatal pit. Not that any repentance can rid me of the stain which has fallen upon my manhood, or make me worthy of the honor of your faintest glance; but it may make me a less debased object in your eyes, and I would secure that much grace for myself even at the expense of what many might consider an unnecessary humiliation. For you have made upon my mind in the short time I have known you a deep, and, as I earnestly believe, a most lasting and salutary impression. Truth, candor, integrity, and a genuine loyalty to all that is noblest and best in human nature no longer seem to me like mere names since I have met you. The selfishness that makes dark deeds possible has revealed itself to me in all its hideous deformity since the light of your pure ideal fell upon it; and while naught on earth can restore me to happiness, or even to that equanimity of mind which my careless boyhood enjoyed, it would still afford me something like relief to know that you recognize the beginning of a new life in me, which, if not all you could desire, still has that gleam of light upon it which redeems it from being what it was before I knew you. I will, therefore, ask not a word from you, but a look. If, when I pass your house to-morrow afternoon at six o'clock, I see you standing in the window, I shall know you grant me the encouragement of your sympathy, a sympathy which will help me to endure the worst of all my thoughts, that indirectly, if not directly, Guy and myself may be guilty of Mr. Barrows' death; that our action may have given him an impetus to destroy himself, or at least have shown him the way to end his life in a seemingly secret manner; though why a man so respected and manifestly happy as he should wish to close his career so suddenly, is as great a mystery to me as it can possibly be to you.

One other word and I am done. If, in the mercy of your gentle and upright nature, you accord me this favor, do not fear that I shall take advantage of it, even in my thoughts. Nor need you think that by so doing you may hamper yourself in the performance of a future duty; since it would be as impossible for me to ask, as for you to grant, the least suppression of the truth on your part; your candor being the charm of all others which has most attracted my admiration and secured my regard.

DWIGHT POLLARD.

Of the emotions produced in me by these, two letters I will say nothing; I will only mention some of my thoughts. The first naturally was, that owing to my illness I had not received the latter letter till a week after it was written; consequently

Dwight Pollard had failed to obtain the slight token of encouragement which he had requested. This was a source of deep regret to me, all the more that I did not know how to rectify the evil without running the risk of rousing suspicion in the breast of Rhoda Colwell. For, unreasonable as it may seem, her words had roused in me a dread similar to that which one might feel of a scorpion in the dark. I did not know how near she might be to me, or when she might strike. The least stir, the least turn of my head towards the forbidden object, might reveal her to be close at my side. I neither dared trust the silence nor the fact that all seemed well with me at present. A woman who could disguise herself as she could, and whom no difficulty deterred from gaining her purpose, was not one to brave with impunity, however clear might seem the outlook. I felt as if my very thoughts were in danger from her intuition, and scarcely dared breathe my intentions to the walls, lest the treacherous breeze should carry them to her ears and awaken that formidable antagonism which in her case was barbed with a power which might easily make the most daring quail. And yet she must be braved; for not to save his life could I let such an appeal as he had made me go unanswered; no, though I knew the possibility remained of its being simply the offspring of a keen and calculating mind driven to its last resource. It was enough that I felt him to be true, however much my reason might recognize the possibility of his falsehood. Rather than slight a noble spirit struggling with a great distress, I would incur any penalty which a possible lapse of judgment might bring; my temperament being such that I found less shame in the thought that I might be deceived, than that, out of a spirit of too great caution and self-love, I should fail an unhappy soul at the moment when my sympathy might be of inestimable benefit to its welfare.

The venomous threats and extreme show of power displayed in Rhoda Colwell's letter had overreached themselves. They roused my pride. They made me question whether it was necessary for us to live under such a dominion of suspense as she had prepared for us. If Dwight Pollard's asseverations were true, it would be a cruel waste of peace and happiness for him or me to rest under such a subjection, when by a little bravery at the outset her hold upon us might be annihilated and her potency destroyed.

The emotions which I have agreed to ignore came in to give weight to this thought. To save myself it was necessary to prove Dwight Pollard true. Not only my sense of justice, but the very life and soul of my being, demanded the settling of all suspicion and the establishment of my trust upon a sure foundation. While a single doubt remained in my mind I was liable to shame before my best self, and shame and Constance Sterling did not mix easily or well, especially with that leaven of self-interest added, to which I have alluded only a few paragraphs back.

But how, with my lack of resources and the apparent dearth of all means for attaining the end I had in view, I was to prove Rhoda Colwell's insinuations false, and Dwight Pollard's assertion true, was a question to which an answer did not come with very satisfactory readiness. Even the simple query as to how I was to explain my late neglect to Dwight Pollard occasioned me an hour of anxious thought; and it was not till I remembered that the simplest course was always the best, and that with a snake in the grass like Rhoda Colwell, the most fearless foot trod with the greatest safety, that I felt my difficulties on that score melt away. I would write to Dwight Pollard, and I would tell Rhoda Colwell I had done so, thus proving to her that I meditated nothing underhanded, and could be trusted to say what I would do, and do what I should say.

This decision taken, I sat down immediately and penned the following two notes:

MISS RHODA COLWELL:—Owing to illness, your letter has just been read by me. To it I will simply reply that you are right in believing my regard could never be given to a guilty man. As long as the faintest doubt of Mr. Pollard remains in my mind we are indeed separated by a gulf. But let that doubt

Anna Katherine Green

in any way be removed, and I say to you frankly that nothing you could threaten or the world perform, would prevent my yielding to him the fullest sympathy and the most hearty encouragement.

I send him to-day, in the same mail which carries this, a few lines, a copy of which I inclose for your perusal.

Yours, CONSTANCE STERLING.

MR. DWIGHT POLLARD:—For two weeks I have been too ill to cross my room, which must account both for this note and the tardiness I have displayed in writing it.

You assert that you know nothing of the causes or manner of a certain catastrophe. I believe you, and hope some day to have more than a belief, viz., a surety of its truth founded on absolute evidence.

Till that time comes we go our several ways, secure in the thought that to the steadfast mind calumny itself loses its sting when met by an earnest purpose to be and do only what is honest and upright.

CONSTANCE STERLING.

If you have any further communication to make to me, let me request that it be allowed to pass through the hands of Miss Colwell. My reasons for this are well founded.

XV

A GOSSIP

This something settled matter in his heart,
Whereon his brains still beating, puts him thus
From fashion of himself.

—HAMLET.

I had not taken this tone with both my correspondents
without a secret hope of being able to do something myself
towards the establishment of Mr. Pollard's innocence. How, I
could not very plainly perceive that day or the next, but as
time elapsed and my brain cleared and my judgment returned,
I at last saw the way to an effort which might not be without
consequences of a satisfactory nature. What that effort was you
may perhaps conjecture from the fact that the first walk that I
took was in the direction of the cottage where Mr. Barrows
had formerly lived. The rooms which he had occupied were for
rent, and my ostensible errand was to hire them. The real
motive of my visit, however, was to learn something more of
the deceased clergyman's life and ways than I then knew; if
happily out of some hitherto unnoticed event in his late
history I might receive a hint which should ultimately lead me
to the solution of the mystery which was involving my
happiness.

I was not as unsuccessful in this attempt as one might

anticipate. The lady of the house was a gossip, and the subject of Mr. Barrows' death was an inexhaustible topic of interest to her. I had but to mention his name, and straightway a tide of words flowed from her lips, which, if mostly words, contained here and there intimations of certain facts which I felt it was well enough for me to know, even if they did not amount to any thing like an explanation of the tragedy. Among these was one which only my fear of showing myself too much interested in her theme prevented me from probing to the bottom. This was, that for a month at least before his death Mr. Barrows had seemed to her like a changed man. A month—that was about the interval which had elapsed between his first visit to the mill and his last; and the evidence that he showed an alteration of demeanor in that time might have its value and might hot. I resolved to cultivate Mrs. Simpson's acquaintance, and sometime put her a question or two that would satisfy me upon this point.

This determination was all the easier to make in that I found the rooms I had come to see sufficiently to my liking to warrant me in taking them. Not that I should have hesitated to do this had they been as unattractive as they were pleasant. It was not their agreeableness that won me, but the fact that Mr. Barrows personal belongings had not yet been moved, and that for a short time at least I should find myself in possession of his library, and face to face with the same articles of taste and study which had surrounded him in his lifetime, and helped to mould, if not to make, the man. I should thus obtain a knowledge of his character, and some day, who knows, might flash upon his secret. For that he possessed one, and was by no means the plain and simple character I had been led to believe was apparent to me from the first glimpse I had of these rooms; there being in every little object that marked his taste a certain individuality and purpose that betrayed a stern and mystic soul; one that could hide itself, perhaps, beneath a practical exterior, but which, in ways like this, must speak, and speak loudly too, of its own inward promptings and tendency.

The evening when I first brought these objects under a close and conscientious scrutiny, was a memorable one to me. I had moved in early that day, and with a woman's unreasoning caprice had forborne to cast more than the most cursory glance around, being content to see that all was as I left it at my first visit, and that neither desk nor library had been disturbed. But when supper was over, and I could set myself with a free mind to a contemplation of my new surroundings, I found that my curiosity could no longer delay the careful tour of inspection to which I felt myself invited by the freshness and beauty of the pictures, and one or two of the statuettes which adorned the walls about me. One painting in especial attracted me, and made me choose for my first contemplation that side of the room on which it hung. It was a copy of some French painting, and represented the temptation of a certain saint. A curious choice of subject, you may think, to adorn a Protestant clergyman's wall, but if you could have seen it, and marked the extreme expression of mortal struggle on the face of the tempted one, who, with eyes shut, and hands clutching till it bent the cross of twigs stuck in the crevices of the rocks beneath which he writhed, waited for the victory over self that was just beginning to cast its light upon his brow, you would have felt that it was good to hang before the eyes of any one in whom conflict of any kind was waging. Upon me the effect was instantaneous, and so real that I have never been able to think of that moment without a sense of awe and rending of the heart. Human passion assumed a new significance in my mind, and the will and faith of a strong man suffering from its power, yet withstanding it to the very last gasp by the help of his trust in God, rose to such an exalted position in my mind, that I felt then, as I feel now whenever I remember this picture, that my whole moral nature had received, from its contemplation, an impetus towards religion and self-denial. While I was still absorbed in gazing at it, my landlady entered the room, and seeing me posed before the picture, quite sympathizingly exclaimed:

"Isn't that a dreadful painting, Miss Sterling, to have in any one's room? I don't wonder Mr. Barrows wanted to cover it up."

Anna Katherine Green

"Cover it up?" I repeated, turning hastily in my surprise.

"Yes," she replied, going to a drawer in his desk and taking out a small engraving, which she brought me. "For nearly a month before his death he had this picture stuck up over the other with pins. You can see the pin-holes now, if you look; they went right through the canvas. I thought it a very sensible thing to do, myself; but when I spoke of it to him one day, remarking that I had always thought the picture unfit for any one to see, he gave me such a look that I thought then he must be crazy. But no one else saw any thing amiss in him, and, as I did not want to lose a good lodger, I let him stay on, though my mind did sometimes misgive me."

The engraving she had handed me was almost as suggestive as the painting it had been used to conceal; but at this remarkable statement front Mrs. Simpson's lips I laid it quickly down.

"You think he was crazy?" I asked.

"I think he committed suicide," she affirmed.

I turned to the engraving again, and took it up. What a change had come over me that a statement against which I had once so honestly rebelled for Ada's sake should now arouse something like a sensation of joy in my breast!

Mrs. Simpson, too much interested in her theme to notice me, went confidently on.

"You see, folks that live in the same house with a person, learn to know them as other folks can't. Not that Mr. Barrows ever talked to me; he was a deal too much absorbed in his studies for that; but he ate at my table, and went in and out of my front door, and if a woman cannot learn something about a man under those circumstances, then she is no good, that is all I have got to say about her."

I was amused and slightly smiled, but she needed no

encouragement to proceed.

"The way he would drop into a brown study over his meat and potatoes was a caution to my mind. A minister that don't eat is—an anomaly," she burst out. "I have boarded them before, and I know they like the good things of life as well as anybody. But Mr. Barrows, latterly at least, never seemed to see what was on the table before him, but ate because his plate of food was there, and had to be disposed of in some way. One day, I remember in particular, I had baked dumplings, for he used to be very fond of them, and would eat two without any urging; but this day he either did not put enough sauce on them, or else his whole appetite had changed; for he suddenly looked down at his plate and shuddered, almost as if he were in a chill, and, getting up, was going away, when I summoned up courage to ask if the dumplings were not as good as usual. He turned at the door—I can see him now,—and mechanically shaking his head, seemed to be trying to utter some apology. But he presently stopped in that attempt, and, pointing quickly at the table, said, in his accustomed tones: 'You need not make me any more desserts, Mrs. Simpson, I shall not indulge in them in the future'; and went out, without saying whether he was sick or what. And that was the end of the dumplings, and of many a good thing besides."

"And is that all—" I began; but she broke in before the words were half out of my mouth.

"But the strangest thing I ever see in him was this: I have not said much about it, for the people that went to his church are a high and mighty lot, and wouldn't bear a word said against his sanity, even by one as had more opportunities than they of knowing him. But you are a stranger in town, and can't have no such foolish touchiness about a person that is nothing to you, so I will just tell you all about it. You see, when he had visitors—and off and on a good many came—I used to seat them in the parlor below, till I was sure he was ready to receive them. This had happened one evening, and I had gone up to his door to notify him that a stranger was down-stairs, when I

Anna Katherine Green

heard such a peculiar noise issuing from his room, that I just stood stock-still on the door-mat to listen. It was a swishing sound, followed by a—Miss Sterling," she suddenly broke in, in a half awe-struck, half-frightened tone, "did you ever *hear* any one whipped? If you have, you will know why I stood shuddering at that door full two minutes before I dared lift my hand and knock. Not that I could believe Mr. Barrows was whipping any body, but the sound was so like it, and I was so certain besides that I had heard something like a smothered cry follow it, that nothing short of the most imperative necessity would have given me the courage to call him; my imagination filling the room with all sorts of frightful images; images that did not fade away in a hurry," she went on, with a look of shrinking terror about her which I am not sure was not reflected in my own face, "when, after the longest waiting I ever had at his door, he slowly came across the room and opened it, showing me a face as white as a sheet, and a hand that trembled so that he dropped the card I gave him and had to pick it up. Had there been a child there—"

"But there wasn't!" I interrupted, shocked and forced to defend him in spite of myself.

"No, nor anybody else. For when he went down-stairs, I looked in and there was no one there, and nothing uncommon about the room, except that I thought his bookcase looked as if it had been moved. And it had; for next day when I swept this room—it did not need sweeping, but one can't wait for ever to satisfy their curiosity—I just looked behind that case, and what do you think I found? A strap—a regular leather strap—just such as—"

"Good God!" I interrupted; "you do not think he had been using it when you went to the door?"

"I do," she said. "I think he had a fit of something like insanity upon him, and had been swinging that strap—Well, I will not say against what, for I do not know, but might it not have been against the fiends and goblins with which crazy people sometimes imagine they are surrounded?"

"Possibly," I acquiesced, though my tone could not have been one of any strong conviction.

"Insane persons sometimes do strange things," she continued; "and that he did not show himself violent before folks is no sign he did not let himself out sometimes when he was alone. The very fact that he restrained himself when he went into the pulpit and visited among his friends, may have made him wilder when he got all by himself. I am sure I remember having heard of a case where a man lived for ten years in a town without a single neighbor suspecting him of insanity; yet his wife suffered constantly from his freaks, and finally fell a victim to his violence."

"But Mr. Barrows was such a brilliant man," I objected. "His sermons up to the last were models of eloquence."

"Oh, he could preach," she assented.

Seeing that she was not to be moved in her convictions, I ventured upon a few questions.

"Have you ever thought," I asked, "what it was that created such a change in him? You say you noticed it for a month before his death; could any thing have happened to disturb him at that time?"

"Not that I know of," she answered, with great readiness. "I was away for a week in August, and it was when I first came back that I observed how different he was from what he had been before. I thought at first it was the hot weather, but heat don't make one restless and unfit to sit quiet in one's chair. Nor does it drive a man to work as if the very evil one was in him, keeping the light burning sometimes till two in the morning, while he wrote and walked, and walked and wrote, till I thought my head would burst with sympathy for him."

"He was finishing a book, was he not? I think I have heard he left a completed manuscript behind him?"

"Yes; and don't you think it very singular that the last word should have been written, and the whole parcel done up and sent away to his publisher, two days before his death, if he did not know what was going to happen to him?"

"And was it?" I inquired.

"Yes, it was; for I was in the room when he signed his name to it, and heard his sigh of relief, and saw him, too, when, a little while afterwards, he took the bundle out to the post-office. I remember thinking, 'Well, now for some rest nights!' little imagining what rest was in store for him, poor soul!"

"Did you know that Mr. Barrows was engaged?" I suddenly asked, unable to restrain my impatience any longer.

"No, I did not," she rather sharply replied, as if her lack of knowledge on that subject had been rather a sore point with her. "I may have suspected there was some one he was interested in, but I am sure nobody ever imagined her as being the one. Poor girl, she must have thought a heap of him to die in that way."

She looked at me as she said this, anticipating, perhaps, a return of the confidences she had made me. But I could not talk of Ada to her, and after a moment of silent waiting she went eagerly on.

"Perhaps a lover's quarrel lay at the bottom of the whole matter," she suggested. "Miss Reynolds was a sweet girl and loved him very devotedly, of course; but they might have had a tiff for all that, and in a nature as sensitive as his, the least thing will sometimes unhinge the mind."

But I could only shake my head at this; the supposition was at once too painful and absurd.

"Well, well," the garrulous woman went on, in no wise abashed, "there are some things that come easy and some things that come hard. Why Mr. Barrows went the way he did is one of the hard things to understand, but that he did go, and that of his own frenzied will, I am as sure as that two and two make four, and four from four leaves nothing."

I thought of all the others who secretly or openly expressed the same opinion, and felt my heart grow lighter. Then I thought of Rhoda Colwell, and then—

"Just what time was it," I asked, "when you were away in August? Was it before the seventeenth, or after? I inquire, because—"

But evidently she did not care why I inquired.

"It was during that week," she broke in. "I remember because it was on the sixteenth that Mr. Pollard died, and I was not here to attend the funeral. I came back—"

But it was no matter to me now when she came back. She had not been at home the night when Mr. Barrows was beguiled into his first visit to the mill, and she had mentioned a name I had long been eager to have introduced into the conversation.

"You knew Mr. Pollard?" I therefore interposed without ceremony. "He was a very rich man, was he not?"

"Yes," she assented. "I suppose the children will have the whole property, now that the old lady is gone. I hope Mr. Harrington will be satisfied. He just married that girl for her money. That, I am sure, you will hear everybody say."

"Yet she is exceedingly pretty," I suggested.

"Oh, yes, too pretty; she makes one think of a wax doll. But these English lords don't care for beauty without there is a deal of hard cash to back it, and if Agnes Pollard had been as poor

Anna Katherine Green

as—what other beauty have we in town?"

"There is a girl called Rhoda Colwell," I ventured.

"Rhoda Colwell! Do you call her a beauty? I know some folks think she is—well, then, let us say as Rhoda Colwell, he would have made her any proposal sooner than that of his hand."

"And is Mr. Harrington a lord?" I asked, feeling that I was lighting upon some very strange truths.

"He is the next heir to one. A nephew I believe, or else a cousin. I cannot keep track of all those fine distinctions in people I never saw."

"They were married privately and right after Mr. Pollard's death, I have heard."

"Yes, and for no other earthly reason that one ever heard of than to have it settled and done; for Mr. Harrington did not take away his wife from the country; nor does he intend to as far as I can learn. Everybody thought it a very strange proceeding, and none too respectful to Mr. Pollard's memory either."

I thought of all I had heard and seen in that house, and wondered.

"Mr. Pollard was such a nice man, too," she pursued, in a musing tone. "Not a commanding person, like his wife, but so good and kind and attentive to poor folks like me. I never liked a man more than I did Mr. Pollard, and I have always thought that if he had had a different kind of mother for his children—but what is the use of criticising the poor woman now. She is dead and so is he, and the children will do very well now with all that money to back them in any caprice they may have."

"You seem to know them well," I remarked, fearful she would

observe the emotion I could not quite keep out of my face.

"No," she returned, with an assumption of grimness, which was evidently meant for sarcasm, "not well. Every one knows the Pollards, but I never heard any one say they knew them well."

"Didn't Mr. Barrows?" I tremblingly inquired, anxious for her reply, yet fearful of connecting those two names.

"Not that I ever saw," she returned, showing no special interest in the question, or in the fact that it was seemingly of some importance to me.

"Didn't they use to come here to see him?" I proceeded, emboldened by her evident lack of perspicuity. "None of them?" I added, seeing her about to shake her head.

"Oh, Dwight or Guy would come here if they had any business with him," she allowed. "But that isn't intimacy; the Pollards are intimate with nobody."

She seemed to be rather proud of it, and as I did not see my way just then to acquire any further information, I sank with a weary air into a chair, turning the conversation as I did so upon other and totally irrelevant topics. But no topic was of much interest to her, that did not in some way involve Mr. Barrows; and after a few minutes of desultory chat, she pleaded the excuse of business and hurriedly left the room.

XVI

THE GREEN ENVELOPE

Sir, you shall understand what hath befall'n,
Which, as I think, you know not. Here is a letter.

—OTHELLO.

Her departure was a relief to me. First, because I had heard so
much, I wanted an opportunity of digesting it; and, secondly,
because of my interest in the engraving she had shown me, and
the impatience I felt to study it more closely. I took it up the
moment she closed the door.

It was the picture of a martyr, and had evidently been cut from
some good-sized book. It represented a man clothed in a long
white garment, standing with his back to the stake, and his
hand held out to the flames, which were slowly consuming it.
As a work of art, it was ordinary; as the illustration of some
mighty fact, it was full of suggestion. I gazed at it for a long
time, and then turned to the bookcase. Was the book from
which it had been taken there? I eagerly hoped so. For,
ignorant as I may seem to you, I did not know the picture or
the incident it represented; and I was anxious to know both.
For Mr. Barrows was not the man to disfigure a work of art by
covering it with a coarse print like this unless he had a motive;
and how could even a suspicion of that motive be mine,
without a full knowledge of just what this picture implied?

But though I looked from end to end of the various shelves before me, I did not succeed in finding the volume from which this engraving had been taken. Large books were there in plenty, but none of the exact size of the print I held in my hand. I own I was disappointed, and turned away from the bookcase at last with a feeling of having been baffled on the verge of some very interesting discovery.

The theory advanced with so much assurance by Mrs. Simpson had not met with much credence on my part. I believed her facts, but not the conclusions she drew from them. Nothing she had related to me convinced me that Mr. Barrows was in any way insane; nor could I imagine for a moment that he could be so without the knowledge of Ada, if not of his associates and friends.

At the same time I was becoming more and more assured in my own mind that his death was the result of his own act, and, had it not been for the difficulty of imagining a reason for it, could have retired to rest that night with a feeling of real security in the justness of a conclusion that so exonerated the man I loved. As it was, that secret doubt still remained like a cloud over my hopes, a doubt which I had promised myself should be entirely removed before I allowed my partiality for Mr. Pollard to take upon itself the character of partisanship. I therefore continued my explorations through the room.

Mr. Barrows' desk presented to me the greatest attraction of any thing there; one that was entirely of the imagination, of course, since nothing could have induced me to open it, notwithstanding every key stood in its lock, and one of the drawers was pulled a little way out. Only the law had a right to violate his papers; and hard as it was to deny myself a search into what was possibly the truest exponent of his character, I resolutely did so, consoling myself with the thought that if any open explanation of his secret had been in these drawers, it would have been produced at the inquest.

As for his books, I felt no such scruples. But then, what could his books tell me? Nothing, save that he was a wide student and loved the delicate and imaginative in literature. Besides, I had glanced at many of the volumes, in my search after the one which had held the engraving. Yet I did pause a minute and run my eye along the shelves, vaguely conscious, perhaps, that often in the most out-of- the-way corners lurks the secret object for which we are so carefully seeking. But I saw nothing to detain me, and after one brief glance at a strong and spirited statuette that adorned the top shelf, I hurried on to a small table upon which I thought I saw a photographic album.

I was not mistaken; and it was with considerable interest I took it up and began to run over its pages in search for that picture of Ada which I felt ought to be there. And which was there; but which I scarcely looked at twice, so much was my attention attracted by an envelope that fell out from between the leaves as I turned them eagerly over. That envelope, with its simple direction, "Miss Ada Reynolds, Monroe Street, S—," made an era in my history. For I no sooner perceived it than I felt confident of having seen it or its like before; and presently, with almost the force of an electric shock, I recollected the letter which I had brought Ada the afternoon of the day she died, and which, as my startled conscience now told me, had not only never been given her, but had not been so much as seen by me since, though all her belongings had passed into my hands, and the table where I had flung it had been emptied of its contents more than once. That letter and this empty envelope were, in style, handwriting, and direction, *facsimiles*. It had, therefore, come from Mr. Barrows; a most significant fact, and one which I had no sooner realized than I was seized by the most intense excitement, and might have done some wild and foolish thing, had not the lateness of the hour restrained me, and kept my passionate hopes and fears within their proper bounds. As it was, I found myself obliged to take several turns up and down the room, and even to open the window for a breath of fresh air, before I could face the subject with any calmness, or ask myself what had become of this letter, with any hope of receiving a rational reply.

That in the startling and tragic events of that day it had been overlooked and forgotten, I did not wonder. But that it should have escaped my notice afterwards, or if mine, that of the landlady who took charge of the room in my absence, was what I could not understand. As far as I could remember, I left the letter lying in plain view on the table. Why, then, had not some one seen and produced it? Could it be that some one more interested than I knew had stolen it? Or was the landlady of my former home alone to blame for its being lost or mislaid?

Had it been daylight I should have at once gone down to my former boarding-place to inquire; but as it was ten o'clock at night, I could only satisfy my impatience by going carefully over the incidents of that memorable day, in the hope of rousing some memory which would lead to an elucidation of this new mystery. First, then, I distinctly recollected receiving the letter from the postman. I had met him at the foot of the steps as I came home from my unsuccessful search for employment, and he had handed me the letter, simply saying: "For Miss Reynolds." I scarcely looked at it, certainly gave it no thought, for we had been together but a week, and I had as yet taken no interest in her concerns. So mechanical, indeed, had been my whole action in the matter, that I doubt if the sight of Mr. Barrows' writing alone, even though it had been used in transcribing her name, would have served to recall the incident to my mind. But the shade of the envelope—it was of a peculiar greenish tint—gave that unconscious spur to the memory which was needed to bring back the very look of the writing which had been on the letter I had so carelessly handled; and I found, as others have found before me, that there is no real forgetfulness in this world; that the most superficial glance may serve to imprint images upon the mind, which only await time and occasion to reappear before us with startling distinctness.

My entrance into my own room, my finding it empty, and the consequent flinging of the letter down on the table, all came back to me with the utmost clearness; even the fact that the letter fell face downwards and that I did not stop to turn it over. But beyond that all was blank to me up to the moment when I found myself confronting Ada standing with her hand on her heart in that sudden spasm of pain which had been the too sure precursor of her rapidly approaching doom.

But wait! Where was I standing when I first became conscious of her presence in the room? Why, in the window, of course. I remembered now just how hot the afternoon sun looked to me as I stared at the white walls of the cottage over the way. And she—where was she?—between me and the table? Yes! She had, therefore, passed by the letter, and might have picked it up, might even have opened it, and read it before the spell of my revery was broken, and I turned to find her standing there before my eyes. Her pallor, the evident distress under which she was laboring, even the sudden pain which had attacked her heart, might thus be accounted for, and what I had always supposed to be a purely physical attack prove to be the result of a mental and moral shock. But, no. Had she opened and read the letter it would have been found there; or if not there, at least upon her person after death. Besides, her whole conduct between the moment I faced her and that of the alarm in the street below precluded the idea that any thing of importance to her and her love had occurred to break her faith in the future and the man to whose care she was pledged. Could I not remember the happy smile which accompanied her offer of assistance and home to me? And was there any thing but hope and trust in the tone with which she had designated her lover as being the best and noblest man in town? No; if she had read his communication and afterwards disposed of it in some way I did not observe, then it was not of the nature I suspected; but an ordinary letter, similar in character to others she had received, foretelling nothing, and only valuable in the elucidation of the mystery before me from the fact of its offering proof presumptive that he did not anticipate death, or at all events did not meditate it.

An important enough fact to establish, certainly; but it was not the fact in which I had come to believe, and so I found it difficult to give it a place in my mind, or even to entertain the possibility of Ada's having seen the letter at all. I preferred rather to indulge in all sorts of wild conjectures, having the landlady, the servant, even Dr. Farnham, at their base; and it was not till I was visited by some mad thought of Rhoda Colwell's possible connivance in the disappearance of this important bit of evidence, that I realized the enormity of my selfish folly, and endeavored to put an end to its further indulgence by preparing stoically for bed.

But sleep, which would have been so welcome, did not come; and after a long and weary night, I arose in any thing but a refreshed state, to meet the exigencies of what might possibly prove to be a most important day.

The first thing to be done was undoubtedly to visit my old home and interview its landlady. If nothing came of that, to hunt up the nurse, Mrs. Gannon, whom, as you will remember, I had left in charge of my poor Ada's remains when sudden duty in the shape of Dr. Farnham carried me away to the bedside of Mrs. Pollard; and if this also came to naught, to burst the bonds of secrecy which I had maintained, and by taking this same Dr. Farnham into my confidence obtain at least an adviser who would relieve me, if only partially, from the weight of responsibility, which I now felt to be pressing rather too heavily upon my strength.

But though I carried out this programme as far as seeking for and procuring an interview with Mrs. Gannon at her place of nursing, I did not succeed in obtaining the least clew to the fate of this mysteriously lost letter. Neither of the women mentioned had seen it, nor was it really believed by them to have been on the table when they arranged the room after my Ada's peaceful death. Yet even to this they could not swear, nor would the landlady admit but that it might still have been lying there when they came to carry Ada away, though she would say that it could not have been anywhere in view the next day, for she had thoroughly cleaned and tidied up the room herself, and as in doing this she had been obliged to shift every article off the table on to the bed and back again, she must not only have seen, but handled the letter twice; and this she was morally certain she did not do.

I was therefore in as great perplexity as ever, and was seriously meditating a visit to Dr. Farnham, when I bethought me of making one final experiment before resorting to this last and not altogether welcome alternative.

This was to examine every thing which had been on the table, in the hope of discovering in some out-of-the-way receptacle the missing letter for which I had such need. To be sure it was an effort that promised little, there having been but few articles on the table capable of concealing even such a small object as this I was in search of; but when one is at their wits' ends, they do not stop to discuss probabilities, or even to weigh in too nice a scale the prospect of success.

Recalling, therefore, just what had been on the table, I went to the trunk in which these articles were packed, and laid them out one by one on the floor. They were as follows: A work-basket of Ada's; a box of writing-paper; a copy of *Harper's Magazine*; an atlas; and two volumes of poetry, one belonging to Ada and one to me.

A single glance into the work-basket was sufficient, also into the box of stationery. But the atlas was well shaken, and the magazine carefully looked through, before I decided it was not in them. As for the two books of poetry, I disdained them so completely, I was about to toss them back unopened, when there came upon me a disposition to be thorough, and I looked at them both, only to find snugly ensconced in my own little copy of Mrs. Browning the long- sought and despaired-of letter, with its tell-tale green envelope unbroken, and its contents, in so far as I could see, unviolated and undisturbed.

XVII

DAVID BARROWS

"I have lived long enough."

—MACBETH.

Before I proceeded to open this letter, I reasoned some time with myself. The will by which I had come into possession of Ada's effects was, as I knew, informal and possibly illegal. But it was the expression of her wishes, and there had been no one to dispute them or question my right to the inheritance she had so innocently bequeathed me. At the same time I felt a hesitation about opening this letter, as I had about using her money; and it was not till I remembered the trust she had reposed in me, and the promise I had given her to support Mr. Barrows' good name before the world, that I summoned up sufficient determination to break its seal. My duty once clear to me, however, I no longer hesitated. This is the result:

September 23d.—*Evening.*

My Beloved Ada:—Could I by any means mitigate the blow which I am forced to deal you, believe me it should be done. But no words can prepare you for the terrible fact I am about to reveal, and I think from what I know of you, and of your delicate but strong soul, that in a matter of life and death like this the most direct language is what you would choose me to employ.

Know then, dearest of all women, that a duty I dare not fly from condemns me to death; that the love we have cherished, the hopes in which we have indulged, can have no fulfilment in this world, but must be yielded as a sacrifice to the inexorable claim of conscience and that ideal of right which has been mine since I took upon myself the lofty vocation of a Christian minister.

You, my people, my own self even, have thought me an honest man. God knows I meant to be, even to the point of requiring nothing from others I was not willing to give myself. But our best friends do not know us; we do not know ourselves. When the hour of trial came, and a sudden call was made upon my faith and honor, I failed to sustain myself, failed ignominiously, showing myself to be no stronger than the weakest of my flock—ay, than the child that flies before a shadow because it is black, and he does not or will not see that it is his father's form that casts it.

Such lapses on the part of men professing to lead others demand heavy penalties. I feared to lose my life, therefore my life must go. Nothing short of this would reinstate me in my own eyes, or give to my repentance that stern and absolute quality which the nature of my sin imperatively demands.

That I must involve you in my sorrow and destruction is the bitterest drop in my cup. But dainty and flower-like as you are, you have a great nature, and would not hold me back from an act necessary to the welfare and honor of my eternal soul. I see you rather urging me on, giving me your last kiss, and smiling upon me with your own inspiring smile. So sure am I of this, that I can bear not to see you again; bear to walk for the last time by your house, leaving only my blessing in the air. For it is a part of my doom that I may not see you; since, were I to find myself in your presence, I could scarcely forbear telling you whither I was going, and that no man must know till all has been accomplished.

I go, then, without other farewell than these poor words can give you. Be strong, and bear my loss as many a noble woman before you has borne the wreck of all her hopes. When I am found—as some day I shall be—tell my people I died in the Christian faith, and for the simple reason that my honor as a man and a minister demanded it. If they love me they will take my word for it; but if questions should arise, and a fuller knowledge of my fate and the reasons which led me to such an act should in your judgment seem to be required, then go to my desk, and, in a secret drawer let into the back, you will find a detailed confession which will answer every inquiry and set straight any false or unworthy suspicions that may arise.

But heed these words and mark them well: Till such a need should arise, the manuscript is to be kept inviolate even from you; and no matter what the seeming need, or by what love or anxiety you may be driven, touch not that desk nor drawer till ten days have elapsed, or I shall think you love my body more than me, and the enjoyment of temporal comfort to the eternal weight of glory which is laid up for those who hold out steadfast to the end.

And now, my dear, my dear, with all the affection of my poor, weak, erring heart, I hold out arms of love towards you. Farewell for a short space. When we meet again may it be on equal terms once more, the heavy sin blotted out, the grievous wrong expiated.

Till then, God bless you.

DAVID.

Do not wonder at my revealing nothing of this in our late interviews. You were so happy, I dared not drop a shadow one day sooner than was necessary into your young life. Besides, my struggle was dark and secret, and could brook no eye upon it save that of the eternal God.

XVIII

A LAST REQUEST

'T is she That tempers him to this extremity.

—Richard III.

The night had fallen. I was in a strange and awe-struck mood. The manuscript, which after some difficulty I had succeeded in finding, lay before, me unopened. A feeling as of an invisible presence was in the air. I hesitated to turn the page, written, as I already felt, with the life-blood of the man in whose mysterious doom the happiness of my own life had become entangled.

Waiting for courage, I glanced mechanically about the room. How strangely I had been led in this affair! How from the first I seemed to have been picked out and appointed for the solving of this mystery, till now I sat in the very room, at the very desk, in front of the very words, of its victim. I thought of Dwight Pollard struggling with his fate, and unconscious that in a few minutes the secret of Mr. Barrows' death would be known; of Rhoda Colwell, confident of her revenge and blind to the fact that I held in my hand what might possibly blunt her sharpest weapon, and make her most vindictive effort useless. Then each and every consideration of a purely personal nature vanished, and I thought only of the grand and tortured soul of him upon whose solemn and awesome history I was about to enter. Was it, as his letter seemed to imply, a martyr's story? I looked at the engraving of Cranmer, which had been a puzzle to me a few days before, and understanding it now, gathered fortitude by what it seemed to suggest, and hastily unrolled the manuscript.

This is what I read:

"He that would save his life shall lose it."

In order that the following tale of sin and its expiation may be understood, I must give a few words to the motives and hopes under which I entered the ministry.

I am a believer in the sacred character of my profession, and the absolute and unqualified devotion of those embracing it to the aims and purposes of the Christian religion. Though converted, as it is called, in my sixteenth year, I cannot remember the time my pulse did not beat with appreciation for those noble souls who had sacrificed every joy and comfort of this temporal life for the sake of their faith and the glory of God. I delighted in Fox's "Book of Martyrs," and while I shuddered over its pages in a horror I did not wholly understand, I read them again and again, till there was not a saint whose life I did not know by heart, with just the death he died and the pangs he experienced. Such a mania did this become with me at one time, that I grew visibly ill, and had to have the book taken away from me and more cheerful reading substituted in its stead.

Feeling thus strongly in childhood, when half, if not all, my interest sprang from the fascination which horrors have upon the impressible mind, what were my emotions and longings when the real meaning of the Christian life was revealed to me, and I saw in this steadfastness of the spirit unto death the triumph of the immortal soul over the weaknesses of the flesh and the terrors of a purely transitory suffering!

That the days for such display of firmness in the fiery furnace were over was almost a matter of regret to me in the first flush of my enthusiasm for the cause I had espoused. I wished so profoundly to show my love, and found all modern ways so tame in comparison to those which demanded the yielding up of one's very blood and life. Poor fool! did I never think that those who are the bravest in imagination fail often the most lamentably when brought face to face with the doom they have invoked.

I have never been a robust man, and consequently have never entered much into those sports and exercises incident to youth and early manhood that show a man of what stuff he is made. I have lived in my books till I came to S—, since which I have tried to live in the joys and sorrows of my fellow-beings.

The great rule of Christian living has seemed to me imperative. Love your neighbor as yourself, or, as I have always interpreted it, more than yourself. For a man, then, to sacrifice that neighbor to save himself from physical or mental distress, has always seemed to me not only the height of cowardice, but a direct denial of those truths upon which are founded the Christian's ultimate hope. As a man myself, I despise with my whole heart such weaklings; as a Christian minister I denounce them. Nothing can excuse a soul for wavering in its duty because that duty is hard. It is the hard things we should take delight in facing; otherwise we are babes and not men, and our faith a matter of expediency, and not that stern and immovable belief in God and His purposes which can alone please Deity and bring us into that immediate communion with His spirit which it should be the end and aim of every human soul to enjoy.

Such are my principles. Let us see how I have illustrated them in the events of the last six weeks.

On the sixteenth of August, five weeks ago to-day, I was called to the bedside of Samuel Pollard. He had been long sinking with an incurable disease, and now the end was at hand and my Christian offices required. I was in the full tide of sermon-writing when the summons came, and I hesitated at first whether to follow the messenger at once or wait till the daylight had quite disappeared, and with it my desire to place on paper the thoughts that were inspiring me with more than ordinary fervor.

But a question to my own heart decided me. Not my sermon, but the secret disinclination I always felt to enter this special family, was what in reality held me back; and this was a reason which, as you will have seen from the words I have already written, I could not countenance. I accordingly signified to the messenger that I would be with Mr. Pollard in a few moments, and putting away my papers, prepared to leave the room.

There, is a saying in the Bible to the effect that no man liveth to himself, nor dieth to himself. If in the course of this narrative I seem to show little consideration for the secrets of others, let this be at once my explanation and excuse: That only in the cause of truth do I speak at all; and that in holding up before you the follies and wrong-doings of persons you know, I subject them to no heavier penalty than that which I have incurred through my own sin. I shall therefore neither gloss over nor suppress any fact bearing upon a full explanation of my fate; and when I say I hesitated to go to Mr. Pollard because of my inherent dislike to enter his house, I will proceed to give as my reason for this dislike, my unconquerable distrust of his wife, who, if a fine-looking and capable woman, is certainly one to be feared by every candid and truth-loving nature.

But, as I said before, I did not yield to the impulse I had within me to stay; and, merely stopping to cast a parting glance about my room—why, I do not know, for I could have had no premonition of the fact that I was bidding good-by to the old life of hope and peace forever—I hastened after the messenger whom I had sent on before me to Mr. Pollard's home.

Small occurrences sometimes make great impressions on the

mind. As I was turning the corner at Halsey Street, the idiot boy Colwell came rushing by, and almost fell into my arms. I started back, shuddering, as if some calamity had befallen me. An invincible repugnance to any thing deformed or half-witted has always been one of my weaknesses, and for him to have touched me—I hate myself as I write it, but I cannot think of it now without a chill in my veins and an almost unbearable feeling of physical contamination. Yet as I would be as just to myself as I hope to be to others, I did not let this incident pass, without a struggle to conquer my lower nature. Standing still, I called the boy back, and deliberately, and with a reverential thought of the Christ, I laid my hand on his arm, and, stooping, kissed him. It cost me much, but I could never have passed that corner without doing it; nor were I to live years on this earth, instead of a few short days, should I ever let another week go by without forcing my body into some such contact with what nature has afflicted and man contemned.

The pallor which I therefore undoubtedly showed upon entering Mr. Pollard's room was owing to the memory of this incident rather than to any effect which the sight of the dying man had upon me. But before I had been many minutes in the room, I found my pulse thrilling with new excitement and my manhood roused to repel a fresh influence more dangerous, if less repulsive, than the last.

Let me see if I can make it plain to you. Mr. Pollard, whom we have all known as an excellent but somewhat weak man, lay with his face turned towards the room, and his gaze fixed with what I felt to be more than the common anxiety of the dying upon mine. At his side sat his wife, cold, formidable, alert, her hand on his hand, her eye on his eye, and all her icy and implacable will set, as I could plainly see, between him and any comfort or encouragement I might endeavor to impart. She even allowed her large and commanding figure to usurp the place usually accorded me on such occasions, and when, after a futile effort or so on my part to break down the barrier of restraint that such a presence necessarily imposed, I arose from my seat at the foot of the bed, and, approaching closer, would have leaned over her husband, she put out her other hand and imperatively waved me aside, remarking:

"The doctor says he must have air."

There are some persons whose looks and words are strangely controlling. Mrs. Pollard is one of these, and I naturally drew back. But a glance at Mr. Pollard's face made me question if I was doing right in this. Such disappointment, such despair even, I had seldom seen expressed in a look; and convinced that he had something of real purport to say to me, I turned towards his wife, and resolutely remarked:

"The dying frequently have communications to make to which only their pastor's ear is welcome. Will you excuse me, then, if I request a moment's solitude with Mr. Pollard, that I may find out if his soul is at rest before I raise my prayers in its behalf?"

But, before I had finished, I saw that any such appeal would be unavailing. If her immovable expression had not given me this assurance, the hopeless closing of his weak and fading eyes would have sufficiently betrayed the fact.

"I cannot leave Mr. Pollard," were the words with which she tempered her refusal. "If he has any communication to make, let him make it in my presence. I am his wife." And her hand pressed more firmly upon his, and her eyes, which had not stirred from his face even when I addressed her, assumed a dark, if not threatening look, which gradually forced his to open and meet them.

I felt that something must be done.

"Mr. Pollard," said I, "is there any thing you wish to impart to me before you die? If so, speak up freely and with confidence, for I am here to do a friend and a pastor's duty by you, even to the point of fulfilling any request you may have to make, so it be only actuated by right feeling and judgment." And determinedly ignoring her quick move of astonishment, I pressed forward and bent above him, striving with what I felt to be a purely righteous motive, to attract his glance from hers, which was slowly withering him away as if it were a basilisk's.

And I succeeded. After an effort that brought the sweat out on his brow, he turned his look on mine, and, gathering strength from my expression, probably, gave me one eager and appealing glance, and thrust his left hand under his pillow.

His wife, who saw every thing, leaned forward with an uneasy gesture.

"What have you there?" she asked.

But he had already drawn forth a little book and placed it in my hand.

"Only my old prayer-book," he faltered. "I felt as if I should like Mr. Barrows to have it."

She gave him an incredulous stare, and allowed her glance to follow the book. I immediately put it in my pocket.

"I shall take a great deal of pleasure in possessing it," I remarked.

"Read it," he murmured; "read it carefully." And a tone of relief was in his voice that seemed to alarm her greatly; for she half rose to her feet and made a gesture to some one I did not see, after which she bent again towards the dying man and whispered in his ear.

But, though her manner had all its wonted force, and her words, whatever they were, were lacking in neither earnestness nor purpose, he did not seem to be affected by them. For the first time in his life, perhaps, he rose superior to that insidious influence, and, nerved by the near approach of death, kept his gaze fixed on mine, and finally stammered:

"Will you do some thing else for me?"

"I will," I began, and might have said more, but he turned from me and with sudden energy addressed his wife.

"Margaret," said he, "bring me my desk."

Had a thunderbolt fallen at her feet, she could not have looked more astonished. I myself was somewhat surprised; I had never heard that tone from him before.

"My desk!" he cried again; "I want it here."

At this repetition of his request, uttered this time with all the vehemence of despair. Mrs. Pollard moved, though she did not rise. At the same moment a quick, soft step was heard, and through the gloom of the now rapidly darkening chamber I saw their younger son draw near and take his stand at the foot of the bed.

"I have but a few minutes," murmured the sick man. "Will you refuse to make them comfortable, Margaret?"

"No, no," she answered hastily, guided as I could not but see by an almost imperceptible movement of her son's hand; and rising with a great show of compliance, she proceeded to the other end of the room. I at once took her place by the side of his pillow.

"Is there no word of comfort I can give you?" said I, anxious for the soul thus tortured by earthly anxieties on the very brink of the grave.

But his mind, filled with one thought, refused to entertain any other.

"Pray God that my strength hold out," he whispered. "I have an act of reparation to make." Then, as his son made a move as if to advance, he caught my hand in his, and drew my ear down to his mouth. "The book," he gasped; "keep it safely—they may try to take it away—don't—"

But here his son intervened with some word of warning; and Mrs. Pollard, hurriedly approaching, laid the desk on the bed in such a way that I was compelled to draw back.

But this did not seem to awaken in him any special distress. From the instant his eyes fell upon the desk, a feverish strength seemed to seize him, and looking up at me with something of his old brightness of look and manner, he asked to have it opened and its contents taken out.

Naturally embarrassed at such a request, I turned to Mrs. Pollard.

"It seems a strange thing for me to do," I began; but a lightning glance had already passed between her and her son, and with the cold and haughty dignity for which she is remarkable, she calmly stopped me with a quiet wave of her hand.

"The whims of the dying must be respected," she remarked, and reseated herself in her old place at his side.

I at once proceeded to empty the desk. It contained mainly letters, and one legal-looking document, which I took to be his will. As I lifted this out, I saw mother and son both cast him a quick glance, as if they expected some move on his part. But though his hands trembled somewhat, he made no special sign of wishing to see or touch it, and at once I detected on their faces a look of surprise that soon took on the character of dismay, as with the lifting of the last paper from the desk he violently exclaimed:

"Now break in the bottom and take out the paper you will find there. It is my last will and testament, and by every sacred right you hold in this world, I charge you to carry it to Mr. Nicholls, and see that no man nor woman touches it till you give it into his hands."

"His will!" echoed Mrs. Pollard, astonished.

"He don't know what he says. This is his will," she was probably going to assert, for her hand was pointing to the legal-looking document I have before mentioned; but a gesture from her son made her stop before the last word was uttered. "He must be wandering in his mind," she declared. "We know of no will hidden away in his desk. Ah!"

The last exclamation was called forth by the sudden slipping into view of a folded paper from between the crevices of the desk. I had found the secret spring. The next instant the bottom fell out, and the paper slipped to the floor. I was quick to recover it. Had I not been, Mrs. Pollard would have had it in her grasp. As it was, our hands met, not without a shock, I fear, on either side. A gasp of intense suspense came from the bed.

"Keep it," the dying eyes seemed to say; and if mine spoke as plainly as his did, they answered with full as much meaning and force:

"I will."

Guy Pollard and his mother looked at each other, then at the pocket into which I had already thrust the paper. The dying man followed their glances, and with a final exertion of strength, raised himself on his elbow.

"My curse on him or her who seeks to step between me and the late reparation I have sought to make. Weaker than most men, I have submitted to your will, Margaret, up to this hour, but your reign is over at last, and—and—" The passionate words died away, the feverish energy succumbed, and with one last look into my face, Samuel Pollard fell back upon his pillow, dead.

XIX

A FATAL DELAY

Would'st thou have that
Which thou esteem'st the ornament of life,
And live a coward in thine own esteem,
Letting "I dare not," wait upon "I would,"
Like the poor cat i' the adage?

—MACBETH.

He was to all appearance immediately forgotten. As with mutual consent we all turned and faced each other, Mrs. Pollard with a stern, inexorable look in her dark eye, which, while it held me enchained, caused me to involuntarily lay my hand upon the document which I had hidden in my breast She noticed the movement, and smiled darkly with a sidelong look at her son. The smile and the look affected me strangely. In them I seemed to detect something deeper than hatred and baffled rage, and when in a moment later her son responded to her glance by quietly withdrawing from the room, I felt such revolt against their secrecy that for a moment I was tempted to abandon an undertaking that promised to bring me in conflict with passions of so deep and unrelenting a nature.

But the impression which the pain and despair of my dead friend had made upon me was as yet too recent for me to yield to my first momentary apprehensions; and summoning up what resolution I possessed, I took my leave of Mrs. Pollard, and was hastening towards the door, when her voice, rising cold and clear, arrested me.

"You think, then, that it is your duty to carry this paper from the house, Mr. Barrows?"

"Yes, madam, I do," was my short reply.

"In spite of my protest and that of my son?"

"Yes, madam."

"Then upon your head be the consequences!" she exclaimed, and turned her back upon me with a look which went with me as I closed the door between us; lending a gloom to the unlighted halls and sombre staircases that affected me almost with an impulse of fear.

I dreaded crossing to where the stairs descended; I dreaded going down them into the darkness which I saw below. Not that I anticipated actual harm, but that I felt I was in the house of those who longed to see me the victim of it; and my imagination being more than usually alert, I even found myself fancying the secret triumph with which Guy Pollard would hail an incautious slip on my part, that would precipitate me from the top to the bottom of this treacherous staircase. That he was somewhere between me and the front door, I felt certain. The deadly quiet behind and before me seemed to assure me of this; and, ashamed as I was of the impulse that moved me, I could not prevent myself from stepping cautiously as I prepared to descend, saying as some sort of excuse to myself: "He is capable of seeing me trip without assistance," and as my imagination continued its work: "He is even capable of putting out his foot to help forward such a catastrophe."

And, indeed, I now think that if this simple plan had presented itself to his subtle mind, of stunning, if not disabling me, and thus making it possible for them to obtain his father's will without an open assault, he would not have hesitated to embrace it. But he evidently did not calculate, as I did, the chances of such an act, or perhaps he felt that I was likely to be too much upon my guard to fall a victim to this expedient, for I met no one as I advanced, and was well down the stairs and on my way to the front door, before I perceived any signs of life in the sombre house. Then a sudden glare of light across my path betrayed the fact that a door had been swung wide in a certain short passage that opened ahead of me; and while I involuntarily stopped, a shadow creeping along the further wall of that passage warned me that some one—I could not doubt it to be Guy Pollard—had come out to meet me.

The profound stillness, and the sudden pause which the shadow made as I inconsiderately stumbled in my hesitation, assured me that I was right in attributing a sinister motive to this encounter. Naturally, therefore, I drew back, keeping my eyes upon the shadow. It did not move. Convinced now that danger of some kind lay ahead of me, I looked behind and about me for some means of escaping from the house without passing by my half-seen enemy. But none presented themselves. Either I must slink away into the kitchen region—a proceeding from which my whole manhood revolted,—or I must advance and face whatever evil awaited me. Desperation drove me to the latter course. Making one bound, I stood before that lighted passage. A slim, firm figure confronted me; but it was not that of Guy, but of his older brother, Dwight.

The surprise of the shock, together with a certain revelation which came to me at the same moment, and of which I will speak hereafter, greatly unnerved me. I had not been thinking of Dwight Pollard. Strange as it may seem, I had not even missed him from the bedside of his father. To see him, then, here and now, caused many thoughts to spring into my mind, foremost among which was the important one as to whether he was of a nature to lend himself to any scheme of violence. The quickness with which I decided to the contrary proved to me in what different estimation I had always held him from what I had his mother and brother.

It was consequently no surprise to me when he leaned forward and spoke to me with consideration and force. I was only surprised at a his words:

"Don't stop, Mr. Barrows," said he. "Go home at once; only"—and here he paused, listened, then proceeded with increased emphasis, "don't go by the way of Orchard Street." And without waiting for my reply, he stepped back and noiselessly regained the apartment he had left, while I, in a confusion of emotions difficult to analyze at the moment, hastily accepted his advice, and withdrew from the house.

The relief of breathing the fresh air again was indescribable. If I had not escaped the miasma and oppression of a prison, I certainly had left behind me influences of darkness and sinister suggestion, which, in the light of the calm moonbeams that I found flooding the world without, had the effect upon me of a vanished horror. Only I was still haunted by that last phrase which I had heard uttered, "Don't go by the way of Orchard Street," an injunction which simply meant, "Don't go with that document to the lawyer's to-night."

Now was this order, given as it was by Dwight Pollard, one of warning or of simple threat? My good-will toward this especial member of the Pollard family inclined me to think it the former.

There was danger, then, lurking for me somewhere on the road to Mr. Nicholls' house. Was it my duty to encounter this danger? It appeared to me not, especially as it was not necessary for me to acquit myself so instantly of the commission with which I had been intrusted. I accordingly proceeded directly home.

But once again in my familiar study, I became conscious of a strong dissatisfaction with myself. Indeed, I may speak more forcibly and say I was conscious of a loss of trust in my own manhood, which was at once so new and startling that it was as if a line had been drawn between my past and present. This was due to the discovery I had made at the moment I had confronted Dwight Pollard—a discovery so humiliating in its character that it had shaken me, body and soul. I had found in the light of that critical instant that I, David Barrows, was *a coward!* Yes, gloss it over as I would, the knowledge was deep in my mind that I lacked manhood's most virile attribute; that peril, real or imaginary, could awaken in me fear; and that the paling cheek and trembling limbs of which I had been so bitterly conscious at that instant were but the outward signs of a weakness that extended deep down into my soul.

It was a revelation calculated to stagger any man, how much more, then, one who had so relied upon his moral powers as to take upon himself the sacred name of minister. But this was not all. I had not only found myself to be a coward, but I had shown myself such to another's eyes. By the searching look which Dwight Pollard had given me before he spoke, and the quiet, half-disdainful curve which his lips took at the close of his scrutiny, I was convinced that he saw the defect in my nature, and despised me for it, even while he condescended to offer me the protection which my fears seemed to demand. Or—the thought could come now that I was at home, and had escaped the dangers lying in wait for me on the road to my duty—he had made use of my weakness to gain his own ends. The carrying of that document to Mr. Nicholls meant loss of property to them all perhaps, and he had but taken means, consistent with his character, to insure the delay which his brother had possibly planned to gain in some more reprehensible manner. And I had yielded to my fears and let his will have its way. I hated myself as I considered my own weakness. I could find no excuse either for my pusillanimity or for that procrastination of my duty into which it had betrayed me. I found I could not face my own scorn; and, rising from my study-chair, I took my hat and went out. I had determined to make amends for my fault by going at once to Orchard Street.

And I did; but alas! for the result! The half-hour I had lost was fatal. To be sure I met with no adventure on my way, but I found Mr. Nicholls out. He had been summoned by a telegram to Boston, and had been absent from the house only fifteen minutes. I meditated following him to the station, but the whistle sounded just as I turned away from his door, and I knew I should be too late. Humiliated still further in my own estimation, I went home to wait with what patience I could for the two or three days which must elapse before his return.

Before I went to bed that night I opened the book which Mr. Pollard had given me, in the expectation of finding a letter in it, or, at least, some writing on the title-page or the blank pages of the book. But I was disappointed in both regards. With the exception of some minute pencil-marks scattered here and there along the text—indications, doubtless, of favorite passages—I perceived nothing in the volume to account for the extreme earnestness with which he had presented it.

XX

THE OLD MILL

Whither wilt thou lead me? speak; I'll go no farther.

—HAMLET.

I did not sleep well that night, but this did not prevent me from beginning work early in the morning. The sermon I had been interrupted in the afternoon before, had to be completed that day; and I was hard at work upon it when there came a knock at my study-door. I arose with any thing but alacrity and opened it. Dwight Pollard stood before me.

It was a surprise that called up a flush to my cheeks; but daylight was shining upon this interview, and I knew none of those sensations which had unnerved me the night before. I was simply on my guard, and saw him seat himself in my own chair, without any other feeling than that of curiosity as to the nature of his errand. He likewise was extremely self-possessed, and looked at me calmly for some instants before speaking.

"Last night," he began, "you refused a request which my mother made of you."

I bowed.

"It was a mistake," he continued. "The paper which my father gave you cannot be one which he in his right senses would wish seen by the public. You should have trusted my mother, who knew my father much better than you did."

"It was not a matter of trust," I protest. "A document had been given me by I a dying man, with an injunction to put it into certain hands. I had no choice but to fulfil his wishes in this regard. Your mother herself would have despised me if I had yielded to her importunities and left it behind me."

"My mother," he commenced.

"Your mother is your mother," I put in. "Let us have respect for her widowhood, and leave her out of this conversation."

He looked at me closely, and I understood his glance.

"I cannot return you your father's will," I declared, firmly.

He held my glance with his.

"Have you it still?" he asked.

"I cannot return it to you," I repeated.

He arose and approached me courteously. "You are doing what you consider to be your duty," said he. "In other words than my mother used, I simply add, on *our* heads must be the consequences." And his grave look, at once half-sad and half-determined, impressed me for the first time with a certain sort of sympathy for this unhappy family. "And this leads me to the purpose of my call," he proceeded, deferentially. "I am here at my mothers wish, and I bring you her apologies. Though you have done and are doing wrong by your persistence in carrying out my poor father's wishes to the detriment of his memory, my mother regrets that she spoke to you in the manner she did, and hopes you will not allow it to stand in the way of your conducting the funeral services."

"Mr. Pollard," I replied, "your father was my friend, and to no other man could I delegate the privilege of uttering prayers over his remains. But I would not be frank to you nor true to myself if I did not add that it will take more than an apology from your mother to convince me that she wishes me well, or is, indeed, any thing but the enemy her looks proclaimed her to be last night."

"I am sorry—" he began, but meeting my eye, stopped. "You possess a moral courage which I envy you," he declared. And waiving the subject of his mother, he proceeded to inform me concerning the funeral and the arrangements which had been made.

I listened calmly. In the presence of this man I felt strong. Though he knew the secret of my weakness, and possibly despised me for it, he also knew what indeed he had just acknowledged, that in some respects I was on a par with him.

The arrangements were soon made, and he took his leave without any further allusion to personal matters. But I noticed that at the door he stopped and cast a look of inquiry around the room. It disconcerted me somewhat; and while I found it difficult to express to myself the nature of the apprehensions which it caused, I inwardly resolved to rid myself as soon as possible of the responsibility of holding Mr. Pollard's will. If Mr. Nicholls did not return by the day of the funeral, I would go myself to Boston and find him.

No occurrence worth mentioning followed this interview with Dwight Pollard. I conducted the services as I had promised, but found nothing to relate concerning them, save the fact that Mrs. Pollard was not present. She had been very much prostrated by her husband's death, and was not able to leave her room, or so it was said. I mistrusted the truth of this, however, but must acknowledge I was glad to be relieved of a presence not only so obnoxious to myself, but so out of tune with the occasion. I could ignore Guy, subtle and secret as he was, but this woman could not be ignored. Where she was, there brooded something dark, mysterious, and threatening; and whether she smiled or frowned, the influence of her spirit was felt by a vague oppression at once impossible to analyze or escape from.

From the cemetery I went immediately to my house. The day was a dreary one, and I felt, chilled. The gray of the sky was in my spirit, and every thing seemed unreal and dark and strange. I was in a mood, I suppose, and, unlike myself on other similar occasions, did not feel that drawing towards the one dear heart which hitherto had afforded me solace and support. I had not got used to my new self as yet, and till I did, the smile of her I loved was more of a reproach to me than consolation.

I was stopped at the gate by Mrs. Banks. She is my next-door neighbor, and in the absence of my landlady who had gone to visit some friends, took charge of any message which might be left for me while I was out. She looked flurried and mysterious.

"You have had a visitor," she announced.

As she paused and looked as if she expected to be questioned, I naturally asked who it was.

"She said she was your sister," she declared. "A tall woman with a thick veil over her face. She went right up to your study, but I think she must have got tired of waiting, for she went away again a few moments ago."

My sister! I had no sister. I looked at Mrs. Banks in amazement

"Describe her more particularly," said I.

"That I cannot do," she returned. "Her veil hid her features too completely for me to see them. I could not even tell her age, but I should say, from the way she walked that she was older than you."

A chill, which did not come entirely from the east wind then blowing, ran sharply through my veins.

"I thank you," said I, somewhat incoherently, and ran hastily upstairs. I had a presentiment as to the identity of this woman.

At the door of my study I paused and looked hurriedly around. No signs of any disturbance met my eye. Crossing over to my desk, I surveyed the papers which I had left scattered somewhat loosely over it. They had been moved. I knew it by the position of the blotter, which I had left under a certain sheet of paper, and which now lay on top. Hot and cold at once, I went immediately to the spot where I had concealed Mr. Pollard's will. It was in my desk, but underneath a drawer instead of in it, and by this simple precaution, perhaps, I had saved it from destruction; for I found it lying in its place undisturbed, though the hand which had crept so near its hiding- place was, as I felt certain, no other than that of Mrs. Pollard, searching for this very document.

It gave me a shuddering sense of disquiet to think that the veiled figure of this portentous woman had glided over my floors, reflected itself in my mirrors, and hung, dark and mysterious in its veiling drapery, over my desk and the papers which I had handled myself so lately.

I was struck, too, by the immovable determination to compass her own ends at any and every risk, which was manifested by this incident; and, wondering more and more as to what had been the nature of the offence for which Mr. Pollard sought to make reparation in his will, I only waited for a moment of leisure in order to make another effort at enlightenment by a second study of the prayer-book which my dying friend had placed so earnestly in my hands.

It came, as I supposed, about eight o'clock that evening. The special duties of the day were done, and I knew of nothing else that demanded my attention. I therefore took the book from my pocket, where I had fortunately kept it, and was on the point of opening its pages, when there came a ring at the door-bell below.

As I have said before, my landlady was away. I consequently went to the door myself, where I was met by an unexpected visitor in the shape of the idiot boy, Colwell. Somewhat disconcerted at the sight of a face so repugnant to me, I was still more thrown off my balance when I heard his errand. He had been sent, he said, by a man who had been thrown from his wagon on the north road, and was now lying in a dying condition inside the old mill, before which he was picked up. Would I come and see him? He had but an hour or so to live, and wished very much for a clergyman's consolation.

It was a call any thing but agreeable to me. I was tired; I was interested in the attempt which I was about to make to solve a mystery that was not altogether disconnected with my own personal welfare, and—let me acknowledge it, since events have proved I had reason to fear this spot—I did not like the old mill. But I was far from conceiving what a wretched experience lay before me, nor did the fact that the unwelcome request came through the medium of an imbecile arouse any suspicion in my mind as to the truth of the message he brought. For, foolish as he is in some regards, his reliability as an errand-boy is universally known, while his partiality for roaming, as well as for excitements of all kinds, fully accounted for the fact of his being upon the scene of accident.

I had, then, nothing but my own disinclinations to contend with, and these, strong as they were, could not, at that time, and in the mood which my late experience had induced, long stand in the way of a duty so apparent.

I consequently testified my willingness to go to the mill, and in a few minutes later set out for that spot with a mind comparatively free from disagreeable forebodings. But as we approached the mill, and I caught a glimpse of its frowning walls glooming so darkly from out the cluster of trees that environed them, I own that a sensation akin to that which had been awakened in me by Mrs. Pollard's threats, and the portentous darkness of her sombre mansion, once again swept with its chilling effect over my nerves.

Shocked, disgusted with myself at the recurrence of a weakness for which I had so little sympathy, I crushed down the feelings I experienced, and advanced at once to the door. A tall and slim figure met me, clothed in some dark enveloping garment, and carrying a lantern.

"The injured man is within," said he.

Something in the voice made me look up. His face was entirely in shadow.

"Who are you?" I asked.

He did not reply.

"Let us go in," he said.

A week before I would have refused to do this without knowing more of my man. But the shame from which I had suffered for the last few days had made me so distrustful of myself that I was ready to impute to cowardice even the most ordinary instinct of self-preservation.

I accordingly followed the man, though with each step that I took I felt my apprehensions increase. To pierce in this manner a depth of sombre darkness, with only the dim outline of an unknown man moving silently before me, was any thing but encouraging in itself. Then the way was too long, and the spot we sought too far from the door. A really injured man would not be carried beyond the first room, I thought, and we had already taken steps enough to be half-way through the building. At last I felt that even cowardice was excusable under these circumstances, and, putting out my hand, I touched the man before me on the shoulder.

"Where are we going?" I demanded.

He continued to move on without reply.

"I shall follow you no longer if you do not speak," I cried again. "This midnight journey through an old building ready to fall into ruins seems to me not only unpleasant but hazardous."

Still no answer.

"I warned you," I said, and stopped, but the next moment I gave an almost frantic bound forward. A form had come up against me from behind, and I found that a man was following as closely upon my steps as I had been following those of the person who stalked before me.

The thrill of this discovery will never be forgotten by me. For a moment I could not speak, and when I did, the sound of my voice only added to my terrors.

"You have me in a trap," said I; "who are you, and what are your intentions with me?"

"We have you where we can reason with you," exclaimed the voice of him who pressed against my back; and at the sound of those gentlemanly tones with their underlying note of sarcasm, I understood that my hour had come. It was the voice and intonation of Guy Pollard.

XXI

THE VAT

Des.—Talk you of killing?'
Oth.—Ay, I do.
Des.—Then, heaven
Have mercy on me!

—OTHELLO.

I quivered with shame, for I felt my heart sink. But there was no pause in the smooth, sarcastic tones behind me. "When a man persists in judging of his duty contrary to the dictates of reason, he must expect restraint from those who understand his position better than he does himself."

"Then," quoth I, with suddenly acquired strength, "I am to understand that the respectable family of Pollard finds itself willing to resort to the means and methods of highwaymen in order to compass its ends and teach me my duty."

"You are," a determined voice returned.

At that word, uttered as it was in a tone inexorable as fate, my last ray of hope went out. The voice was that of a woman.

I however, made a strong effort for the preservation of my dignity and person.

"And will Samuel Pollard's oldest and best-beloved son, the kind-hearted and honest Dwight, lend himself to a scheme of common fraud and violence?" I asked.

The reply came in his brother's most sarcastic tones. "Dwight has left us," he declared. "We have no need of honesty or kind-heartedness here. What we want for this business is an immovable determination."

Startled, I looked up. The lantern which had hitherto swung from the hand of my guide stood on the floor. By its light three things were visible. First, that we stood at the head of a staircase descending into a depth of darkness which the eye could not pierce; secondly, that in all the area about me but two persons stood; and third, that of these two persons one of them was masked and clad in a long black garment, such as is worn at masquerade balls under the name of a domino. Struck with an icy chill, I looked down again. Why had I allowed myself to be caught in such a trap? Why had I not followed Mr. Nicholls immediately to Boston when I heard that he was no longer in town? Or, better still, why had I not manufactured for myself a safeguard in the form of a letter to that gentleman, informing him of the important document which I held, and the danger in which it possibly stood from the family into whose toils I had now fallen? I could have cursed myself for my dereliction.

"David Barrows," came in imperative tones from the masked figure, "will you tell us where this will is?"

"No," I returned.

"Is it not on your person?" the inquisitorial voice pursued.

"It is not," I answered, firmly, thankful that I spoke the truth in this.

"It is in your rooms, then; in your desk, perhaps?"

I remained silent.

"Is it in your rooms?" the indomitable woman proceeded.

"You who have been there should know," I replied, feeling my courage rise, as I considered that they could not assail my honor, while my life without my secret would benefit them so little that it might be said to stand in no danger.

"I do not understand you," the icy voice declared; while Guy, stepping forward, planted his hand firmly on my shoulder and said:

"Wherever it is, it shall be delivered to our keeping to-night. We are in no mood for dallying. Either you will give us your solemn promise to obtain this will, and hand it over to us without delay and without scandal, or the free light of heaven is shut out from you forever. You shall never leave this mill."

"But," I faltered, striving in vain to throw off the incubus of horror which his words invoked, "what good would my death do you? Could it put Mr. Pollard's will in your hands?"

"Yes," was the brief and decided reply, "if it is anywhere in your rooms."

It was a word that struck home. The will was in my rooms, and I already saw it, in my imagination, torn from its hiding-place by the unscrupulous hand that held me.

Mastering my emotion with what spirit I could, I looked quickly about me. Was there no means of escape? I saw none. In the remote and solitary place which they had chosen for this desperate attempt, a cry would be but waste breath, even if we were in that part of the mill which looked toward the road. But we were not; on the contrary, I could see by the aid of the faint glimmer which the lantern sent forth, that the room in which we had halted was as far as possible from the front of the building, for its windows were obscured by the brush-wood which only grew against the back of the mill. To call out, then, would be folly, while to seek by any force or strategy to break away from the two relentless beings that controlled me could only end in failure, unless darkness would come to my aid and hide my road of escape. But darkness could only come by the extinguishing of the lantern, and that it was impossible for me to effect; for I was not strong enough to struggle in its direction with Guy Pollard, nor could I reach it by any stretch of foot or hand. The light must burn and I must stay there, unless—the thought came suddenly—I could take advantage of the flight of steps at the head of which I stood, and by a sudden leap, gain the cellar, where I would stand a good chance of losing myself amid intricacies as little known to them as to myself. But to do this I must be free to move, and there was no shaking myself loose from the iron clutch that held me.

"You see you are in our power," hissed the voice of the woman from between the motionless lips of her black mask.

"I see I am," I acknowledged, "but I also see that you are in that of God." And I looked severely towards her, only to drop my eyes again with an irrepressible shudder.

For, lay it to my weakness or to the baleful influence which emanated from the whole ghostly place, there was something absolutely appalling in this draped and masked figure with its gleaming eyes and cold, thin voice.

"Shall we have what we want before your death or after?" proceeded Guy Pollard, with a calm but cold ignoring of my words that was more threatening than any rudeness.

I did not answer at first, and his grip upon me tightened; but next moment, from what motive I cannot say, it somewhat relaxed; and, startled, with the hope of freedom, I exclaimed with a vehemence for which my former speech must have little prepared them:

"You shall not have it at all. I cannot break my word with your father, and I will not stay here to be threatened and killed;" and making a sudden movement, I slipped from his grasp, and plunged down the steps into the darkness below.

But, scarcely had my feet touched the cellar floor, before I heard the warning cry shrill out from above:

"Take care! There is an open vat before you. If you fall into that, we shall be free of your interference without lifting a hand."

An open vat! I had heard of the vats in the old mill's cellar. Instinctively recoiling, I stood still, not knowing whether to advance or retreat. At the same moment I heard the sound of steps descending the stairs.

"So you think this a better place for decision than the floor above?" exclaimed Guy Pollard, drawing up by my side. "Well, I not sure but you are right," he added; and I saw by the light of the lantern which his companion now brought down the stairs, the cold glimmer of a smile cross his thin lips and shine for a moment from his implacable eyes. Not knowing what he meant, I glanced anxiously about, and shrank with dismay as I discerned the black hole of the vat he had mentioned, yawning within three feet of my side. Was it a dream, my presence in this fearful spot? I looked at the long stretch of arches before me glooming away into the darkness beyond us, and felt the chill of a nameless horror settle upon my spirit.

Was it because I knew those circles of blackness held many another such pit of doom as that into which I had so nearly stumbled? Or was it that the grisly aspect of the scene woke within me that slumbering demon of the imagination which is the bane of natures like mine.

Whatever it was, I felt the full force of my position, and scarcely cared whether my voice trembled or not as I replied:

"You surely have me in your hands; but that does not mean that it is I who must make a decision. If I understand the situation, it is for you to say whether you will be murderers or not."

"Then you do not intend to put us in possession of my father's will?"

"No," I murmured, and bowed my head for the blow I expected from him.

But he dealt me no blow. Instead of that he eyed me with a look which grew more and more sinister as I met his glance with one which I meant should convey my indomitable resolution. At last he spoke again:

"I think you will reconsider your determination," said he, with a meaning I did not even then fathom, and exchanging a quick glance with the silent figure at his right, he leaned towards me and—what happened? For a moment I could not tell, but soon, only too soon, I recognized by my stunned and bleeding body, by the closeness of the air I suddenly breathed, and by the circle of darkness that shut about me, and the still more distinct circle of light that glimmered above, that I had been pushed into the pit whose yawning mouth had but a few short moments before awakened in me such dismay.

Aghast, almost mad with the horror of a fate so much more terrible than any I had anticipated, I strove to utter a cry; but my tongue refused its office, and nothing but an inarticulate murmur rose from my lips. It was not piercing enough to clear the edge of the vat, and my soul sunk with despair as I heard its fruitless gurgle and realized by the sound of departing steps, and the faint and fainter glimmer of the circle of light which at my first glance had shone quite brightly above my hideous prison-house, that my persecutors had done their worst and were now leaving me alone in my trap to perish.

God! what an instant it was! To speak, to shriek, to call, nay plead for aid, was but the natural outcome of the overwhelming anguish I felt, but the sound of steps had died out into an awful stillness, and the glimmering circle upon which my staring eyes were fixed had faded into a darkness so utter and complete, that had the earth been piled above my head, I could not have been more wholly hidden from the light.

I had fallen on my knees, and desperate as I was, had made no attempt to rise. Not that I thought of prayer, unless my whole dazed and horrified being was a prayer. The consolations which I had offered to others did not seem to meet this case. Here was no death in the presence of friends and under the free light of heaven. This was a horror. The hand of God which could reach every other mortal, whatever their danger or doom, seemed to stop short at this gate of hell. I could not even imagine my soul escaping thence. I was buried; body and soul, I was buried and yet I was alive and knew that I must remain alive for days if not for weeks.

I do not suppose that I remained in this frightful condition of absolute hopelessness for more than five minutes, but it seemed to me an eternity. If a drowning man can review his life in an instant, what was there not left for me to think and suffer in the lapse of those five horrible minutes? I was young when the unscrupulous hand of this daring murderer pushed me into this pit; I was old when with a thrill of joy such as passes over the body but once In a life-time, I heard a voice issue from the darkness, saying severely, "David Barrows, are you prepared for a decision now?" and realized that like the light which now sprang into full brilliance above my head, hope had come again into my life, and that I had to speak but a dozen words to have sunshine and liberty restored to me.

The rush of emotion which this startling change brought was almost too much for my reason. Looking up into the sardonic face, I could now discern peering over the edge of the vat, I asked with a frantic impulse that left me no time for thought, if an immediate restoration to freedom would follow my compliance with his wishes, and when he answered: "Yes," I beheld such a vision of sunshiny fields and a happy, love-lighted home, that my voice almost choked as I responded, that I did not think his father would have wished me to sacrifice my life or force a son of his into the crime of murder, for the sake of any reparation which money could offer. And as I saw the face above me grow impatient, I told in desperate haste where I had concealed the will and how it could be obtained without arousing the suspicions of my neighbors.

He seemed satisfied and hastily withdrew his face; but soon returned and asked for the key of my house. I had it in my pocket and hurriedly pitched it up to him, when he again disappeared.

"When shall I be released?" I anxiously called out after him.

But no answer came back, and presently the light began to fade as before, and the sound of steps grow fainter and fainter till silence and darkness again settled upon my dreadful prison-house.

But this time I had hope to brighten me, and shutting my eyes, I waited patiently. But at last, as no change came and the silence and darkness remained unbroken, I became violently alarmed and cried to myself: "Am I the victim of their treachery? Have they obtained what they want and now am I to be left here to perish?"

The thought made my hair stand on end and had I not been a God-fearing man I should certainly have raised my voice in curses upon my credulity and lack of courage. But before my passion could reach its height, hope shone again in the shape of returning light. Some one had entered the cellar and drawn near the edge of the vat; but though I strained my gaze upward, no face met my view, and presently I heard a voice which was not that of Guy Pollard utter in tones of surprise and apprehension:

"Where is the clergyman? Guy said I should find him here in

good condition?"

The masked figure, who was doubtless the one addressed, must have answered with a gesture towards the hole in which I lay, for I heard him give vent to a horrified exclamation and then say in accents of regret and shame: "Was it necessary?" and afterwards: "Are you sure he is not injured?"

The answer, which I did not hear, seemed to satisfy him, for he said no more, and soon, too soon, walked away again, carrying the light and leaving me, as I now knew, with that ominous black figure for my watch and guardian,—a horror that lent a double darkness to the situation which was only relieved now by the thought that Dwight Pollard's humanity was to be relied on, and that he would never wantonly leave me there to perish after the will had been discovered and destroyed.

It was well that I had this confidence, for the time I now had to wait was long. But I lived it through and at last had the joy of hearing footsteps and the voice of Guy saying in a dry and satisfied tone: "It is all right," after which the face of Dwight looked over the edge of the vat and he gave me the help which was needed to lift me out.

I was a free man again. I had slipped from the gates of hell, and the world with all its joys and duties lay before me bright and beautiful as love and hope could make it. Yet whether it was the gloom of the cellar in which we still lingered, or the baleful influence that emanated, from the three persons in whose presence I once more stood, I felt a strange sinking at my heart and found myself looking back at the pit from which I had just escaped, with a sensation of remorse, as if in its horrid depths I had left or lost something which must create a void within me forever.

My meditations in this regard were interrupted by the voice of Guy.

"David Barrows," said he, "we hold the paper which was given you by my father."

I bowed with a slight intimation of impatience.

"We have looked at it and it is as he said, his will. But it is not such a one as we feared, and to-morrow, or as soon as we can restore the seal, we shall return it to you for such disposition as your judgment suggests."

I stared at him in an amazement that made me forget my shame.

"You will give it back?" I repeated.

"To-morrow," he laconically replied.

XXII

THE CYPHER

Ah, my false heart, what hast thou done?

This is a story of fact; it is also a story of mental struggle. I shall not, therefore, be considered too diffuse if I say that this unlooked for ending to my unhappy adventure threw me into a strange turmoil of feeling, from which I had no rest until the next day came. That they should promise to restore the will, to obtain which they had resorted to measures almost criminal in their severity, awoke in me the greatest astonishment. What could it mean? I waited to see the will before replying.

It came, as Guy Pollard had promised, at noon of the following day. It was in a new envelope, and was sealed just as it had been before it left my possession. Had I not known into what unscrupulous hands it had fallen, I should have doubted if it had ever been opened. As it was, I was not only confident that it had been read from end to end, but fearful that it had been tampered with, and perhaps altered. To get it out of my hands, and if possible, my mind also, I carried it at once to Mr. Nicholls, who, I had ascertained that morning, had returned to town the day before.

He received me with affability, but looked a little surprised when he learned my errand.

"I was just going to call on the family," said he; "I drew up Mr. Pollard's will myself, and—"

"You drew up Mr. Pollard's will?" I hastily interrupted. "You know, then, its contents, and can tell me—"

"Pardon me," he as hastily put in, "the family have the first right to a knowledge of what Mr. Pollard has done for them."

I felt myself at a loss. To explain my rights and the great desire which I experienced to ascertain whether the tenor of the paper he now held coincided with that which he had submitted to Mr. Pollard for his signature, necessitated a full relation of facts which I was not yet certain ought to be made public. For if the will had not been meddled with, and Mr. Pollard's wishes stood in no danger of being slighted or ignored, what else but a most unhappy scandal could accrue from the revelation which I should be forced to make? Then, my own part in the miserable affair. If not productive of actual evil, it was still something to blush for, and I had not yet reached that stage of repentance or humility which made it easy to show the world a weakness for which I had no pity nor sympathy myself. Yet to guard the interests with which I had been entrusted, it was absolutely necessary that the question which so much disturbed me should be answered. For, if any change had been made in this important paper by which the disposition of Mr. Pollard's property should be turned aside from the channel in which he had ordered it, I felt that no consideration for the public welfare or my own good fame should hinder me from challenging its validity.

My embarrassment evidently showed itself, for the acute lawyer, after a momentary scrutiny of my face, remarked:

"You say Mr. Pollard gave you this will to hand to me. Do you know the cause of this rather extraordinary proceeding, or have you any suspicion why, in the event of his desiring me to have in charge a paper which ought to be safe enough in his own house, he choose his pastor for his messenger instead of one of

Anna Katherine Green

his own sons?"

"Mr. Nicholls," I returned, with inward satisfaction for the opportunity thus given me for reply, "the secrets which are confided to a clergyman are as sacred as those which are entrusted to a lawyer. I could not tell you my suspicions if I had any; I can only state the facts. One thing, however, I will add. That owing to circumstances which I cannot explain, but greatly regret, this paper has been out of my hands for a short time, and in speaking as I did, I wished merely to state that it would be a satisfaction to me to know that no harm has befallen it, and that this is the very will in spirit and detail which you drew up and saw signed by Mr. Pollard."

"Oh," exclaimed the lawyer, "if that is all, I can soon satisfy you." And tearing open the envelope, he ran his eye over the document and quietly nodded.

"It is the same," he declared. "There has been no meddling here."

And feeling myself greatly relieved, I rose without further conversation and hastily took my leave.

But when I came to think of it all again in my own room, I found my equanimity was not yet fully restored. A doubt of some kind remained, and though, in consideration of the manifold duties that pressed upon me, I relentlessly put it aside, I could not help its lingering in my mind, darkening my pleasures, and throwing a cloud over my work and the operations of my mind. The sight which I now and then caught of the Pollards did not tend to allay my anxieties. There was satisfaction in their countenances, and in that of Guy, at least, a certain triumphant disdain which could only be partly explained by the victory which he had won over me through my fears. I awaited the proving of the will with anxiety. If there were no seeming reparation made in it, I should certainly doubt its being the expression of Mr. Pollard's wishes.

What was my surprise, then, when the will having been proved, I obtained permission to read it and found that it not only contained mention of reparation, but that this reparation was to be made to Margaret his wife.

"For sums loaned by her to me and lost, I desire to make reparation by an added bequest—" so it read; and I found myself nonplussed and thrown entirely out in all my calculations and conjectures. The anxiety he had shown lest the will should fall into this very woman's hands, did not tally with this expression of justice and generosity, nor did the large sums which he had left to his three children show any of that distrust which his countenance had betrayed towards the one who was present with him at the time of his death. Could it be that he had given me the wrong paper or was he, as Mrs. Pollard had intimated, not responsible for his actions and language at that time. I began to think the latter conjecture might be true, and was only hindered in the enjoyment of my old tranquility by the remembrance of the fearful ordeal I had been subjected to in the mill, and the consideration which it brought of the fears and suspicions which must have existed to make the perpetration of such an outrage possible.

But time, which dulls all things, soon began to affect my memory of that hideous nightmare, and with it my anxiety lest in my unfaithfulness to my trust, I had committed a wrong upon some unknown innocent. Life with its duties and love with its speedy prospect of marriage gradually pushed all unpleasant thoughts from my mind, and I was beginning to enjoy the full savor of my happy and honorable position again, when my serenity was again, and this time forever, destroyed by a certain revelation that was accidentally made to me.

The story of it was this. I had taken by mistake with me to a funeral the prayer-book with which Mr. Pollard had presented me. I was listening to the anthem which was being sung, and being in a nervous frame of mind, was restlessly fingering the leaves of the book which I held in my hand, when my eye, running over the page that happened to open before me, caught sight of some of the marks with which the text was plentifully bestowed. Mechanically I noticed the words under which they stood, and mechanically I began reading them, when, to my great astonishment and subsequent dismay, I perceived they made sense, in short had a connection which, when carried on from page to page of the book, revealed sentences which promised to extend themselves into a complete communication. This is the page I happened upon, with its lines and dots. Note the result which accrues from reading the marked words alone.

THE EPIPHANY.

with haste, and found Mary and Joseph, and the babe lying in a manger. And when they had seen it, they made known *abroad* the saying which told them concerning this child. And all they that heard it wondered at those things which were told them by the shepherds. But Mary kept all these things, and pondered them in her heart. And the shepherds returned, glorifying and praising God for all the things that they had heard and seen, as it was told unto them. And when eight days were accomplished for the circumcising of the child, his name was called JESUS, which was so named of the angel before he was conceived in the womb.

The same Collect, Epistle, and Gospel shall serve for every day after, unto the Epiphany.

The Epiphany,

Or the Manifestation of Christ to the Gentiles.

THE COLLECT.

O God, who by the leading of *a* star didst manifest thy only-begotten Son to the Gentiles, Mercifully grant that we, who know thee now by faith, may after this life have the fruition of thy glorious Godhead through Jesus Christ our Lord. *Amen.*

THE EPISTLE. Eph iii. I.

For this cause, I Paul the *prisoner* of Jesus Christ for you Gentiles, if ye have heard of the dispensation of the grace of God, which is given me to you ward. How that by *revelation* he *made known* unto me the mystery (as I wrote afore *in few words, whereby, when ye read, ye may understand* my knowledge in *the mystery* of Christ) *which* in other ages *was* not *made known unto the sons* of men, as it is now revealed unto his holy Apostles and Prophets by the Spirit, that the Gentiles should be *fellow-heirs,* and *of* the same body, and partakers of his promise in Christ, by the Gospel whereof I was made a minister, according to the gift of the *grace* of God given unto me by the effectual working of his power. Unto me, who am less than the least of all saints is this grace given, that I should preach among the Gentiles the unsearchable riches of Christ, and to make all men see what is the fellowship of the mystery, which from the beginning of the world hath been hid in God, who created all things by Jesus Christ: to the intent that now unto the principalities and powers in heavenly]

It was but one of many, and you can imagine how difficult I found it to continue with the service and put the subject from my mind till the funeral was over and I could return to solitude and my third and final examination into the meaning of this mysterious gift.

You can also imagine my wonder when by following out the plan I have indicated, the subjoined sentences appeared, which, if somewhat incoherent at times—as could only be expected from the limited means at his command—certainly convey a decided meaning, especially after receiving the punctuation and capital letters, which, after long study and some after-knowledge of affairs, I have ventured upon giving them:

"My sin is ever before me."

"Correct, lest thou bring me to nothing."

"Do those things which are requisite and necessary for a pure and humble one, Grace by name, begotten by son, he born of first wife and not obedient to the law abroad, a prisoner."

"Revelation made known in few words whereby when ye read ye may understand the mystery which was made known unto the sons, fellow-heirs of Grace."

"Go and search diligently for the young child."

"The higher powers resist and are a terror to good works."

"Do that which is good and thou shalt have praise, minister of God."

"Wherefore ye must needs be subject for wrath, for they are attending continually upon this thing."

"Render therefore to all their dues; tribute to whom tribute; honor to whom honor."

"Two possessed of devils, exceeding fierce of the household, hope Grace may evermore be cast away."

"They murmur against the good man of the house, and do not agree to mercifully defend against perils in the city an honest and good heart."

"My will leave(s) heritage to Grace."

"The devil is against me."

"Behold a woman grievously vexed with lost sheep of the house."

"Then came she, saying: 'It is not mete to take the children's bread and to cast it to the dogs. Be unto, us an offering named as becometh saints. For this ye know, that no unclean person hath any inheritance because of disobedience and fellowship with works of darkness. For it is a shame to speak of those things which are done of them in secret.'

"Beelzebub, the chief of devils, and sons cast out man; taketh from him all wherein he trusteth and divideth the spoils against me."

"To purge conscience, the new testament means redemption of the transgressions under first testament."

"Said a devil: 'Father, ye do dishonor me. Say ye know him not, thy son, and suffer that a notable prisoner, his wife and child, were not called by thy name.' 'I will,' said I. But I deny all here. My soul is sorrowful unto death, as I bear false witness against them.

"The hand that betrayeth me is with me."

"I appoint you to sift as wheat."

"This must be accomplished, for the things concerning me have an end."

"Words sent unto me out of prison, said: 'Daughter weep(s). Beseech thee graciously to fetch home to thee my child in tribulation. For lo, the ungodly bend their bow and make ready their arrows within the quiver, that they may privily shoot at them which are true of heart. Show I thy marvellous loving-kindness unto an undefined soul forsaken on every side of mother and friendly neighbors. Make haste to deliver and save. I am clean forgotten, as a dead man out of mind. I am become as a broken vessel.'"

"Whilst I held my tongue, my bones consumed away daily."

"I will inform thee and teach thee ill the way wherein thou shalt go."

"Blessed are folk chosen to inheritance; the children of them that dwell under the king."

"Poor Grac(e) come over the see (sea), unaware that I were sick."

"Deliver my darling from the lions, so will I give thee thanks."

"O let not them that are mine enemies triumph that hate me."

"They imagine deceitful words against them that are quiet in the land."

"Child is in thy land."

"Look after daughter among honorable women. House in City of the East Wind."

[Footnote: Number omitted for obvious reasons.]"—C-H-A-R-L-E-S-S- T-R-E-E-T.

"Child I have looked upon not."

"I promised with my lips and spake with my mouth, but God turned his mercy upon me, and upon health hath sent forth his voice, yea, and that a mighty voice."

"I sink, and the deep waters drown me."

"Mine adversaries hath broken my heart."

"Let the things that should have been for them be for the poor prisoner's posterity."

"Break down the carved work and search out my will."

"Walk to table under southwest borders of room, take the wood that hath in it operations of the law, and cleave."

"For my days are gone like a shadow, and I am withered as grass."

Anna Katherine Green

XXIII

TOO LATE

What fear is this, which startles in our ears?

—ROMEO AND JULIET.

The conclusion which I drew from these sentences after a close and repeated perusal of them was to this effect:

That Mr. Pollard instead of possessing only two sons, as was generally supposed, had in reality been the father of three. That the eldest, born in all probability before Mr. Pollard's removal to this country (he was an Englishman by birth), had, by some act of violence or fraud, incurred the penalty of the law, and was even now serving out a term of imprisonment in his native land. That this son had a daughter innocent and virtuous, whom he desired to commit to the care of her grandfather; that he had even sent her over here for that purpose, but that Mr. Pollard, taken down with the illness which afterwards ended in death, had not only failed to be on hand to receive her, but that, surrounded and watched by his wife and sons, who, in their selfish pride, were determined to ignore all claims of kinship on the part of one they despised, he had not even had the chance to take such measures for her safety and happiness as his love and regard for her lonely and desolate position seemed to demand. That the will, whose concealment in his desk he had managed to describe, had been made in recompense for this neglect, and that by it she would receive that competence and acknowledgment of her rights which the hatred of her unscrupulous relatives would otherwise deny her.

And this was the will I had weakly given up, and it was upon the head of this innocent child that the results of my weakness must fall.

When I first recognized this fact I felt stupefied. That I, David Barrows, should be the cause of misery and loss to a guileless and pure soul! I could not realize it, nor believe that consequences so serious and irremediable could follow upon an act into which I had been betrayed by mere cowardice. But soon, too soon, the matter became plain to me. I saw what I had done and was overwhelmed, for I could no longer doubt that the real will had been destroyed and that the one which had been returned to me was a substituted one, perhaps the very same which I had seen among the papers of Mr. Pollard's desk.

The result of my remorse was an immediate determination on my part to search out the young girl, left in this remarkable manner to my care, and by my efforts in her behalf do what I could to remedy the great evil which, through my instrumentality, had befallen her.

The purpose was no sooner taken than I prepared to carry it out. S—could hold no duty for me now paramount to this. I was a father and my child lingered solitary and uncared-for in a strange place. I took the first train the next morning for the "city of the east-wind."

The hour at which I arrived at number—Charles Street, was one of deep agitation to me, I had thought so continually upon my journey of the young waif I was seeking. Would she be the embodiment of ingenuousness which her grandfather had evidently believed her to be? Should I find her forgiving and tractable; or were the expectations I had formed false in their character and founded rather upon Mr. Pollard's wishes than any knowledge he had of her disposition and acquirements?

The house was, as far as I could judge from the exterior, of a most respectable character, and the lady who answered my somewhat impatient summons was one of those neat and intelligent-looking persons who inspire confidence at first glance. To my inquiries as to whether there was living in her house a young English lady by the name of Grace—I did not like to venture upon that of Pollard, there being some phrases in the communication I have shown you which led me to think that Mr. Pollard had changed his name on coming to this country,—she gave me a look of such trouble and anxiety that I was instantly struck with dismay.

"Miss Merriam?" she exclaimed; then, as I bowed with seeming acquiescence, continued in a tone that conveyed still more disquiet than her face, "She *was* here; but she is gone, sir; a woman took her away."

A woman! I must have grown pale, for she swung wide the door and asked me to come in.

"We can talk better in the hall," she remarked, and pointed to a chair into which I half fell.

"I have a great interest in this young lady," I observed; "in short, I am her guardian. Can you tell me the name of the person with whom she went away, or where she can be found now?"

"No sir," she answered, with the same expression of trouble. "The woman gave us no name nor address, and the young lady seemed too much frightened to speak. We have felt anxious ever since she went, sir; for the letter she showed us from the captain of the ship which brought her over, told us to take great care of her. We did not know she had a guardian or we should not have let her go. The woman seemed very pleasant, and paid all the bills, but—"

"But what?" I cried, too anxious to bear a moment's delay.

"She did not lift her veil, and this seemed to me a suspicious circumstance."

Torn with apprehension and doubt, I staggered to my feet.

"Tell me all about this woman," I demanded. "Give me every detail you can remember. I have a dreadful fear that it is some one who should never have seen this child."

"Well, sir, she came at about eleven in the morning—"

"What day?" I interrupted her to ask.

"Thursday," she replied, "a week ago yesterday."

The very day after the will was returned to me. If she were the woman I feared, she had evidently lost no time.

"She asked for Miss Merriam," the lady before me pursued, evidently greatly pitying my distress, "and as we knew no reason why our young boarder should not receive visitors, we immediately proceeded to call her down. But the woman, with a muttered excuse, said she would not trouble us; that she knew the child well, and would go right up to her room if we would only tell her where it was. This we did and should have thought no more of the matter, if in a little while she had not reappeared in the hall, and, inquiring the way to my room, told me that Miss Merriam had decided to leave my house; that she had offered her a home with her, and that they were to go immediately.

"I was somewhat taken aback by this, and inquired if I could not see Miss Merriam. She answered 'What for?' and when I hinted that money was owing me for her board, she drew out her pocket-book and paid me on the spot. I could say nothing after this, 'But are you a relative, ma'am?' to which her quick and angry negative, hidden, however, next moment, by a suave acknowledgment of friendship, gave me my first feeling of alarm. But I did not dare to ask her any further questions,

Anna Katherine Green

much as I desired to know who she was and where she was going to take the young girl. There was something in her manner that overawed me, at the same time it filled me with dread. But if I could not speak to her I meant to have some words with Miss Merriam before she left the house. This the woman seemed to wish to prevent, for she stood close by me when the young girl came down, and when I stepped forward to say good-by, pushed me somewhat rudely aside and took Miss Merriam by the arm. 'Come, my dear,' she cried, and would have hurried her out without a word. But I would not have that. The sorrow and perplexity in Miss Merriam's face were too marked for me to let her depart in silence. So I persisted in speaking, and after saying how sorry I was to have her go, asked her if she would not leave her new address with me in case any letters should come for her. Her answer was a frightened look at her companion who immediately spoke for her. 'I have told you,' said she, 'that Miss Merriam goes home with me. It is not likely she will have any letters, but if she should, you can send them to the place mentioned on this card,' and she pulled a visiting card from her bag and gave it to me, after which she immediately went away, dragging Miss Merriam after her."

"And you have that card?" I cried. "Why did you not show it to me at once?"

"O, sir," she responded with a sorrowful shake of her head, "it was a fraud, a deception. The card was not hers but another person's, and its owner don't even know Miss Merriam."

"How do you know this?" I asked. "Have you seen this other person?"

"Yes, sir, I had occasion to, for a letter did come for Miss Merriam only a short time after she left. So thinking it a good opportunity to see where she had gone, I carried it to the address which was on the card given me, and found as I have told you that it was not the same lady at all who lived there, and that there was not only no Miss Merriam in the house but that her name was not even known there."

"And you saw the lady herself?"

"Yes, sir."

"And are you sure it was not the same as the one who was here?"

"Oh yes; she was short and stout and had a frank way of speaking, totally unlike that of the veiled woman."

"And the latter? How was she shaped? You have not told me."

I asked this in trembling tones. Though I was sure what the answer would be, I dreaded to have my fears confirmed.

"Well, sir, she was tall and had a full commanding figure, very handsome to look at. She was dressed all in gray and had a way of holding her head that made an ordinary sized woman like myself feel very small and insignificant. Yet she was not agreeable in her appearance; and I am sure that if I could have seen her face I should have disliked her still more, though I do not doubt it was in keeping with her figure, and very handsome."

I could have no doubts as to whom this described, yet I made one final effort to prove my suspicions false.

"You have given me the description of a person of some pretensions to gentility," I remarked, "yet from the first you have forborne to speak of her as a lady."

"An involuntary expression of my distrust and dislike I suppose. Then her dress was very plain, and the veil she wore quite common."

I thought of the dress and veil which my self-designated "sister" had worn in the visit she paid to my rooms and wondered if they would not answer to the description of these.

"What was the color of her veil?" I inquired.

"Dark blue."

That was the color of the one which had been worn by my mysterious visitor, as I had found from subsequent questions put to my neighbor, and I could no longer have the least uncertainty as to who the woman was who had carried off Mr. Pollard's grandchild. Sick at heart and fearing I scarcely knew what, I asked for the letter which had been left for Miss Merriam, and receiving it from the hand of this amiable woman in whom I appeared to have inspired as much confidence as her former visitor had alarm, I tore it open, and in my capacity of guardian read what it contained. Here it is:

MY DEAR MISS MERRIAM:

The gentleman, in the hope of whose protection you came to this country, is dead. I am his son and naturally feel it incumbent upon me to look after your interests. I am therefore, coming shortly to see you; but till I do so, remember that you are not to receive any one who may call, no matter what their name, sex, or apparent business. If you disobey me in this regard you may do yourself a permanent injury. Wait till my card is brought you, and then judge for yourself whether I am a person in whom you can trust. Hoping to find you in good health, and as happy as your bereaved condition will admit of, I remain sincerely yours,

DWIGHT GAYLORD POLLARD.

"Ah, he wrote a day too late!" I involuntarily exclaimed; then perceiving the look of curiosity which this unguarded expression had awakened on the face of my companion, folded the letter up and put it quietly in my pocket. "It is an unhappy piece of business," I now observed, "but I shall hope to find Miss Merriam very soon, and place her where she will be both safe and happy."

And feeling that I ought to know something of the appearance and disposition of one I so fully intended to befriend, I inquired whether she was a pretty girl.

The reply I received was almost enthusiastic.

"I do not know as you would call her pretty, sir, she is so pale and fragile; but if her features are not regular nor her color good, she has something unusually attractive in her face, and I have heard more than one gentleman here say, 'Miss Merriam is lovely.'"

"And her manners?"

"Very modest, sir, and timid. She seems to have a secret sorrow, for I have often seen her eyes fill when she thought no one was looking at her."

"Do you know her history or connections?"

"No, sir."

"Then she never talked to you about herself?"

"No, sir; though so young, she was strangely like a woman in many things. An uncommonly sweet child, sir, an uncommonly sweet child."

I felt the sting of a great reproach in my heart, and, anxious to hide the depth of my emotion, rose to leave. But the good woman, detaining me, Inquired what she should do with Miss Merriam's trunk.

"What," I exclaimed, "is that still here?" "Yes, sir; she took, as I noticed, a bag of some size with her, but she left her trunk. In the flurry of their departure I forgot to speak about it. I have expected an expressman after it every day, but none has come.

That is another reason why I have felt anxious."

"I do not wonder," I exclaimed. "Sometimes," she observed, "I have thought it was my duty to speak to the police about the matter; it would be such a dreadful thing if any harm had come to her."

"I will speak to the police if necessary," said I. And determined as I had never been before in my life, I left the house and proceeded directly to the depot, where I took the first train for S—.

XXIV

CONFRONTED

Stop up the access and passage to remorse;
That no compunctious visitings of nature
Shake my fell purpose, nor keep peace between
The effect and it!

—MACBETH.

Being in the confessional, I have not forborne to tell the worst
of myself; I will not, therefore, hesitate to tell the best. When
on that very afternoon I entered Mrs. Pollard's grounds, it was
with a resolve to make her speak out, that had no element of
weakness in it. Not her severest frown, nor that diabolical look
from Guy's eye, which had hitherto made me quail, should
serve to turn me aside from my purpose, or thwart those
interests of right and justice which I felt were so deeply at
stake. If my own attempt, backed by the disclosures which had
come to me through the prayer-book I had received from Mr.
Pollard, should fail, then the law should take hold of the
matter and wrench the truth from this seemingly respectable
family, even at the risk of my own happiness and the consideration which I had always enjoyed in this town.

The house, when I approached it, struck me with an odd sense
of change. I did not stop at the time to inquire why this was,
but I have since concluded, in thinking over the subject, that

the parlor curtains must have been drawn up, something which I do not remember ever having seen there before or since. The front door also was ajar, and when I rang the bell it was so speedily answered that I had hardly time to summon up the expression of determination which I felt would alone gain me admittance to the house. But my presence instead of seeming unwelcome, seemed to be almost expected by the servant who opened to me. He bowed, smiled, and that, too, in almost a holiday fashion; and when I would have asked for Mrs. Pollard, interrupted me by a request to lay off my overcoat in a side room, which he courteously pointed out to me.

There was something in this and in the whole aspect of the place which astonished me greatly. If this sombre dwelling with its rich but dismally dark halls and mysterious recesses could be said to ever wear an air of cheer, the attempt certainly had been made to effect this to-day. From the hand of the bronze figure that capped the newel-post hung wreaths of smilax and a basket full of the most exquisite flowers; while from a half-open door at my right came a streak of positive light, and the sound of several voices animated with some sentiment that was strangely out of accord with the solemn scene to which this very room had so lately been a witness. Can they be having a reception? I asked myself; and almost ashamed of the surmise, ever in the house of one so little respected, I, nevertheless, turned to the civil servant before me and remarked:

"There is something going on here of which I was ignorant. Is Mrs. Pollard entertaining guests to-day?"

"Did you not know, sir?" he inquired. "I thought you had been invited, perhaps; Miss Pollard is going to be married this afternoon."

Miss Pollard going to be married! Could any thing have been worse? Shocked, I drew back; Miss Pollard was a beautiful girl and totally innocent, in as far as I knew, of any of the wrong which had certainly been perpetrated by some members of her family. It would never do to mortify her or to mar the pleasure of her wedding-day by any such scene as my errand probably involved. She must be saved sorrow even if her mother—But at that instant the vague but pathetic form of another young girl flitted in imagination before my eyes, and I asked myself if I had not already done enough injury to the helpless and the weak, without putting off for another hour even that attempt at rescue, which the possibly perilous position of Mr. Pollard's grandchild so imperatively demanded. As I thought this and remembered that the gentleman to whom Miss Pollard was engaged was an Englishman of lordly connections and great wealth, I felt my spirit harden and my purpose take definite form. Turning, therefore to the servant before me I inquired if Mrs. Pollard was above or below; and learning that she had not yet come down-stairs, I tore a leaf out of my note-book and wrote on it the following lines:

I know your daughter is on the point of descending to her marriage. I know also that you do not want to see me. But the interests of Miss Merriam demand that you should do so, and that immediately. If you do not come, I shall instantly enter the parlor and tell a story to the assembled guests which will somewhat shake your equanimity when you come to appear before them. My moral courage is not to be judged by my physical, madam, and I shall surely do this thing.

David Barrows

The servant, who still lingered before me, took this note.

"Give it to Mrs. Pollard," I requested. "Tell her it is upon a matter of pressing importance, but do not mention my name, if you please; she will find it in the note." And seeing by the man's face that my wishes would be complied with, I took up my stand in a certain half-curtained recess and waited with loudly beating heart for the issue.

She came. I saw her when she first put foot on the stairs, and notwithstanding my strong antipathy, I could not repress a certain feeling of admiration from mixing with the dread the least sight of her always occasioned me. Her form, which was of the finest, was clad in heavy black velvet, without a vestige of ornament to mar its sombre richness, and her hair, now verging towards gray, was piled up in masses on the top of her haughty head, adding inches to a height that in itself was almost queenly. But her face! and her cruel eye and the smile of her terrible lip. I grew cold as I saw her approach, but I did not move from my place or meditate the least change in the plan I had laid for her subjection.

She stopped just two feet from where I stood, and without the least bend of her head or any gesture of greeting, looked at me. I bore it with quietude, and even answered glance with glance, until I saw her turn pale with the first hint of dismay which she had possibly ever betrayed; then I bowed and waited for her to speak. She did so with a hiss like a serpent.

"What does this mean?" she cried. "What do you hope to gain from me, that you presume to write me such a letter on an occasion like this?"

"Madam," I rejoined, "you are in haste, and so am I; so, without expressing any opinion of the actions which have driven me to this step, I will merely say that I want but one thing of you, but that I want immediately, without hesitation and without delay. I allude to Miss Merriam's address, which you have, and which you must give me on the spot."

She shrank. This cold, confident, imperious woman shrank, and this expression of emotion, while it showed she was not entirely without sensation, awoke within me a strange fear, since how dark must be her secret, if she could tremble at the thought of its discovery. She must have seen that I was affected, for her confidence immediately returned.

"I do not know,—" she began to say.

But I mercilessly interrupted her.

"But *I* know," said I, with an emphasis on the pronoun, "and know so much that I am sure the company within would be glad to hear what I could tell them. Mr. Harrington, for instance, who I hear is of a very honorable family in England, would be pleased to learn—"

"Hush!" she whispered, seizing my wrist with a hand of steel. "If I must tell you I will, but no more words from you, do you hear, no more words."

I took out my note-book and thrust it into her hand.

"Write," I, commanded; "her full address, mind you, that I may find her before the day is over."

She gave me a strange glance but took the book and pencil without a word.

"There!" she cried, hurriedly writing a line and passing the book back to me. "And now go; our time for further conversation will come later."

But I did not stir. I read aloud the line she had given me and then said:

"Madam, this address is either a true or a false one. Which, I shall soon know. For upon leaving here, I shall proceed immediately to the telegraph-office, from which I shall telegraph to the police station nearest to this address, for the information I desire. I shall receive an answer within the hour; and if I find you have deceived me I shall not hesitate to return here, and so suitably accompanied that you will not only open to me, but rectify whatever mistake you may have made. Your guests will not be gone in an hour," I ruthlessly added.

Her face, which had been pale, turned ghastly. Glancing up at a clock which stood a few feet from the recess in which we stood, she gave an involuntary shudder and looked about for Guy.

"Your son, fertile as he is in resources, cannot help you," I remarked. "There is no pit of darkness here; besides I have learned a lesson, madam; and not death itself would deter me now from doing my duty by this innocent child. So if you wish to change this address—"

I stopped; a strain of music had risen from the parlor. It was Mendelssohn's Wedding March. Mrs. Pollard started, cast a hurried look above and tore the note-book out of my hands.

"You are a fiend," she hissed, and hurriedly scratching out the words she had written, she wrote another number and name. "You will find she is there," she cried, "and since I have complied with your desire, you will have no need to return here till you bring the young girl *home*."

The emphasis she placed on the last word startled me. I looked at her and wondered if Medea wore such a countenance when she stabbed her children to the heart. But it flashed and was gone, and the next moment she had moved away from my side and I had stepped to the door. As I opened it to pass out I caught one glimpse of the bride as she came down the stairs. She looked exquisite in her simple white dress, and her face was wreathed in smiles.

XXV

THE FINAL BLOW

It was a deadly blow! A blow like that
Which swooping unawares from out the night,
Dashes a man from some high starlit peak
Into a void of cold and hurrying waves.

The distrust which I felt for Mrs. Pollard was so great that I was still uncertain as to whether she had given me the right address. I therefore proceeded to carry out my original design and went at once to the telegraph-office. The message I sent was peremptory and in the course of half an hour this answer was returned.

Person described, found. Condition critical. Come at once.

There was a train that left in fifteen minutes. Though I had just come from Boston, I did not hesitate to return at once. By six o'clock of that day I stood before the house to which I had been directed. My first sight of it struck me like death. God, what was I about to encounter! What sort of a spot was this, and what was the doom that had befallen the child committed to my care. Numb with horror, I rang the door-bell with difficulty, and when I was admitted by a man in the guise of an officer, I felt something like an instantaneous relief, though I saw by his countenance that he had any thing but good news to give me.

"Are you the gentleman who telegraphed from S—?" he asked.

I bowed, not feeling able to speak.

"Relative or friend?" he went on.

"Friend," I managed to reply.

"Do you guess what has happened?" he inquired.

"I dare not," I answered, with a fearful look about me on walls that more than confirmed my suspicions.

"Miss Merriam is dead," he answered.

I drew a deep breath. It was almost a relief.

"Come in," he said, and opened the door of a room at our right. When we were seated and I had by careful observation made sure we were alone, I motioned for him to go on. He immediately complied. "When we received your telegram, we sent a man here at once. He had some difficulty in entering and still more in finding the young lady, who was hidden in the most remote part of the house. But by perseverance and some force he at last obtained entrance to her room where he found—pardon my abruptness, it will be a mercy to you for me to cut the story short—that he had been ordered here too late; the young lady had taken poison and was on the point of death."

The horror in my face reflected itself faintly in his.

"I do not know how she came to this house," he proceeded; "but she must have been a person of great purity and courage; for though she died almost immediately upon his entrance, she had time to say that she had preferred death to the fate that threatened her, and that no one would mourn her for she had no friends in this country, and her father would never hear how she died."

I sprang wildly to my feet.

"Did she mention no names?" I asked.

"Did she not say who brought her to this hell of hells, or murmur even with her dying breath, one word that would guide us in fixing this crime upon the head of her who is guilty of it?"

"No," answered the officer, "no; but you are right in thinking it was a woman, but what woman, the creature below evidently does not know."

Feeling that the situation demanded thought, I composed myself to the best of my ability.

"I am the Rev. David Barrows of S—," said I, "and my interest in this young girl is purely that of a humanitarian. I have never seen her. I do not even know how long she has been in this country. But I learned that a girl by the name of Grace Merriam had been beguiled from her boarding-place here in this city, and fearing that some terrible evil had befallen her, I telegraphed to the police to look her up."

The officer bowed.

"The number of her boarding-place?" asked he.

I told him, and not waiting for any further questions, demanded if I might not see the body of the young girl.

He led me at once to the room in which it lay, and stood respectfully at the door while I went in alone. The sight I saw has never left me. Go where I will, I see ever before me that pure young face, with its weary look hushed in the repose of death. It haunts me, it accuses me. It asks me where is the noble womanhood that might have blossomed from this sweet bud, had it not been for my pusillanimity and love of life? But when I try to answer, I am stopped by that image of death, with its sealed lips and closed eyes never to open again—never, never, whatever my longing, my anguish, or my despair.

But the worst shock was to come yet. As I left the room and went stumbling down the stairs, I was met by the officer and led again into the apartment I had first entered on the ground floor.

"There is some one here," he began, "whom you may like to question."

Thinking it to be the woman of the house, I advanced, though somewhat reluctantly, when a sight met my eyes that made me fall back in astonishment and dread. It was the figure of a woman dressed all in gray, with a dark-blue veil drawn tightly over her features.

"Good God!" I murmured, "who is this?"

"The woman who brought her here," observed the officer. "Farrell, there, has just found her."

And then I perceived darkly looming in the now heavy dusk the form of another man, whose unconscious and business-like air proclaimed him to be a member of the force.

"Her name is Sophie Preston," the officer continued, motioning to the woman to throw up her veil. "She is a hard character, and some day will have to answer for her many crimes."

Meanwhile, I stood rooted to the ground; the name, the face were strange, and neither that of her whom I had inwardly accused of this wrong.

"I should like to ask the woman—" I commenced, but here my eyes fell upon her form. It was tall and it was full, but it was not by any means handsome. A fearful possibility crossed my mind. Approaching the woman closely, I modified my question.

"Are you the person who took this young lady from her boarding place?" I asked.

"Yes, sir," was the reply, uttered in smooth but by no means cultivated tones.

"And by what arts did you prevail upon this young and confiding creature to leave her comfortable home and go out into the streets with you?"

She did not speak, she smiled. O heaven! what depths of depravity opened before me in that smile!

"Answer!" the officer cried.

"Well, sir, I told her," she now replied, "that I was such and such a relative, grandmother, I think I said; and being a dutiful child—"

But I was now up close to her side, and, leaning to her very ear I interrupted her.

"Tell me on which side of the hall was the parlor into which you went."

"The right," she answered, without the least show of hesitation.

"Wrong," I returned; "you have never been there."

She looked frightened.

"O, sir," she whispered, "hush! hush! If you know—" And there she stopped; and instantly cried aloud, in a voice that warned me I should make nothing by pressing my suspicions at this time and in this place, "I lured the young lady from her home and I brought her here. If it is a criminal act I shall have to answer for it. We all run such risks now and then."

To me, with my superior knowledge of all the mysteries which lay behind this pitiful tragedy, her meaning was evident. Whether she had received payment sufficient for the punishment possibly awaiting her, or whether she had been frightened into assuming the responsibility of another, she was evidently resolved to sustain her role of abductress to the end.

The look she gave me at the completion of her words intensified this conviction, and not feeling sufficiently sure of my duty to dispute her at the present time, I took advantage of her determination, and outwardly, if not inwardly, accepted her confession as true.

I therefore retreated from her side, and being anxious to avoid the coroner, who was likely to enter at any minute, I confined myself to asking a few leading questions, which being answered in a manner seemingly frank, I professed myself satisfied with the result, and hastily withdrew.

XXVI

A FELINE TOUCH

Thou hast not half the power to do me harm,
as I have to be hurt.

—OTHELLO.

The tumult in my mind and heart were great, but my task was
not yet completed, and till it was I could neither stop to
analyze my emotions nor measure the depths of darkness into
which I had been plunged by an occurrence as threatening to
my peace as it was pitiful to my heart. Mrs. Pollard was to be
again, interviewed, and to that formidable duty every thing
bowed, even my need of rest and the demand which my whole
body made for refreshment.

It was eight o'clock when I stood for the second time that day
at her door; and, contrary to my expectations, I found as little
difficulty in entering as I had before. Indeed, the servant was
even more affable and obliging than he had been in the
afternoon, and persisted in showing me into a small room off
the parlor, now empty of guests, and going at once for Mrs.
Pollard.

"She will see you, sir, I am sure," was his last remark as he
went out of the door, "for, though she is so very tired, she told
me if you called to ask you to wait."

I looked around on the somewhat desolate scene that presented itself, and doubtingly shook my head. This seeming submission on the part of a woman so indomitable as she, meant something. Either she was thoroughly frightened or else she meditated some treachery. In either case I needed all my self-command. Happily, the scene I had just quitted was yet vividly impressed upon my mind, and while it remained so, I felt as strong and unassailable as I had once felt weak and at the mercy of my fears.

I did not have to wait long. Almost immediately upon the servant's call, Mrs. Pollard entered the room and stood before me. Her first glance told me all. She was frightened.

"Well?" she said, in a hard whisper, and with a covert look around as if she feared the very walls might hear us. "You have found the girl and you have come to ask for money. It is a reasonable request, and if you do not ask too much you shall have it. I think it will heal all wounds."

My indignation flared up through all my horror and dismay.

"Money?" I cried, "money? what good will money do the dead; you have killed her, madam."

"Killed her?" No wonder she grew pale, no wonder she half gasped. "Killed her?" she repeated.

"Yes," I returned, not giving her time to think, much less speak. "Lured by you to a den of evil, she chose to die rather than live on in disgrace. The woman who lent you her clothes has been found, and—I see I have reached you at last," I broke in. "I thought God's justice would work."

"I—I—" She had to moisten her lips before she could speak. "I don't understand what you mean. You say I lured her, that is a lie. I never took her to this den of evil as you call it."

"But you knew the street and number of the house, and you

gave her into the hand of the woman who did take her there."

"I knew the number of the house but I did not know it was a den of evil. I thought it was a respectable place, cheaper than the one she was in. I am sorry—"

"Madam," I interrupted, "you will find it difficult to make the world believe *you* so destitute of good sense as not to know the character of the house to which such a woman as you entrusted her with would be likely to lead her. Besides, how will you account for the fact that, you wore a dress precisely like that of this creature when you enticed Miss Merriam away from her home. Is there any jury who will believe it to be a coincidence, especially when they learn that you kept your veil down in the presence of every one there?"

"But what proof have you that it was I who went for Miss Merriam? The word of this woman whom you yourself call a *creature?*"

"The word of the landlady, who described Miss Merriam's visitor as tall and of a handsome figure, and my own eyesight, which assured me that the woman who came with her to her place of death was not especially tall nor of a handsome figure. Besides, I talked to the latter, and found she could tell me nothing of the interior of the house where Miss Merriam boarded. She did not even know if the parlors were on the right or the left side of the hall."

"Indeed!" came in Mrs. Pollard's harshest and most cutting tones. But the attempted sarcasm failed. She was shaken to the core, and there was no use in her trying to hide it. I did not, therefore, seek to break the silence which followed the utterance of this bitter exclamation; for the sooner she understood the seriousness of her position the sooner I should see what my own duty was. Suddenly she spoke, but not in her former tones. The wily woman had sounded the depths of the gulf upon the brink of which she had inadvertently stumbled, and her voice, which had been harsh? and biting, now took on all the softness which hypocrisy could give it.

But her words were sarcastic as ever.

"I asked you a moment ago," said she, "what money you wanted. I do not ask that now, as the girl is dead and a clergyman is not supposed to take much interest in filthy lucre. But you want something, or you would not be here. Is it revenge? It is a sentiment worthy of your cloth, and I can easily understand the desire you may have to indulge in it."

"Madam," I cried, "can you think of no other motive than a desire for vengeance or gain? Have you never heard of such a thing as justice?"

"And do you intend—" she whispered.

"There will be an inquest held," I continued. "I shall be called as a witness, and so doubtless will you. Are you prepared to answer all and every question that will be put you?"

"An inquest?" Her face was quite ghastly now. "And have you taken pains to publish abroad my connection with this girl?"

"Not yet."

"She is known, however, to be a grandchild of Mr. Pollard?"

"No," said I.

"What is known?" she inquired.

"That she was Mr. Pollard's protege."

"And you, you alone, hold the key to her real history?"

"Yes," I assented, "I."

She advanced upon me with all the venom of her evil nature

sparkling in her eye. I met the glance unmoved. For a reason I
will hereafter divulge, I no longer felt any fear of what either
she or hers might do.

"I alone know her history and what she owes to you," I
repeated. She instantly fell back. Whether she understood me
or not, she saw that her hold upon me was gone, that the
cowardice she had been witness to was dead, and that she, not
I, must plead for mercy.

"Mr. Barrows," said she; "what is this girl to you that you
should sacrifice the living to her memory?"

"Mrs. Pollard," I returned with equal intensity, "shall I tell
you? She is the victim of my pusillanimity. That is what she is
to me, and that is what makes her memory more to me than
the peace or good name of her seemingly respectable
murderers."

Was it the word I used or did some notion of the effect which
a true remorse can have upon a conscientious soul, pierce her
cold heart at last? I cannot tell; I only know that she crouched
for an instant as if a blow had fallen upon her haughty head,
then rising erect again—she was a proud woman still and
would be to her death, whatever her fate or fortune—she gave
me an indescribable look, and in smothered tones remarked:

"Your sympathies are with the innocent. That is well; now
come with me, I have another innocence to show you, and
after you have seen it tell me whether innocence living or
innocence dead has the most claim upon your pity and
regard." And before I realized what she was doing, she had led
me across the room to a window, from which she hastily
pulled aside the curtain that hung across it.

The sight that met my eyes was like a dream of fairyland let
into the gloom and terror of a nightmare. The window
overlooked the conservatory, and the latter being lighted, a
vision of tropical verdure and burning blossoms flashed before

us. But it was not upon this wealth of light and color that the gaze rested in the fullest astonishment and delight. It was upon two figures seated in the midst of these palm-trees and cacti, whose faces, turned the one towards the other, made a picture of love and joy that the coldest heart must feel, and the most stolid view with delight. It was the bridegroom and his bride, Mr. Harrington and the beautiful Agnes Pollard.

I felt the hand that lay upon my arm tremble.

"Have you the heart to dash such happiness as that?" murmured a voice in my ear.

Was it Mrs. Pollard speaking? I had never heard such a tone as that from her before. Turning, I looked at her. Her face was as changed as her voice; there was not only softness in it but appeal. It was no longer Mrs. Pollard who stood beside me, but *the mother*.

"*She* has never made a mistake," continued this terrible being, all the more terrible to me now that I saw capabilities of feeling in her. "She is young and has her whole life before her. If you pursue the claims of justice as you call them, her future will be wrecked. It is no fool she has married but a proud man, the proudest of his race. If he had known she had for a brother one whom his own country had sentenced to perpetual imprisonment, he would not have married her had his love been ten times what it is. It was because her family was honored and could bestow a small fortune upon her in dowry that he braved his English prejudices at all. What then do you think would be the result if he knew that not only was her brother a convict, but her mother—" She did not finish, but broke in upon herself with a violence that partook of frenzy. "He would first ignore her, then hate her. I know these Englishmen well."

It was true. The happiness or misery of this young creature hung upon my decision. A glance at her husband's face made this evident. He would love her while he could be proud of her; he would hate her the moment her presence suggested shame or opprobrium.

My wily antagonist evidently saw I was impressed, for her face grew still softer and her tone more insinuating.

"She was her father's darling," she whispered. "He could never bear to see a frown upon her face or a tear in her eye. Could he know now what threatened her do you think he would wish you to drag disgrace upon her head for the sake of justice to a being who is dead?"

I did not reply. The truth was I felt staggered.

"See what an exquisite creature she is," the mother now murmured in my ear. "Look at her well—she can bear it—and tell me where in the world you will find beauty more entrancing or a nature lovelier and more enticing?"

"Madam," said I, turning upon her with a severity the moment seemed to deserve, "In a den of contamination, amid surroundings such as it will not do for me to mention even before her who could make use of them to destroy the innocence that trusted in her, there lies the dead body of one as pure, as lovely, and as attractive as this; indeed her beauty is more winning for it has not the stamp of worldliness upon it."

The mother before me grew livid. Her brows contracted and she advanced upon me with a menacing gesture almost as if she would strike me. In all my experience of the world and of her I had never seen such rage; it was all but appalling. Involuntarily I raised my hand, in defence.

But she had already remembered her position and by a violent change now stood before me calm and collected as of old.

"You have been injured by me and have acquired the right to insult me," cried she. Then as I made no move, said: "It is not of the dead we were speaking. It was of her, Samuel Pollard's *child*. Do you intend to ruin her happiness or do you not?

Speak, for it is a question I naturally desire to have settled."

"Madam," I now returned, edging away from that window with its seductive picture of youthful joy, "before I can settle it I must know certain facts. Not till I understand how you succeeded in enticing her from her home, and by what means you transferred her into the care of the vile woman who took your place, will I undertake to consider the possibility of withholding the denunciation which it is in my power to make."

"And you expect me to tell—" she began.

"Every thing," I finished, firmly.

She smiled with a drawing in of her lips that was feline. Then she glared; then she looked about her and approached nearer to me by another step.

"I wish I could kill you," her look said. "I wish by the lifting of my finger you would fall dead." But her lips made use of no such language. She was caught in the toils, and lioness as she was, found herself forced to obey the will that ensnared her.

"You want facts; well, you shall have them. You want to know how I managed to induce Miss Merriam to leave the house where my husband had put her. It is a simple question. Was I not her grandfather's wife, and could I not be supposed to know what his desires were concerning her?"

"And the second fact?"

She looked at me darkly.

"You are very curious," said she.

"I am," said I.

Her baleful smile repeated itself.

"You think that by these confessions I will place myself in a position which will make it impossible for me, to press my request. You do not understand me, sir. Had I committed ten times the evil I have done, that would not justify you in wantonly destroying the happiness of the innocent."

"I wish to know the facts," I said.

"She went with me to a respectable eating house," Mrs. Pollard at once explained. "Leave her to eat her lunch, I went to a place near by, where the woman you saw, met me by appointment, and putting on the clothes I had worn, went back for the girl in my stead. As I had taken pains not to raise my veil except just at the moment when I wanted to convince her I was her natural guardian, the woman had only to hold her tongue to make the deception successful. That she did this is evident from the result. Is there any thing more you would like to know?"

"Yes," I replied, inwardly quaking before this revelation of an inconceivable wickedness, yet steadily resolved to probe it to the very depths. "What did you hope to gain by this deliberate plan of destruction? The girl's death, or simply her degradation?"

The passion in this woman's soul found its vent at last.

"I hoped to lose her; to blot her out of my path—and hers," she more gently added, pointing with a finger that trembled with more than one fierce emotion, at the daughter for whom she had sacrificed so much. "I did not think the girl would die; I am no murderess whatever intimation you may make to that effect. I am simply a mother."

A mother! O horrible! I looked at her and recoiled. That such a one as this should have the right to lay claim to so holy a title and asperse it thus!

She viewed my emotion but made no sign of understanding it.

Her words poured forth like a stream of burning liquid.

"Do you realize what this girl's living meant? It meant recognition, and consequently disgrace and a division of our property, the loss of my daughter's dowry, and of all the hopes she had built on it. Was I, who had given to Samuel Pollard the very money by means of which he had made his wealth, to stand this? Not if a hundred daughters of convicts must perish."

"And your sons?"

"What of them?"

"Had they no claim upon your consideration. When you plunged them into this abyss of greed and deceit did no phantom of their lost manhood rise and confront you with an unanswerable reproach?"

But she remained unmoved.

"My sons are men; they can take care of themselves."

"But Dwight—"

Her self-possession vanished.

"Hush!" she whispered with a quick look around her. "Do not mention him. I have sent him away an hour ago but he may have come back. I do not trust him."

This last clause she uttered beneath her breath and with a spasmodic clutch of her hand which showed she spoke involuntarily. I was moved at this. I began to hope that Dwight at least, was not all that his mother would have him.

"And yet I must speak of him," said I, taking out the letter he had written to Miss Merriam. "This letter addressed to one you have so successfully destroyed seems to show that he returns your mistrust."

She almost tore it out of my hands.

"When was this letter received?" she asked, reading it with burning eyes and writhing lips.

"The day after Miss Grace left her home."

"Then she never saw it?"

"No."

"Who has seen it?"

"Myself and you."

"No one else?"

"No one but the writer."

She laughed.

"We will destroy it," she said; and deliberately tore it up.

I stooped and picked up the fragments.

"You forget," said I, "this letter may be called for by the coroner. It is known that I took it in charge."

"I might better have burnt it," she hissed.

"Not so, I should then have had to explain its loss."

Her old fear came back into her eyes.

"Now I have merely to give it up and leave it to Mr. Dwight Pollard to explain it. He doubtless can."

"My son will never betray his mother."

"Yet he could write this letter."

She frowned.

"Dwight has his weakness," said she.

"It is a pity his weakness did not lead him to send this letter a few hours sooner."

"That is where his very weakness fails. He struggles because he knows his mother partly, and fails because he does not know her wholly."

"And Guy?"

"He knows me better."

The smile with which this was said was the culminating point in a display of depravity such as I had never beheld, even in hovels of acknowledged vice. Feeling that I could not endure much more, I hastened to finish the interview.

"Madam," said I, "by your own acknowledgment you deserve neither consideration nor mercy. What leniency I then show will be for your daughter alone, who, in so far as I can see, is innocent and undeserving of the great retribution which I could so easily bring upon this family. But do not think because I promise to suppress your name from the account I may be called upon to give the coroner, that your sin will be forgotten by Heaven, or this young girl's death go unavenged. As sure as you are the vilest woman I ever met, will suffering and despair overtake you. I do not know when, and I do not know by what means, but it will be bitter when it comes, and the hand of man will not be able to save you."

But it was as if I had not spoken. All she seemed to hear, all, at least, that she paid the least attention to, was the promise I had made.

"You are decided, then, upon secrecy?" she asked.

"I am decided upon saying nothing that will bring your name into public notice."

Her proud manner immediately returned. You would have thought she had never suffered a humiliation.

"But how will you account for your interest in this young person?"

"By telling a portion of the truth. I shall say that my attention was called to her by a letter from Mr. Pollard requesting me to hunt her up and take care of her after he was dead. I shall not say he called her his grandchild unless I am positively forced to do so, nor will I mention the treatment I have received at your hands."

"And the woman you saw?"

"Is your business. I have nothing to do with her."

The shadow which till this moment rested upon her haughty brow, cleared away. With a quick gesture, from which she could not entirely exclude a betrayal of triumph, she dropped the curtain across that charming picture of bridal felicity by which she had won so much, and turning upon me with all the condescension of a conqueror, she exclaimed:

"I once did you an injustice, Mr. Barrows, and called you a name that was but little complimentary to your cloth. Allow me to make such amends as I can and call you what you most surely are—the most generous and least vindictive of men."

This was intolerable. I made haste to leave the room.

"Mrs. Pollard," said I, "no amenities can take place between us. From this hour on we are strangers, till the time conies when we shall appear before the judgment-seat of God. In that day, neither you nor I can hold back one iota of the truth. Think of this, and repent your part in this awful tragedy of sin, if you can." And I turned away toward the door.

But just as I was about to open it, it swung slowly aside, and in the frame-work made by the lintels, I saw Guy Pollard standing with a quiet look of inquiry on his face.

"Mother," said he, in the calmest and most courteous of tones, "shall I let this gentleman pass?"

The reply came in accents equally calm and courteous:

"Certainly, my son."

And Guy Pollard made me a deep bow, and drew softly aside from my path.

I had been within an inch of my death, but it scarcely ruffled me.

XXVII

REPARATION

If hearts are weak, souls should at least be strong.
I will be brief, for my short date of breath
Is not so long as is a tedious tale.

—ROMEO AND JULIET.

Let me hasten to the end.

When I told Mrs. Pollard that I would suppress that portion of the truth which connected her name with this fatal affair, I did not of course mean that I would resort to any falsehood or even prevarication. I merely relied upon the improbability of my being questioned close enough to necessitate my being obliged to reveal the astounding facts which made this matter a destructive one for the Pollards. And I was right in my calculations. Neither socially, nor at the formal inquiry before the coroner, was any question raised of relationship between the dead girl and the family in S—; and this fact, taken with the discreet explanations accorded by Dwight Pollard of his father's, and afterwards of his own interest in her, as shown in the letter which he had sent to her address, is the reason why this affair passed without scandal to the parties concerned.

But not without results for deep down in the heart of one person an influence was at work, destined ere long to eventuate in the tragedy to which these lines are the clue. Remorse deep as my nature and immovable as my sin, has gotten hold upon me, and nothing short of death, and death in the very shape from which I fled in such a cowardly manner, will ever satisfy my soul or allay that burning sense of shame and regret which makes me fear the eye of man and quake at the thought of eternal justice.

For in a final interview with Dwight Pollard I have become convinced that, however unprincipled his brother might be, it was with no intention of carrying out his threats that he plunged me into the vat on that fatal night; that, recognizing the weakness in me, he had resorted to intimidation to ensure his ends; and that all the consequences which followed might have been averted, if I had but remained true to my trust.

Being a Christian minister, and bound by my creed and faith to resist the devil and face the wrath of men, my dereliction in this regard acquires an importance not to be measured by the ordinary standard of law or social usage. For, when I failed to support my principles under trial, Christian faith was betrayed and the avowed power of God put to mockery and shame. I go, therefore, to the death I then shunned, deliberately, conscientiously, determinedly. For the sake of God, for the sake of honor, for the sake of those higher principles which it should be the glory of men to sustain at all risk and in every furnace of affliction, I lay down youth, love, and life, confident that if in so doing I rob one sweet soul of its happiness, I sow anew in other hearts the seed of that stern belief in God and the requirements of our faith which my cowardly act must have gone so far to destroy.

May God accept the sacrifice in the spirit in which I perform it, and in His gracious mercy make light, not the horrors of the pit into which I am about to descend, but the heart of him who must endure them. Whether long or short, they will be such as He sends me, and the end must be peace.

XXVIII

TWO OR ONE

How all the other passions fleet to air,
As doubtful thoughts and rash embrac'd despair,
And shuddering fear, and green-ey'd jealousy.
O love, be moderate; allay thy ecstasy.

—MER. OF VENICE.

I had finished it; the last line had been read, and I sat in a
maze of astonishment and awe. What my thoughts were, what
my judgment upon this astounding act of self-destruction for
conscience sake, it will not interest you to know. In a matter so
complicated with questions of right and wrong, each man
must feel for himself, and out of his own nature adjudge
praise, or express censure; I, Constance Sterling, shall do
neither; I can only wonder and be still.

One point, however, in this lengthy confession I will allude to,
as it involves a fact. Mr. Barrows says that he goes to his death,
the same death from which he fled when he yielded to the
threats of Guy Pollard and gave up the will. He expected,
therefore, to find the vat dry, and looked forward to hours, if
not days, of long-drawn suffering in a spot devoid of warmth,
light, water, and food. His injunction to Ada in that last letter
of his—not to make any move to find him for ten days—
favors this idea, and proves what his expectations were.

But, by the mercy of God, the vat had been half filled with water in the interim which had elapsed between his first and last visit to the mill, and the prison thus becoming a cistern, he must have come to his end in a few moments after his fatal plunge. It was the one relief which a contemplation of this tragedy brought to my overwrought mind.

But with the next day came a reaction; and with a heart full of rejoicing, I prepared to communicate to Dwight Pollard the fact of his release from the dominion of Rhoda Colwell. For whether this record of the past showed him to be a man worthy of full honor or not, it certainly sufficed to exonerate him from all suspicion of being the direct cause of David Barrow's death, and I knew her well enough, or thought I did, to feel certain that no revenge, unless the greatest, would ever satisfy her, and that in losing her hold upon his life and love, she would make no attempt that would merely darken his name before the world. It was therefore with a fearless heart I penned the following lines.

MISS COLWELL:

Your suspicions were unfounded. I have Mr. Barrows' own words to the effect that he meditated death by imprisonment in the vat. I go to acquaint Dwight Pollard with the fact that any accusation on your part must fail before the minute and circumstantial confession which Mr. Barrows has left behind him.

Signing this letter, I despatched it at once to its destination; then taking the important manuscript in my hand, I set out for the Pollard mansion.

It was a day full of sunshine and promise. As I sped through the streets and approached that end of the town which hitherto it had taken all my courage to face, I was astonished at the lightness of my own heart and the beneficent aspect which every object about me seemed to have acquired. Even the place I had come to visit looked less dreary than usual, and I found myself in the grounds and half way up the stoop, before I realized the least falling of that shadow which seemed inseparable from this particular spot. And even now it only came with the thought of Guy, whose possible presence at the door would be any thing but desirable. But my errand being one of peace I was enabled to contemplate even this contingency with equanimity, and was about to ring the bell with a trembling but determined hand, when the door suddenly opened and Dwight Pollard stood before me.

The look of surprise and delight which he gave me brought the color to my cheeks.

"Ah, what a pleasure!" he murmured. Then with a quick look in my face, added earnestly, "You bring good news."

"The best," I answered cheerily, and following him in, I took my stand once more in that dismal parlor where weeks ago I had received my first intimation of the feeling which his every look and gesture now conveyed.

"Mr. Pollard," I now managed to say with a certain dignity, "you see me here because Providence has lately put into my hands a document which completely exonerates you from the charges which Rhoda Colwell has threatened to make against you. Read it, and when you understand the tragedy we so much deplore, we will see how much or how little can be done with the lives it has so deeply affected." And placing the thickly written sheets in his hands I withdrew to the first window I saw and mechanically threw aside the curtains that hid it.

The sight that met my gaze made me for an instant forget the importance of what I had just done. The window I had chosen was the one which looked into the conservatory, and the picture which Mr. Barrows describes as having seen from this spot was then and there before my eyes. The tropical growth, the gorgeous blossoms, even the beautiful woman and the sturdy man. Mr. and Mrs. Harrington were lovers, then, still.

The mother's death and that of the devoted clergyman had not served to reveal the secret which secured the happiness of this bright, attractive, if somewhat worldly, pair. I own I was glad of this, little as I felt myself in sympathy with the radiant but superficial Agnes. Youth, love, and joy are so precious that it lightens the heart to behold their sunshine even on the faces of those whose characters we do not envy.

Nevertheless, the thoughts suggested by this unexpected scene did not long serve to distract me from the more serious matter in hand. Dropping the curtains, I cast one look, toward Mr. Pollard. He was sitting with his face bent over the manuscript, a deep corrugation marked his brow, and a settled look of pain his mouth. I turned away again; I could not bear that look; all my strength was needed for the effort which it might possibly be my duty to make. I sat down in a remote corner and diligently set my soul to patience.

It was well, for my suspense was long, so long that hope and courage began to fail and an inward trembling to take the place of the joyous emotions with which I had placed this confession in his hands. Nevertheless, it came to an end at last, and, with an agitation easy to conceive, I heard him roll the manuscript up, rise, and approach to where I sat. I did not look up, I could not; but I felt his gaze burning through my half-closed lids, and terrified lest I should reveal my weakness and my hopes, I set my lips together, and stilled the beatings of my heart, till I must have struck his sense with the chill and immobility of a totally insensible woman. The despair which the sight caused him, showed itself in his tone when he spoke.

"You share my own opinion of myself," said he. "You consider me the destroyer of Mr. Barrows."

I looked up. What grief, what shame, what love I beheld in the face above me. Slowly I shook my head.

"Mr. Barrows does not accuse you," said I. Then, determined to be truthful to the core at all risks and at all hazards, I added earnestly, "But you were to blame; greatly to blame; I shall never hide that fact from you or from myself. I should be unworthy of your esteem if I did."

"Yes," he earnestly assented, "and I would be less than a man if I did not agree with you." Then, in a lower tone and with greater earnestness yet, continued, "It is not pleasant for a man to speak ill of his own flesh and blood; but after having read words as condemnatory as these, it may be pardoned me, perhaps, if I speak as much of the truth as is necessary to present myself in a fair light to the woman upon whose good opinion rests all my future happiness. Constance, I love you—"

But at this word I had hurriedly risen.

"Oh!" I somewhat incoherently exclaimed; "not here! not under your own roof!"

But at his look I sank back.

"Yes," he imperatively cried, "here and now. I cannot wait another day, another hour. My love for you is too great, too absorbing, for any paltry considerations to interpose themselves upon my attention now. I must tell you what you are to me, and ask you, as you are a just and honest woman, to listen while I lay bare to you my life—the life I long to consecrate to your happiness, Constance."

I looked up.

"Thank you," he murmured; but whether in return for my look or the smile which his look involuntarily called up, I cannot say, for he went on instantly in continuation of his former train of thought, "Constance, you have read this confession from Mr. Barrows which you have just placed in my hands?"

"Yes," I nodded gravely.

"You can, then, understand what a dilemma we were in some three months ago. My sister had attracted the notice of an English aristocrat. He loved her and wished to marry her. We admired him—or rather we admired his position (I would be bitterly true at this hour) and wished to see the union effected. But there was a secret in our family, which if known, would make such a marriage impossible. A crime perpetrated before my birth had attached disgrace to our name and race, and Mr. Harrington is a man to fly disgrace quicker than he would death. Miss Sterling, it would be useless for me to try to make myself out better than I am. When I heard that my father, whom I am just beginning to revere but of whom in those days I had rather a careless opinion, was determined to acknowledge his convict son through the daughter which had been sent over here, I revolted. Not that I begrudged this young girl the money he wished to leave her,—though from a somewhat morbid idea of reparation which my father possessed, he desired to give her an amount that would materially affect our fortunes—but that I loved my sister, and above all loved the proud and isolated position we had obtained in society, and could not endure the results which the revelation of such a stain in, our family must produce. Not my mother, whose whole life since her marriage had been one haughty protest against this secret shame, nor Guy, with all his cynicism and pride, felt stronger on this point than I. To my warped judgment any action within the bounds of reason seemed justifiable that would prevent my dying father from bringing this disgrace upon his children; and being accustomed to defer to my mother's judgments and desires,—she was not only a powerful woman, Constance, but possessed of a strange fascination for those she loved and sought to govern—I lent myself sufficiently to her schemes to stand neutral in the struggle between my father's wishes and her determination, though that father would often turn upon me with a gaze of entreaty that went to my heart. That he had taken advantage of his last journey to Boston to have a new will drawn, and that his only desire now was for an opportunity to get this same safely transferred into the hands of his lawyer, I never suspected any more than did my mother or brother. We thought that as far as the past was concerned we were secure, and that if we could prevent an interview between him and Mr. Nicholls, the future would likewise be safe from a discovery of our secret It was therefore a terrible shock to my mother and afterwards to me when we learned that he had already accomplished the act we so much dreaded and that the clergyman we had called in at my father's urgent request, had been entrusted with the paper that was to proclaim our shame to the world. But the disappointment, great as it was, had little time to exert its force on me, for with my brother's recital of what had taken place at my father's death-bed there came a new dread which I find it difficult to name but which you will understand when I say that it led me to give Mr. Barrows the warning of which he has spoken. My brother—I cannot speak of him with calmness—is a man to be feared, Miss Sterling. Not that I would not be a match for him in all matters of open enmity; but in ways of secrecy and deep dealing, he is master, and all the more to be dreaded that he makes it impossible for one to understand him or measure the depths of turpitude to which he would descend. When, therefore I heard him say he should have that will back before it could pass into the hands of Mr. Nicholls, I trembled; and as the night passed and morning came without showing any diminution in the set determination of his expression, I decided upon visiting Mr. Barrows, in the hope of influencing him to return the will of his own accord. But I soon saw that in spite of the weakness I detected in him there was small prospect of his doing this; and turning my steps home again, I confronted my mother and my brother and asked them what they meant to do; they told me, that is, they told me partly; and I, with that worse dread in my soul, was fain to be satisfied with the merely base and dishonorable scheme they meditated. To take Mr. Barrows at a disadvantage, to argue with him, threaten him, and perhaps awe him by place and surroundings to surrender to them the object of their desires, did not seem to me so dreadful, when I thought of what they might have done or might yet attempt to do if I stood in their way too much. So, merely stipulating that they would allow me to accompany them to the mill, I let matters take their course, and true to my own secret desire to retain their confidence and so save him, and if possible them, from any act that would entail consequences of a really serious nature, I gave them my assistance to the extent of receiving Mr. Barrows at the door and conducting him through the mill to the room which my brother had designated to me as the one in which they proposed to hold their conference.

"But the task was uncongenial, and at the first words which Guy chose to employ against Mr. Barrows, I set down my lantern on the floor and escaped to the outer air again. Money, station, fame before the world, seemed to me but light matters at that moment, and if I had followed my first impulse I should have rushed back to the assistance of Mr. Barrows. But considerations terrible and strange prevented me from following this impulse. In the first place I was not myself free from a desire to see the contents of the will and judge for myself to what extent my father had revealed our disgrace to the world; and secondly, the habit of years is not broken in an instant, and this mother who gave her countenance to an act I so heartily disapproved, had for all her reserve and a nature seriously differing from my own, ever been the dominator of my actions and the controlling force of my life. I could not brave her, not yet, not while any hope remained of righting matters, without a demonstration that would lead to open hostilities. So with a weakness I now wonder at, I let the minutes go by till the sound of coming steps warned me that my brother was at hand. What he told me was brief and to the point He had obtained the clergyman's consent to read the will and was on his way to get it. "But, Mr. Barrows?" I inquired. "Is in the cellar there with mother." "The cellar!" I repeated. But he was already in the yard, on his way to the town. I was disturbed. The calmness of his tone had not deceived me. I felt that something was wrong; what I could not tell. Taking the lantern he had left behind him, I made my way to the cellar. It seemed empty. But when I had reached the other end I found myself confronted by a ghostly figure in which I was forced to recognize my mother, though the sight of her in the masquerade costume she had adopted; gave me a shock serious as the interests involved. But this surprise, great as it was, was soon lost in that of finding her alone; and when to my hurried inquiry as to where Mr. Barrows was, she pointed to the vat, you can imagine the tide of emotions that swept over me. But no, that is impossible. They were not what you would have felt, they were not what I would feel now. Mingled with my shame and the indignant protest of my manhood against so unworthy an exercise of power, was that still dominating instinct of dread which any interference with my mother's plans or wishes had always inspired; and so when I learned that the worst was over and that Mr. Barrows would be released on Guy's return, I subdued my natural desire to rescue him and went away, little realizing that in thus allying myself with his persecutors, I had laid the foundations of a remorse that would embitter my whole after existence. The return of my brother with the will caused me fresh emotions. As soon as I saw him I knew there was a struggle before me; and in handing him back the lantern, I took occasion to ask if he had opened the document. He looked at me a moment before replying and his lip took a sinister curl. 'I have,' he said. 'And what does it contain?' 'What we wish,' he answered, with a strange emphasis. I was too much astonished to speak. I could not believe this to be true, and when, Mr. Barrows having been released, we had all returned home, I asked to see the will and judge for myself. But Guy refused to show it. 'We are going to return it,' he said, and said no more. Nor would my mother give me any further information. Either I had betrayed myself in the look I gave Guy on his return to the mill, or else some underlying regard for my feelings had constrained her to spare me actual participance in a fraud. At all events, I did not know the truth till the real will had been destroyed and the substituted one placed in Mr. Nicholls' hands, and then it was told to me in a way to confound my sense of right and make me think it would be better to let matters proceed to this false issue, than by a public acknowledgment of the facts, bring down upon me and mine the very disgrace from which I had been so desirous of escaping. I was caught in the toils you see, and though it would have been a man's part to have broken through every constraint and proclaimed myself once and for all on the side of right, I had nothing whereby to show what the last wishes of my father had been, and could only say what would ruin us without benefiting the direct object of those wishes. I therefore kept their counsel and my own; stilling my conscience when it spoke too loud, by an inward promise to be not only a friend to my older brother's child, but to part with the bulk of my fortune to her. That she would need my friendship I felt, as the letter I wrote to her shows, but that such evil would come upon her as did, or that my delay to see her would make it impossible for me ever to behold her in this world, I had yet too much filial regard to imagine. I was consequently overwhelmed by the news of her death, and though I never knew the whole truth till now, I was conscious of a distrust so great that from that day to the worser ones which followed, I never looked at those nearest to me without a feeling of deep separation such as is only made by some dark and secret crime. I was alone, or so I felt, and was gradually becoming morbid from a continual brooding on this subject, when the great blow fell which changed whatever vague distress I felt into an active remorse and positive fear. Mr. Barrows was found dead, drowned in the very vat into which my brother had forced him a month or so before. What did it mean? It was impossible for me to guess the truth, but I could not but recognize the fact that we were more or less responsible for his death; that the frenzy which had doubtless led to this tragedy was the outcome of the strain which had been put upon his nerves, and though personally I had had nothing to do with placing him in the vat, I was certainly responsible for allowing him to remain there a moment after I knew where he was. It was, therefore, with the deepest horror and confusion that I rushed home with this news, only to find that it had outstripped me, and that my mother, foreseeing the dangers which this death might bring upon us, had succumbed to the shock, and lay, as you know, in a most alarming condition herself. The perilous position into which we were thrown by these two fatal occurrences necessitated a certain confidence between my brother and myself. To watch our mother, and stifle any unguarded expressions into which she might be betrayed, to watch you, and when we saw it was too late to prevent your sharing our secret, to make our hold upon you such that you would feel it to your own advantage to keep it with us, was perhaps only pardonable in persons situated as we were. But, Constance, while with Guy the feeling that made this last task easy was one of selfish passion only, mine from the first possessed a depth and fervency which made the very thought of wooing you seem a desecration and a wrong. For already had your fine qualities produced their effect, and in the light of your high and lofty nature, my own past looked deformed and dark. And when the worst came, and Rhoda Colwell's threats put a seemingly immovable barrier between us, this love which had sprung up in a very nightmare of trouble, only seemed to take deeper and more lasting root, and I vowed that whether doomed to lifelong regret or not, I would live worthy of you, and be in misery what I could so easily be in joy, the man you could honor, if not love. That this hour would ever come I dared not dream, but now that it has, can you, will you give me so much as you have, and not give me more? I know I have no right to ask any thing from you; that the secrets of our family are a burden which any woman might well shrink from sharing, but if you do not turn from me, will you turn from them? Love is such a help to the burdened, and I love you so fondly, so reverently."

He was on his knees; his forehead was pressed against my arm. The emotion which shook his whole body communicated itself to me. I felt that whatever his past weaknesses had been, he possessed a character capable of the noblest development, and, yielding to the longing with which my whole being was animated, I was about to lay my hand upon his head, when he lifted his face and, gazing earnestly at me, said:

"One moment; there is yet a cloud which ought to be blown away from between us—Rhoda Colwell. I loved her; I sought her love; but once gained, my eyes opened. I saw her imperfections; I felt the evil in her nature. I knew if I married her, I should ruin my life. I left her. I seemed to have no choice, for my love died with my esteem, and she was not a woman to marry without love. Could I have done differently, Constance?"

I answered as my whole heart inclined me to. I could not refuse this love coming into my desolate life. It seemed to be mine. Whatever trials, fear, or disquietude it might bring, the joy of it was great enough to make these very trials desirable, if only to prove to him and me that the links which bound us were forged from truest metal, without any base alloy to mar their purity and undermine their strength.

And so that spot of gloom, which had been the scene of so much that was dark and direful, became the witness of a happiness which seemed to lift it out of the veil of reserve in which it had been shrouded for so long, and make of the afternoon sun, which at that moment streamed in through the western windows, a signal of peace, whose brightness as yet has never suffered change or eclipse.

Choose from Thousands of 1stWorldLibrary Classics By

A. M. Barnard
Ada Leverson
Adolphus William Ward
Aesop
Agatha Christie
Alexander Aaronsohn
Alexander Kielland
Alexandre Dumas
Alfred Gatty
Alfred Ollivant
Alice Duer Miller
Alice Turner Curtis
Alice Dunbar
Allen Chapman
Alleyne Ireland
Ambrose Bierce
Amelia E. Barr
Amory H. Bradford
Andrew Lang
Andrew McFarland Davis
Andy Adams
Angela Brazil
Anna Alice Chapin
Anna Sewell
Annie Besant
Annie Hamilton Donnell
Annie Payson Call
Annie Roe Carr
Annonaymous
Anton Chekhov
Archibald Lee Fletcher
Arnold Bennett
Arthur C. Benson
Arthur Conan Doyle
Arthur M. Winfield
Arthur Ransome
Arthur Schnitzler
Arthur Train
Atticus
B.H. Baden-Powell
B. M. Bower
B. C. Chatterjee
Baroness Emmuska Orczy
Baroness Orczy
Basil King
Bayard Taylor
Ben Macomber
Bertha Muzzy Bower
Bjornstjerne Bjornson

Booth Tarkington
Boyd Cable
Bram Stoker
C. Collodi
C. E. Orr
C. M. Ingleby
Carolyn Wells
Catherine Parr Traill
Charles A. Eastman
Charles Amory Beach
Charles Dickens
Charles Dudley Warner
Charles Farrar Browne
Charles Ives
Charles Kingsley
Charles Klein
Charles Hanson Towne
Charles Lathrop Pack
Charles Romyn Dake
Charles Whibley
Charles Willing Beale
Charlotte M. Braeme
Charlotte M. Yonge
Charlotte Perkins Stetson
Clair W. Hayes
Clarence Day Jr.
Clarence E. Mulford
Clemence Housman
Confucius
Coningsby Dawson
Cornelis DeWitt Wilcox
Cyril Burleigh
D. H. Lawrence
Daniel Defoe
David Garnett
Dinah Craik
Don Carlos Janes
Donald Keyhoe
Dorothy Kilner
Dougan Clark
Douglas Fairbanks
E. Nesbit
E. P. Roe
E. Phillips Oppenheim
E. S. Brooks
Earl Barnes
Edgar Rice Burroughs
Edith Van Dyne
Edith Wharton

Edward Everett Hale
Edward J. O'Biren
Edward S. Ellis
Edwin L. Arnold
Eleanor Atkins
Eleanor Hallowell Abbott
Eliot Gregory
Elizabeth Gaskell
Elizabeth McCracken
Elizabeth Von Arnim
Ellem Key
Emerson Hough
Emilie F. Carlen
Emily Bronte
Emily Dickinson
Enid Bagnold
Enilor Macartney Lane
Erasmus W. Jones
Ernie Howard Pie
Ethel May Dell
Ethel Turner
Ethel Watts Mumford
Eugene Sue
Eugenie Foa
Eugene Wood
Eustace Hale Ball
Evelyn Everett-green
Everard Cotes
F. H. Cheley
F. J. Cross
F. Marion Crawford
Fannie E. Newberry
Federick Austin Ogg
Ferdinand Ossendowski
Fergus Hume
Florence A. Kilpatrick
Fremont B. Deering
Francis Bacon
Francis Darwin
Frances Hodgson Burnett
Frances Parkinson Keyes
Frank Gee Patchin
Frank Harris
Frank Jewett Mather
Frank L. Packard
Frank V. Webster
Frederic Stewart Isham
Frederick Trevor Hill
Frederick Winslow Taylor

Friedrich Kerst
Friedrich Nietzsche
Fyodor Dostoyevsky
G.A. Henty
G.K. Chesterton
Gabrielle E. Jackson
Garrett P. Serviss
Gaston Leroux
George A. Warren
George Ade
Geroge Bernard Shaw
George Cary Eggleston
George Durston
George Ebers
George Eliot
George Gissing
George MacDonald
George Meredith
George Orwell
George Sylvester Viereck
George Tucker
George W. Cable
George Wharton James
Gertrude Atherton
Gordon Casserly
Grace E. King
Grace Gallatin
Grace Greenwood
Grant Allen
Guillermo A. Sherwell
Gulielma Zollinger
Gustav Flaubert
H. A. Cody
H. B. Irving
H.C. Bailey
H. G. Wells
H. H. Munro
H. Irving Hancock
H. R. Naylor
H. Rider Haggard
H. W. C. Davis
Haldeman Julius
Hall Caine
Hamilton Wright Mabie
Hans Christian Andersen
Harold Avery
Harold McGrath
Harriet Beecher Stowe
Harry Castlemon
Harry Coghill
Harry Houidini

Hayden Carruth
Helent Hunt Jackson
Helen Nicolay
Hendrik Conscience
Hendy David Thoreau
Henri Barbusse
Henrik Ibsen
Henry Adams
Henry Ford
Henry Frost
Henry James
Henry Jones Ford
Henry Seton Merriman
Henry W Longfellow
Herbert A. Giles
Herbert Carter
Herbert N. Casson
Herman Hesse
Hildegard G. Frey
Homer
Honore De Balzac
Horace B. Day
Horace Walpole
Horatio Alger Jr.
Howard Pyle
Howard R. Garis
Hugh Lofting
Hugh Walpole
Humphry Ward
Ian Maclaren
Inez Haynes Gillmore
Irving Bacheller
Isabel Cecilia Williams
Isabel Hornibrook
Israel Abrahams
Ivan Turgenev
J.G.Austin
J. Henri Fabre
J. M. Barrie
J. M. Walsh
J. Macdonald Oxley
J. R. Miller
J. S. Fletcher
J. S. Knowles
J. Storer Clouston
J. W. Duffield
Jack London
Jacob Abbott
James Allen
James Andrews
James Baldwin

James Branch Cabell
James DeMille
James Joyce
James Lane Allen
James Lane Allen
James Oliver Curwood
James Oppenheim
James Otis
James R. Driscoll
Jane Abbott
Jane Austen
Jane L. Stewart
Janet Aldridge
Jens Peter Jacobsen
Jerome K. Jerome
Jessie Graham Flower
John Buchan
John Burroughs
John Cournos
John F. Kennedy
John Gay
John Glasworthy
John Habberton
John Joy Bell
John Kendrick Bangs
John Milton
John Philip Sousa
John Taintor Foote
Jonas Lauritz Idemil Lie
Jonathan Swift
Joseph A. Altsheler
Joseph Carey
Joseph Conrad
Joseph E. Badger Jr
Joseph Hergesheimer
Joseph Jacobs
Jules Vernes
Julian Hawthrone
Julie A Lippmann
Justin Huntly McCarthy
Kakuzo Okakura
Karle Wilson Baker
Kate Chopin
Kenneth Grahame
Kenneth McGaffey
Kate Langley Bosher
Kate Langley Bosher
Katherine Cecil Thurston
Katherine Stokes
L. A. Abbot
L. T. Meade

L. Frank Baum
Latta Griswold
Laura Dent Crane
Laura Lee Hope
Laurence Housman
Lawrence Beasley
Leo Tolstoy
Leonid Andreyev
Lewis Carroll
Lewis Sperry Chafer
Lilian Bell
Lloyd Osbourne
Louis Hughes
Louis Joseph Vance
Louis Tracy
Louisa May Alcott
Lucy Fitch Perkins
Lucy Maud Montgomery
Luther Benson
Lydia Miller Middleton
Lyndon Orr
M. Corvus
M. H. Adams
Margaret E. Sangster
Margret Howth
Margaret Vandercook
Margaret W. Hungerford
Margret Penrose
Maria Edgeworth
Maria Thompson Daviess
Mariano Azuela
Marion Polk Angellotti
Mark Overton
Mark Twain
Mary Austin
Mary Catherine Crowley
Mary Cole
Mary Hastings Bradley
Mary Roberts Rinehart
Mary Rowlandson
M. Wollstonecraft Shelley
Maud Lindsay
Max Beerbohm
Myra Kelly
Nathaniel Hawthrone
Nicolo Machiavelli
O. F. Walton
Oscar Wilde

Owen Johnson
P.G. Wodehouse
Paul and Mabel Thorne
Paul G. Tomlinson
Paul Severing
Percy Brebner
Percy Keese Fitzhugh
Peter B. Kyne
Plato
Quincy Allen
R. Derby Holmes
R. L. Stevenson
R. S. Ball
Rabindranath Tagore
Rahul Alvares
Ralph Bonehill
Ralph Henry Barbour
Ralph Victor
Ralph Waldo Emmerson
Rene Descartes
Ray Cummings
Rex Beach
Rex E. Beach
Richard Harding Davis
Richard Jefferies
Richard Le Gallienne
Robert Barr
Robert Frost
Robert Gordon Anderson
Robert L. Drake
Robert Lansing
Robert Lynd
Robert Michael Ballantyne
Robert W. Chambers
Rosa Nouchette Carey
Rudyard Kipling
Saint Augustine
Samuel B. Allison
Samuel Hopkins Adams
Sarah Bernhardt
Sarah C. Hallowell
Selma Lagerlof
Sherwood Anderson
Sigmund Freud
Standish O'Grady
Stanley Weyman
Stella Benson
Stella M. Francis

Stephen Crane
Stewart Edward White
Stijn Streuvels
Swami Abhedananda
Swami Parmananda
T. S. Ackland
T. S. Arthur
The Princess Der Ling
Thomas A. Janvier
Thomas A Kempis
Thomas Anderton
Thomas Bailey Aldrich
Thomas Bulfinch
Thomas De Quincey
Thomas Dixon
Thomas H. Huxley
Thomas Hardy
Thomas More
Thornton W. Burgess
U. S. Grant
Upton Sinclair
Valentine Williams
Various Authors
Vaughan Kester
Victor Appleton
Victor G. Durham
Victoria Cross
Virginia Woolf
Wadsworth Camp
Walter Camp
Walter Scott
Washington Irving
Wilbur Lawton
Wilkie Collins
Willa Cather
Willard F. Baker
William Dean Howells
William le Queux
W. Makepeace Thackeray
William W. Walter
William Shakespeare
Winston Churchill
Yei Theodora Ozaki
Yogi Ramacharaka
Young E. Allison
Zane Grey

Lightning Source UK Ltd.
Milton Keynes UK
UKOW04n2204300915